To Michele—
Enjoy!
Liliana Hart

KILL SHOT

A COLLECTIVE NOVEL

D1557551

LILIANA HART

DEDICATION

For my readers, because you let me have the best job ever.

And for Dallas, because you've gotten really good at grabbing take out to feed the kids.

CONTENTS

ACKNOWLEDGMENTS

Many thanks to the Author Life Support Group—Jana DeLeon, Tina Folsom, Colleen Gleason, Jane Graves, Dorien Kelly, Jasinda Wilder, Theresa Ragan and Denise Grover-Swank. You guys are absolutely the best!

And to Team MacKenzie, because you brighten my day.

PROLOGUE

Kidal, Africa

William Sloane was a killer. And he liked it.

He stepped off his private jet into the hot African desert, adjusted his wide-brimmed hat, and curled his lip in disgust at the sight before him. Dust swirled in devilish whirls, and the fine grains lodged themselves in places not meant for sand. His eyes watered, and though his mouth stayed closed, the gritty particles crunched like bits of broken shell between his molars.

Ramshackle huts sat in drunken rows, pieced together with worn cloth and brittle wood. Crude chairs were scattered around the remains of long-cold fires, and a thick iron stew pot lay haphazardly on its side, thickly crusted with old food.

God, how did people live in such filth?

The horrendous conditions weren't likely to bother the people of this tiny village anymore. The body count was just shy of a hundred—a paltry sum in comparison to some of the other sites—but every death brought him closer to finding the original components of the formula.

Each test only improved his chances of succeeding— the rush of power almost overwhelming with every death. He walked through the wasteland of scattered bodies, stepped over emaciated limbs, and barely spared a glance at the remains of a group of children. There were no consequences to face if the experiments failed as this one had. William's reach was vast—his influence unparalleled—and his pockets were deep.

The cleanup was already underway. It would take only hours for the bodies to be incinerated. For the crude huts to be leveled and the ground swept clean of any reminder that humans had once lived there. His smile of grim satisfaction had more than one of the workers in grey jumpsuits with the black logo over the breast pocket heading in the opposite direction.

"Mr. Sloane…Mr. Sloane?"

William started at the high-pitched, nasally voice of his head scientist and watched with hidden revulsion as Dr. Alan Standridge lumbered over. Standridge was as wide as he was short. Sweat stains yellowed his too-small lab coat, and a white button hung limply by a lone thread, as if it knew its days were numbered and it would never have the satisfaction of penetrating a buttonhole again. Standridge's disheveled hair was dampened at the temples, and his glasses sat crooked on his pug nose. But under the layers of fat and distaste was the mind of a genius.

"Standridge," William acknowledged with a nod, not bothering to extend his hand. "Are we getting closer?"

"It's all trial and error at this point. Every test brings new results." He pushed his glasses up higher on the bridge of his nose so his muddy eyes bugged out in their nervous sockets.

That's what William liked about Standridge. Morals never got in the way of an experiment, which was exactly why Standridge had been let go from his position at MIT. The chemicals for healing were never quite as fascinating as the chemicals for killing.

"So what you're saying is we're no goddamned closer to having the formula than we were the last time."

A cold bead of sweat dripped from the nape of his neck down William's spine, and the red haze of anger clouded his vision. Nothing would be more satisfying than putting his hands around Standridge's pudgy neck and squeezing.

"What you're telling me is that The Passover Project is useless."

"Yes…I mean, no." Standridge grimaced and shrunk as far as he could into the enormity of his lab coat.

"My patience grows thin, Dr. Standridge. Failure to complete this experiment is not an option. Do you think there aren't other scientists who could do this for me? I already have your replacement lined up should you continue to fail. And you won't be sent to your retirement with benefits, if you understand my meaning."

William nodded in satisfaction as Standridge's pasty complexion turned even paler.

"You've got to give me another chance, Mr. Sloane. I know I'm getting closer. Maybe two more experiments. I swear," the scientist whined. "We can't rush a weapon of this magnitude. It has an enormous number of variables, and it's going to take time. There's never been anything like this. The man who created it has no equal."

"Obviously," Sloane derided. "I have appointments to keep, Standridge. And I believe you need to get back to the lab. I've picked out a Native American tribe in Central Mexico for your next experiment. I want you to target the chief. If you manage not to fuck it up, he'll die a quick death. If you do manage to fuck it up...well, let's just say you and the chief will have a lot in common."

William Sloane boarded the plane with a smile on his face.

CHAPTER ONE

By her calculations, Grace Meredith had exactly five and a half seconds to take out six targets before an alarm sounded. She had a round in the chamber and five in the magazine of her M40A5. Piece of cake.

She ignored the mosquitoes the size of hummingbirds searching for exposed flesh, and she ignored the sweat that dripped steadily down her spine as she looked through the scope of her rifle. The temperature was in the mid-nineties, but the canopy of trees that blanketed the area held the heat in like an oven and slowly baked anyone who didn't have shelter. Her body and mind were disciplined, so the discomforts didn't register.

Colombia wasn't known for its gentle climate. Or gentle anything for that matter. Gemino Vasquez was

Colombia's baddest arms dealer, and lately his biggest client had been North Korea. But Vasquez had something Grace wanted very badly. Something that would bring in a big, fat paycheck from the South Korean government.

She shifted slightly, and the bark of the large tree branch she'd lain on for the last four hours ground against her stomach. But her focus was absolute. Not even the hundred-and-fifty-foot drop to the ground could distract her.

The orange sun blazed just over the tops of the trees, but it would disappear completely in another twenty minutes. By the time it was gone, she'd have the flash drive in hand and already be across the border to Venezuela.

Grace did one final check of all her equipment and took a deep, steadying breath, slowing her heartbeat so her pulse would be in time with each shot. She'd hit the sentry at the top of the Vasquez compound first and then take the rest in order from left to right. She pushed her feet against the tree for balance. The clock ticked in the background of her mind as she put the slightest amount of pressure on the trigger.

"One," she whispered. She didn't wait to watch him fall but moved to the next target. Five seconds until the report from her rifle reached their ears. Five seconds for five more kills.

Two…

Three…

Four…

Five…

Six…

Grace didn't stop to check the accuracy of her shots. She never missed. She hung her rifle on a tree branch, already missing the feel of it in her hands. Time was of the essence now, and she couldn't afford to be burdened with too much equipment; she'd have to leave it behind. The new guards would be driving up soon for the shift change, and she had to be long gone by then.

She unzipped her supply pack, pulling out a lightweight pipe no longer than her forearm that looked completely worthless at first glance. In reality, it was a military prototype she'd borrowed from her former life. She hit the button on each end of the pipe and it expanded in length until it was almost as tall as she was, and then she hit the button in the center and waited as wings made out of a synthetic material unfurled to complete the hang-glider.

"No time like the present," she said, swallowing as she perched on the edge of the tree and looked out across the jungle. She had a straight shot into the compound, but any shift in wind would have her hurtling into trees. Falling to her death wouldn't bring her the money she needed, so she had no choice but to take a leap of faith. Literally.

Fifteen minutes until all hell broke loose.

Grace grasped the bar and jumped. The bottom dropped out of her stomach as she free fell for just a brief moment, and then the air caught beneath the wings and she soared through the treetops like a phantom. It took all her strength and concentration to keep the glider on a straight path to the compound roof, and when her feet touched the ground her muscles were fatigued and her skin coated with perspiration.

She hit another button on the long metal tube and the glider folded itself back up until it was small enough to fit back in her pack.

The body of the first sentry she'd shot lay face down in the greenish-blue water of the swimming pool. A hazy cloud of blood ballooned from under him, and his arms and legs floated like waving ribbons.

Her eyes and ears were alert, but all that greeted her was growing darkness and silence. Even the animals and birds in the jungle knew bad shit was about to go down.

Grace unhooked the harness and pulled her Sig from a thigh holster. She stood silently next to the gray door that led from the roof down a set of stairs to the main floors of the house. Two heartbeats passed before she opened the door and slipped inside. It was quiet, but that wasn't unusual at this time of the day according to her intel—six sentries on duty surrounding the compound, only two guarding Vasquez's private suite of rooms.

Vasquez's stupidity only made her job easier.

Grace walked silently down the thickly carpeted hallway as if she weren't about to steal the schematics for a new superweapon—a weapon that used state-of-the-art laser technology—and sell it to another country. But the closer she got to Vasquez, the more her spine tingled in awareness that something was wrong. That tingle had saved her life more than once, and she never ignored it. The hallway opened up into a landing just as she reached Vasquez's private rooms. Weak light filtered through the windows and cast rainbows as it pierced the glass chandelier that hung overhead.

She saw firsthand exactly why her spine was tingling.

Both sentries were slumped against each other—a dead man's embrace—one with a broken neck and the other with a hunting knife in his carotid. Efficient work considering the size of the sentries.

She pushed the bodies out of her way with her foot and eased the door open, her finger on the trigger of her Sig. All that mattered was the flash drive. If she didn't produce it, then she didn't get paid.

The smells of new death were thick and cloying in the heat, and she could taste the fresh blood in the back of her throat with every breath she took. Dust mites danced in the air, and long shadows were cast in the fading sunlight.

Grace waited for her eyes to adjust and listened for sounds of footsteps, but all she heard was the gentle whir of the wicker fans that rotated slowly on the ceiling. She moved silently, staying close to the wall as she checked each room.

Vasquez's bedroom was bigger than her whole apartment—the furniture oversized and ornate, the colors garishly red. He was set up for sex. The interesting kind of sex by the looks of it. Restraints and various whips and other tools lined one whole wall, and torn condom packages littered the floor. It looked like Vasquez had had a busy morning. Too bad his afternoon hadn't turned out so hot.

Gemino Vasquez's body lay spread eagle on his bed. He was naked, and his eyes were open and unseeing. A single gunshot wound to the heart bled sluggishly. He hadn't been dead long. She couldn't stop the bitter disappointment when she saw the flash drive was gone from the chain on his right wrist.

"Dammit," she whispered and moved to check the covers of his bed just to make sure it hadn't come off in the struggle. But she knew in her heart it was long gone. She knew the signs of a professional hit, and this job reeked of it. What pissed her off even more was that whoever did it managed to sneak in right under her nose. He had to have known she was watching and snuck in through the one blind spot she had at the back of the compound.

The stir of air behind her was the only warning she had before an arm locked around her throat.

"Looking for this?" a deep voice whispered in her ear, holding the flash drive in front of her face.

He pressed close against her back and squeezed his arm tighter around her throat so she had to breathe shallowly through her nose. Grace winced as he pressed his fingers against the pressure points of her wrist, and her pistol fell uselessly to the floor with a dull thunk.

Fear never had a chance to take hold. It was anger that drove Grace. Anger that had kept her alive the last couple of years. And she knew how to wield it. She threw her head back and aimed her heel at his knee simultaneously. He dodged her blows as if he'd been expecting them, but the distraction was enough for him to loosen his grip. She swept her leg and brought him to his knees, reaching down for the knife in her boot. The blade gleamed once in the fading sunlight just before it was knocked out of her hand and across the room.

He outweighed her by close to eighty pounds, and he had a good eight inches on her in height. They grappled and rolled, each one blocking the other's strikes with only seconds to spare. It was a well-choreographed dance.

A familiar dance.

The surprise of recognition took her off guard, and she looked up into laughing blue eyes framed by thick, dark lashes she'd always been jealous of. She had time to register that he'd let his hair grow—a shaggy mane of ink black that curled just over his ears and collar, and a face that was covered in a short, stubbled beard—just before her legs went out from under her. She hit the carpet with a thud. A hard body pressed her into the floor, and he held her wrists captive above her head.

"Hello, Grace." His breath whispered against her skin, and she couldn't stop her traitorous body from reacting to his familiar scent. Her nipples hardened, and she arched against him. "You've been practicing. Who's your new sparring partner?"

"What do you want, Gabe?" She tried to act as if his growing erection against her thigh wasn't having any effect, but she could tell by the way he shifted against her that her attempt failed. She bit her lip to stifle a moan as he pressed against the very heat of her. He knew exactly how to weaken her resolve. They'd always been able to read each other much too well.

"I want you, of course." His lips glanced across her cheek to the corner of her mouth, and she sucked in a breath that brought her body even closer to his. After everything he'd done, he was still the only man who could make her feel less than whole when their bodies weren't fused together. She hated him for it. She hated herself for it.

"Go to hell." She struggled against him, but he just shifted his weight to hold her down.

"I've been there, thanks. Christ you feel good. Stop wiggling and we'll talk. Don't you want to at least hear my offer?"

She stilled her body and relaxed, hoping he'd get distracted long enough for her to make a move. "I don't want anything you have to offer. Just give me the flash drive."

"I figure we have exactly four minutes to get out of this place before the new guards show up for the shift change and Armageddon begins. All I'm asking is that you come back with me and listen to my offer. If you hear me out and still turn me down, then I'll give you the flash drive with no hard feelings, and you can claim your bounty."

Grace stared at him and tried to decide if he was bluffing. "I don't trust you."

"You never have. But what I'm offering will pay you more than double any of the jobs you've recently taken. Just hear me out."

"Fine. Just move your hard-on and let's get the hell out of here."

"Darlin', I have scars on my back from the last time you asked me to move my hard-on. Be careful what you wish for."

"You son of a bitch."

"So you've told me before. Let's go before Vasquez's

men get here. I've got a pickup scheduled in twenty on the other side of the border."

Grace had no choice but to follow him out of one hell and into another.

***

The woman hadn't changed a bit in seven years. She still kept her deep auburn hair braided tightly down her back while she was working. But he knew what it looked like spread across his pillow, and he knew what it felt like as it slithered like silk across his chest—glorious. He couldn't have helped his body's instant arousal at the touch of her if he'd wanted to.

He looked at her critically, trying to decipher exactly why his cock always stood at full attention when she was near. It wasn't just one thing, but the entire package. Her face was thinner now—her cheekbones more pronounced—but it was still the face of a sea goddess. Eyes the color of emeralds, slightly tilted at the corners, and full lips that he'd dreamed about for the past two years. She was every desire he'd ever had wrapped in one tiny package.

He let his gaze drift down her body. She was thinner all over. The lush curves that had haunted his memory were gone, replaced by a compact body of pure muscle and athleticism. She glanced back at him and raised her brow at where his eyes were glued.

Gabe smiled, but it didn't reach his eyes. He'd been wrong. She'd changed a lot. There was a hardness about her now that hadn't been there before. When she'd first started with the CIA, there had been hope and an ideal of the greater good. Now there was just emptiness—a cold, green stare that didn't believe in anything, and it scared the hell out of him. Because it was no one's fault but his own.

"We've just crossed the border into Venezuela by my calculations," she said, slowing to a jog. "How much farther is your rendezvous point?"

"About another mile. Keep the sound of water to your immediate left." He put his hand on her arm before she could take off again. "Wait."

She stopped dead in her tracks, and Gabe could tell she was trying to hear what he had. They were silent for a few more seconds before the sound came again.

"Shit," she said. "It's the new guards. You always did have ears like a bat."

"What do you have on you?"

"My Sig and a hunting knife. How many do you think there are?"

"No more than a dozen. They're noisy bastards. And not too fast." He pulled his own pistol from the small of his back and checked the clip. "I'll give you a boost." He replaced his weapon in his pants and laced his fingers together. He arched a brow as she just stared at him.

"I'm really tired of trees." She blew out a breath and put her foot into his hands. He launched her up so she could reach the lowest branch, and she swung herself up like a monkey.

"Do you have good visibility?" Gabe asked.

"Yeah, I see them. You'll have to draw them close enough so I'm within range."

"Try not to hit me by mistake."

"Oh, it wouldn't be a mistake," she said.

Gabe smiled and left her there to go meet trouble head-on. He found cover behind a tree trunk the size of a small car and waited patiently. Heavy footsteps crunched over twigs, and he stuck out his foot as two of them passed by. One of the guards tripped and went sprawling to the ground, and Gabe struck out at the other with a palm to the chest, stopping his heart instantly. He broke the neck of the one who was already down before the man could rise off his knees.

Gabe ignored the steady stream of fire that came from behind him, trusting Grace to not let anyone too close, and he went searching for his next victim. Only a few minutes passed before he stood in the middle of a ring of twelve guards—all of them dead. None of them had had a chance to fire a shot.

Grace was waiting for him on the ground when he caught up to where he'd left her. They both picked up their pace and ran the last mile in silence. They slowed as they came to a winding dirt road with deeply rutted tire tracks, making footing tricky. Less than a minute later, a forest-green Humvee coated with a thick layer of dust pulled up beside them. Gabe opened the back door and Grace slid across the hot leather seat.

The driver turned and looked at Gabe, waiting for instructions. Logan Grey had worked with him on other missions. He was a quiet man, tall and sinewy with muscle.

He wore his dark blond hair long, not as a fashion statement, but to help cover the terrible scars on the back of his neck. Logan was former MI6, but an almost fatal accident had gained him retirement before he was ready. Gabe hadn't hesitated at snatching Logan up to join the team. No one knew explosives better than Logan Grey.

"Get us out, and in a hurry," Gabe said. Logan glanced once at Grace and then nodded.

Gabe closed the window that divided the front and back seat so he and Grace had complete privacy.

"Who's your friend?" Grace asked.

"Logan Grey. Don't worry. He's heard all about you and still agreed to help me find you."

"I'm sure he's a real stand-up guy."

"He'll grow on you. So what do you think? This was just like old times. We always made a hell of a team."

"Tell me what you want, and then let me go. I've got a schedule to keep."

"You don't have another job lined up once you deliver the flash drive to the South Koreans. Looks like you're at loose ends." Gabe watched for a reaction closely, but she showed no surprise that he'd been keeping up with her movements. She just waited him out with silence and a hard look, and he decided to give in to the unspoken standoff just this once.

"I've left the CIA," he told her.

"I heard. Congratulations. Let me go."

Gabe smiled and stretched out across the seat, crowding her with the length of his legs, but she didn't budge an inch. "Did you hear I'd joined the private sector and opened my own agency?"

She laughed, low and sexy, and the smoky sound swirled around him until he was dizzy with desire. "So, good boy Gabriel Brennan has decided to become a bad boy and go rogue. I assume the agency is displeased by your decision?"

"Not at all. They know when something is out of their control. My agency is privately funded. Even the CIA recognizes the benefits unknown money can buy. Government agencies are still hampered by rules. Sometimes there are jobs where the rules need to be broken. That's when they call me."

"Well, bully for you. You always did manage to get what you wanted."

"Nothing could be further from the truth, and you know it," he said quietly. Gabe waited patiently for her to make eye contact. It didn't take her long. She'd never been a coward.

"I don't know anything about you, Gabe. I never did. Our life was a lie."

"How long are you going to pretend she's not sitting here between us?"

"Don't mention her!" The quiver in her voice was quickly controlled. "I'll get out of this car and disappear off the face of the planet. If you want me to stay, then the past stays in the past. It's nonnegotiable."

"Fine. Whatever you say."

The SUV slowed to a stop, and Gabe pushed the door

open, not waiting to see if she'd follow. It was a stupid idea to think he could fix things—to heal the wounds that had been bleeding for the last two years.

Gabe's Gulfstream sat ready for takeoff on the hard-packed dirt the small Venezuelan city called an airport. He went up the stairs and then turned to face Grace, sure she'd still be in the car. But she stood at the bottom of the steps, her face carefully blank.

"You can either come with me or you can leave. The choice is yours," Gabe said without emotion, tossing her the flash drive.

She caught it one handed and stared at him, studying him, trying to read every angle of the situation as she'd been trained to do at the agency. She finally nodded and started up the steps. "I'll come."

Gabe let out a breath he didn't know he'd been holding and nodded before boarding the plane. He had a feeling that before this job was over, she'd have one more reason to hate him.

CHAPTER TWO

The Gulfstream was a luxury Gabe was glad he didn't have to do without. The interior was set up like an apartment—a living area, kitchen, bathroom, and bedroom—and was comfortably decorated in muted shades of gray and navy blue. He'd spent more time in the comfortable space the last two years than he had in his actual apartment. International terrorism and intelligence had kept him busy, and working constantly helped him to forget Grace. At least he liked to think it did.

Logan climbed aboard, ignoring both of them, and immediately went to seat himself in the cockpit. A smile twitched at Gabe's lips. Logan was a man of few words.

Grace had already fastened her seat belt by the time Gabe took his own place across from her. She stared out the window as they taxied before takeoff, doing her damnedest to ignore him. A table sat between them, but it might as well have been a brick wall.

"Grace," Gabe said softly. Her gaze met his—her eyes filled with pain and coldness—and he decided she needed no less than complete honesty from him. "I want you to join my team." She opened her mouth to say something, but he hurried on before she could deny him. "You're the best there is, and I only want top agents working with me. I need you. Even if it's just for this one mission, I need you. It's important. More important than anything we've done before."

She was the best sniper he'd ever known. Her eyes could focus on a target from a thousand yards and she was brilliant enough to calculate terrain and angles in her head in a matter of seconds before taking the fatal shot. She never missed. And they'd worked well together once. She'd saved his life and the lives of others on more than one occasion.

"If I agree, I want something in return." She gripped the armrest of her seat tightly as the nose of the plane tipped up and then left the safety of solid ground behind. She'd always hated flying. A weakness he knew she despised in herself.

"I've already told you I'd double what you're getting for the jobs you're doing now. I know what you've been doing with the money, Grace, and how important it is to you. I'll give you what you need."

"I won't need the money anymore if I work for you. I want something else."

He looked at her warily, a feeling of dread curling in his stomach. He knew what she was going to ask before the words left her mouth.

"I want your help and your resources hunting down Kamir Tussad. I want his head on a platter. Take it or leave it."

The hatred in her eyes knifed through him, but he understood it. Gabe stared at her intently, all the impotent rage he'd kept bottled inside at the terrorist's name threatening to claw its way out and slash him to ribbons. He couldn't afford to be ruled by anger as she was. Anger made him less than useless. They were fire and ice, and cold logic was the only thing that worked for him. He knew if he wanted to get her on his team then he had to agree to her demand. And then they'd face the past. Together.

"Agreed. But you'll not take any side jobs while you're working for me. My company has an international reputation. A good one."

"Fine. Tell me about the job."

Gabe handed her a thick file folder. "Take a look and tell me what you see."

He waited patiently while Grace flipped through pictures and let out a long, low whistle. "It's a clean job," she finally said. "Too clean. Land this smooth doesn't occur naturally. What was in these places before they were leveled?"

"Whole communities. Houses, people, animals, children. You name it. Six tribes, sparsely populated by traditional standards, fallen off the face of the earth. South America, Central Mexico, Africa, and Australia. The fingerprint is the same at each place."

She raised a brow but didn't say anything else as she

looked through the rest of the documentation. She held up a picture of a couple, both with pale blonde hair and the kind of creases in their faces that said they spent a lot of time smiling. "Who are they?"

"John and Esther Norris. Missionaries with a Tuareg Tribe in Africa. They came back to the states because she had pregnancy complications four months ago. They arrived back with the Tuareg last week and were greeted with this." He pointed to the aerial picture that showed nothing more than a flat square of smooth dirt. "The U.S. Embassy told the Norris's they'd check into it."

"Which means they've decided to ignore it for some reason."

"You got it."

"Which is where you come in, I assume. Who hired you?"

"Frank Bennett." Deputy Director Frank Bennett had been a mentor to Gabe for fifteen of his sixteen years at the CIA.

"Very funny, Gabe. Frank Bennett is dead. Even I heard that news, and I was in a third world country with very limited communications at the time."

"He's dead because he had information he wasn't supposed to have."

"And now you have it?" Grace asked, holding up the file in question.

"That's part of it. You haven't seen the rest yet." Gabe unbuckled his seatbelt and went to the fridge to grab a couple of waters. He handed one to Grace and sat back down. "Are you curious enough to stay on board?"

"You knew I would be." Grace rotated her neck and used her water to wet a cloth napkin. She wiped the grime from her face and neck, and the action was unguarded for only a split second, but it was long enough for Gabe to see a glimpse of the vulnerability she kept hidden.

"Good. Go take a shower, and feel free to use whatever is in the closet. Everything you need is on board. We'll have plenty of time for me to tell you the rest on the way to London."

"Why the hell are we going to London?"

"Because that's where The Collective headquarters is."

"The Collective?"

"Your new employer. The rest of the team will be waiting for us there." He held up a hand before she could argue. "Yes, a team. A five-man unit all hand selected. The others have been with me awhile. It took some time to track you down. Be nice. You're the new guy."

"Great," she said, standing. "We'll be one big, happy family."

Grace went into the small bathroom and he heard the shower turn on. He knew exactly what she looked like naked, and the thought of her pale, wet body made him ache with desire. He knew without a shadow of a doubt that he was tempting fate in more ways than one. Grace was a different person than she'd been two years ago—harder—colder—but he loved her still.

He just had to prove it to her. And pray to God that she might forgive him.

CHAPTER THREE

London, England

Gabe was exhausted—his thirty-eight years felt closer to a hundred—but at least his life wasn't tied to the CIA any longer. He was free. Of course, the reason he no longer worked for the CIA was that his life had turned to shit, so he wasn't sure the levels of bad canceled each other out in the long run. Shit was still shit, no matter how you labeled it.

If his cover hadn't been blown two years ago, he'd still be accepting missions. And he knew with absolute certainty he'd be dead. He was used up. A man could only live that way so long before he lost his soul or his life. He'd come close to losing both.

But now there was Grace.

He spent the flight back to London trying to keep his

mind focused on anything but her, but it was impossible when he could smell the scent of his soap on her skin teasing his already-primed senses. All he wanted to do was sink into her wet heat and chase away the memories of the last two years with every thrust. He'd be lucky if she didn't stab him in the back in the middle of his orgasm.

He shook his head at his foolish fantasies and got up to check on her, only to find her dead to the world in his bed—her hair lying like wet ropes against her pale skin and her body restless even in sleep. She wore a pair of his sweats that swallowed her whole, and her feet were bare and delicate.

Gabe covered her with a blanket and touched the curve of her cheek with his fingers. She curled into his hand, nuzzling against him. He couldn't stop the pain that clutched his heart as he remembered how their daughter had always done the same thing. He turned and walked away before he could do something stupid like get in bed beside her and just hold her.

Gabe took his own shower and changed into black cargo pants and a black T-shirt. He spent the rest of the flight buried in work and keeping his personal life locked away. And when Grace woke a few hours later—so they could refuel the plane and their stomachs—her hair was rebraided, she was dressed in the black jeans and green silk blouse he'd put in the closet for her, and she sat across from him without uttering a word, content to pass the time with a book she'd found on his desk.

It was dusk when they left Heathrow. A gloomy drizzle settled over the city and gleamed in the streetlights like dirty diamonds. Logan handled the black Mercedes with ease, weaving in and out of the London streets with familiarity. Gabe sat with Grace in the backseat, answering questions as she read through the files again.

"We've got company, boss," Logan said, meeting his eyes in the rearview mirror. "They're trained. Two cars— one black, one tan—trading off positions since we left the airport."

"Open the screen," Gabe said and turned to stare at Grace. "Who have you been pissing off lately?"

"This tail isn't for me. I've been off the grid for two years."

"Yeah, but I was able to find you."

"Fine, maybe they're here for me. Pull over and I'll ask them nicely before I put a bullet between their eyes."

"You've always been a charmer, Grace."

"If shooting them is out, maybe you should ask yourself if anyone knows Frank Bennett sent you this information." She held up the file in question. "There are obviously leaks in Frank's office, or he wouldn't be dead."

Gabe grunted in agreement and waited while Logan flipped a switch on the dashboard. A 6 x 6 television screen came into view, showing a full view of the traffic behind them.

"Do you want me to lose them?"

"Not yet. Let's see if we can get an identification. Slow down a little."

Logan did as he was told while Gabe opened his satellite phone and pressed a number on speed dial. He switched on speakerphone and kept his eyes on the screen as it rang. The voice that answered was amused. "This is Dragon at command. Looks like you brought back trouble, Ghost. I've been watching the drama unfold from my laptop."

"Do you have a visual?" Gabe asked.

"I've got a partial face of the driver of a black Audi. The windows are tinted, so that might delay things a bit until I can get the image cleaned up. I'll run it through the system and see if we get lucky first, though. The plates are bogus."

"What about the second vehicle?"

"I don't see the secondary vehicle. Are you sure there's another?"

"We're coming up to an exit off the motorway," Logan said. "They'll switch places."

The inside of the car was tense with silence as they all watched the black sedan take the next exit.

"I still don't have a visual on the replacement vehicle," Dragon said.

"He'll be there," Logan growled. "I know how to spot a tail, boy."

"Settle down, Grim Reaper," Dragon said. "You're too uptight. When was the last time you got laid?"

"I've got a visual," Gabe said before his two agents could get into an argument. "Tan sedan at five o'clock."

"Hot damn. I guess Grim Reaper really does know what he's talking about."

"Dragon, shut up before Logan kills you," Gabe said,

rolling his eyes.

"Sure thing, Ghost. I'm real agreeable like that. I'm running the second face through the recognition program. The plates on the tan sedan are also fake."

"What do you want me to do, Ghost?" Logan asked. "We'll be at headquarters soon."

"Go ahead and lose them," Gabe said.

"What's the point?" Grace asked. "It'll only be a matter of time before they find your headquarters if they were able to track you from the airport."

"Yes, but I prefer to make them work for it. If they use computers, then Dragon might be able to lock in on their location."

A low whistle echoed through the phone line. "Damn, that's the sexiest voice I've ever heard," Dragon said. "Please tell me it belongs to the package you went to pick up. Is she single? What color is her hair?"

"Goodbye, Dragon," Gabe said and disconnected the line. Gabe caught Grace's snicker out of the corner of his eye.

"Somebody is going to kill that wanker someday," Logan muttered.

"Meaning you?" Grace asked.

"I can only hope."

Grace held on to the seat as Logan accelerated across four lanes of traffic. Horns blared, and she turned to watch the tail cars scramble to keep up. They exited onto a roundabout that had just enough traffic to make things confusing, and they disappeared into the heart of London, no trace of their followers behind them.

Half an hour later, Logan drove them up to the front gate of the building Gabe owned on Chapel Street. It was six stories of dark red brick and beveled bulletproof windows. Wet ivy drooped in planter boxes and snaked across the front of the building—a green so dark it looked black against the red of the brick.

"What's your cover?" Grace asked.

"Worthington Financial Services. It's solid. Licensed and taxed to the max. Owned by Edgar Harris. Me," he said, giving her a wolfish grin. "Your cover is Maggie Fitzpatrick, my new analyst. You'll only need the cover when you go outside the safety of the building. No one's allowed inside except for agents."

"Am I staying here?"

"You have an apartment on the sixth floor. It's furnished, and a wardrobe has been supplied, though the clothes might be too big. You've lost weight."

"I figured you'd take the top floor."

"I did," he said, smiling at the mutinous look that crossed her face. "I'm across the hall from you."

"As long as you stay on your side, we won't have a problem."

"You can't hide forever, Grace."

"I find that incredibly ironic coming from you."

Logan cleared his throat, and they all fell into an uncomfortable silence. The car was scanned, and the wrought iron gate opened smoothly. Logan parked on the short, graveled drive and turned off the ignition. Grace was out of the car before the entry guard could open the door for her, and Gabe came around and took her by the elbow. She stiffened against his touch, but he held firm as he faced the head of Worthington Financial's security team. As far as his guards were concerned, Worthington Financial was exactly what they portrayed it to be. No one except the immediate team under Gabe's command really knew what went on inside the building.

"Good evening, Mr. Harris," said the guard. He wore a dark suit and crisp tie and an earpiece was barely visible in his ear. He wasn't trying to hide the gun at his waist.

"Good evening, George. This is Ms. Fitzpatrick. She's new to Worthington Financial."

"Very good, sir." George looked Grace over dispassionately, as if memorizing her features, before turning back to his post.

"You've got a lot of security," Grace said, studying the façade of the building. "Cameras, motion detectors, retinal and thumbprint scanners once you get past the guard. Not bad."

"Financial service is a dangerous business."

"I could still get in."

"Which is one of the many reasons I want you on my side."

"Who puts in all the bells and whistles? You're good, but not that good."

"Ethan Thomas. Or Dragon, as he likes to call himself."

Grace shook her head and said, "You're kidding me.

Isn't Ethan Thomas that kid the agency was trying to recruit just before I left? The one who hacked into the Pentagon from his basement in Hoboken?"

"The one and only."

"Christ, he's an infant. What is he, fifteen?"

"He's eighteen. And he's still the best."

Grace shook her head in disbelief. "That doesn't make it any better that you have an agent who probably has to check in with his mother once a week. How'd you get him away from agency clutches?"

"I told him he could either go to prison, since he would now be tried as adult, or he could work for me as a kind of community service. The CIA didn't know what to do with him. He has a bit of an attitude problem. All I had to do was buy his mom a new house and promise he'd get to keep hacking. The kid is fucking brilliant. You'll like working with him. Eventually."

Grace's lips twitched. "Can't wait to meet him in person."

Gabe nodded to another guard at the front door and scanned himself in—first the thumbprint, then the retinal scan.

"Your thumb and retinal imprints are already in the system, and your new identity badge with photo ID is on your kitchen counter. Do me a favor and wear the badge whenever you leave the premises. You don't want the security guards to get antsy."

Grace stopped him from going inside by putting a hand on his shoulder. Gabe froze in his tracks, the heat from her fingers burning through his clothes, straight to his groin.

"You were pretty damn sure I'd come back with you. Why?"

He shifted his body so they stood facing each other. So close that he could feel her erect nipples through the thin silk of her shirt against his chest.

"Because I know the one thing that turns you on more than anything else." He whispered the words against her ear and smiled in triumph as she shivered. Her fingers clutched the fabric of his shirt, and he could see her pulse thumping wildly at the base of her neck.

"What's that?"

"Danger."

Even saying the word made her pupils dilate and her breath hitch with excitement. Gabe bit back a groan as his cock grew impossibly hard and the urge to take and conquer beat at the base of his skull. She was his woman. He knew that on the most primal level.

He nipped at her ear as he tortured them both. "The more dangerous the better. Isn't that right, Grace? The higher the stakes, the wetter you get. Remember when we were on that mission in Siberia and had to hide in that cave? Land mines and grenades were going off all around us, and you were so hot for me that I made you come with a whisper of breath and a diamond the size of my fist."

Her eyes glazed with desire before she could get herself under control, and he knew then and there that she would give him her body again before too much longer. The pull had always been too strong between them. But she wasn't quite ready yet. They still had things to deal with.

Her hands pushed against his chest, and Gabe backed away, giving her the space she wanted.

"Let's just make sure that history doesn't repeat itself," she said shakily.

Gabe smiled tightly and motioned for her to precede him into the building. Dark hardwood floors gleamed with polish, and a Persian rug in muted colors lay in the middle of the room. Fresh flowers sat on a round table in the center of the rug. To the left of the entryway was a large, glass-enclosed conference room. A mahogany table that sat twelve dominated the room, and empty bookshelves lined one wall. There were no scattered papers. No electronics. And no people anywhere in sight.

"We'll do most of our team briefings down here," Gabe said, pointing to the conference room. "All of the upper floors are for personal use by whoever's in the country at the time, or when I add new agents."

"Are you planning on expanding?"

"I've got some ideas. I don't plan on working in the field forever. I'd like to slow down a little in my old age."

"I hope it works out for you," she said, dismissing the thought. "What are those rooms?"

"The whole right side of this floor is offices. You're welcome to one if you'd like."

"No, thanks. My job's in the field. I never sit behind a desk, and I have no plans of slowing down."

"You can only go on so long in our line of business before you either slow down or get taken down. Is that what you're looking for, Grace? The easy way out?"

"I died a long time ago, Gabe. Everything from here on is just paving the way to hell."

They were stopped in front of the elevators, and he wanted nothing more than to take her by the shoulders and shake her until he rattled some sense back into her brain. But she had that stubborn look in her eye that told him the only thing he was going to get was a fight if he kept pushing.

He pulled a key card from his pocket and handed it to her, watching as some of the tension left her shoulders. He decided to lighten things up a bit for both their sakes.

"The elevator needs a key card and a palm print to open and another to take you to whatever floor you want. The fifth floor is a full gym and sauna, and there's also a lap pool. You're free to use it whenever you'd like. I wouldn't want you to get slow and sloppy. You're not getting any younger, you know."

"Jackass. I'm in my prime, and you know it." She smiled, and he literally felt his heart stumble in his chest. Her eyes were brilliant green, and it was the first time in twenty-four hours he'd seen a sign of life in them.

"Yeah, you are," he said softly.

He lifted his hand to touch her—just one touch to douse the fierce need that was building inside of him—but the elevator doors opened and ruined the moment. He stepped back and put plenty of space between them so he wouldn't be tempted to act on the lust that zinged between them like a ricocheting bullet and carry her upstairs to his bed.

***

"Mmm, mmm, mmm," a deep voice said. "You told me there'd be perks with this job, Ghost, but I had no idea. I've always been partial to redheads."

The sound of Jack Donovan's southern drawl brought Grace out of the trance Gabe seemed to have her in. He'd almost touched her. And she'd almost let him. How many times could she make the same mistake in a lifetime? Apparently, every time Gabe Brennan was in the vicinity.

"You're partial to every damned hair color on the planet," Gabe said, rolling his eyes.

"It's true. I'm a real cad. Want to be the one to reform me, sugar?"

"Well, well," Grace said. "Jack Donovan, big as life."

Last time she'd heard, Jack had been the commanding officer of a group of Navy Seals conducting Visit, Board, Search and Seizure missions in the Persian Gulf, but that had been two years ago. She remembered he'd sent pink roses to the funeral. It was weird how some memories were so clear during a time that was for the most part an absolute haze.

"Don't tell me Gabe's talked you out of the adrenaline rush of VBSS operations just to come twiddle your thumbs for him. Friendship should only go so far."

"I figure he needed someone to keep him out of trouble," Jack said, pointing to Gabe with a charming grin. "And since you're here, I have a feeling I'm going to have my hands full with that job. You two always manage to find trouble no matter where you are."

"What can I say? It's a talent."

He laughed. "Damn, it's good to see you, Grace." He pulled her into a tight hug, and she burrowed into the hardness of his chest. He was a large man, a couple of inches taller than Gabe, and thickly muscled. His dark brown hair was cut close to the scalp, and his angular face was freshly shaven. Misty green eyes made women think romantic thoughts of sonnets and white picket fences, but they got over that notion soon enough. Jack was a womanizer, plain and simple, and he was proud of it.

Tears stung her eyes, but she willed them away and held onto him a little more desperately than she'd intended. She hadn't held anyone in her arms for so long. Hadn't even touched anyone. She was a master at keeping her distance, not getting too involved or too close to anyone. It was the only way she knew how to survive. She pulled back so she wouldn't cling too long.

Gabe stared at her intently, his face blank of any thought. She already regretted her mistake of coming back with him. She wasn't ready for whatever he had in mind. Her solitude and her trigger finger were the two things that had been most important to her the last couple of years. Gabe had managed to take one of them away so far.

The elevator opened again, and a fresh-faced kid wearing sweatpants and a Halo T-shirt bounded out of the elevator. His hair was dark brown and shaggy, and she'd bet money he'd never shaved a day in his life.

"Hellooo, beautiful. What do you say you and I do a

little extra-hours work this evening?"

"Don't be obnoxious, runt," Jack said, smacking him on the back of the head. "Grace, this is Ethan Thomas. Try not to kill him. As hard as it is to believe, he actually proves himself useful every once in a while."

The kid was cute, Grace thought, trying not to laugh so she wouldn't hurt his feelings. In another ten years he'd be a good-looking man. Right now, though, he was still awkward arms and legs, his body on the thin side. Horn-rimmed glasses lay crooked on his nose, and a slow flush of anger at the way Jack had scolded him was working its way up his neck and into his cheeks.

"Listen, sweetheart. I might be young, but that doesn't mean I don't have experience. You know what I mean? I know how to treat a lady."

"Good thing I've never claimed to be a lady," she said, ignoring Gabe and Jack's laughter. "The last man who thought he wanted to share his experience with me ended up with a bullet between his eyes."

Ethan waggled his eyebrows, and he put a hand over his heart. "I think I'm in love. I've been looking for a woman who could be my protector. I've always thought I would adjust well to being a kept man. This is like kismet. Tell me your name, sweetheart, and make all my dreams come true."

Grace held out her hand, and Ethan took it automatically. Her grip was strong but nonthreatening, and it gave Ethan plenty of time to feel the ridge of callous along her finger. His eyes widened, and she gave him a smile that made the smirk on his lips and the teasing sparkle in his eyes fade.

"Grace Meredith," she said. "Gabe tells me I'll get used to working with you. I'm sure it will be a pleasure."

He snapped his hand back as if she'd burned him and looked at Gabe with an anger she wouldn't have guessed someone so young would possess.

Silence lay heavily across the room. Grace wasn't used to being the center of attention. She was used to hiding behind the rocks and taking the long, hard shots. She used Gabe as her center and didn't break his stare as Ethan analyzed her closely.

"Seriously, Gabe?" Ethan asked. "Have you lost your fucking mind?"

"Are you questioning my authority, Ethan?"

Grace winced as Gabe turned cold blue eyes toward Ethan, and she shook her head as Ethan tried to bluster his way through. The kid had a lot to learn, that was for sure, and he'd probably be lucky to seen twenty-one with the way he was going.

"She's a fucking mercenary," Ethan said, backing up a step as Gabe's expression grew more menacing. "You can't trust someone who's only in it for the money. And from the things I've heard lately, she should probably be rotting in a prison somewhere."

Jack stepped in front of Gabe before things got too far out of hand, and Grace breathed a sigh of relief. No one really knew the kind of people they'd had to be over the last decade. The kills that had to be justified, the lies and subterfuge. She and Gabe and Jack had seen and done unimaginable things. Ethan Thomas couldn't possibly know what he was dealing with when he tested Gabe like he was doing. Gabe was a good man—a fair man. But he lived by his own code and his own rules, and if Ethan Thomas overstepped himself or put any other agents in jeopardy with his smart mouth and careless ways, then Gabe wouldn't hesitate to take him out. She would have done the same thing.

"She served her country just like the rest of us did," Jack said, trying to calm things down. "And what she's done with her life since she left the CIA is her business and no one else's. You know how rumors fly. You've never stepped foot out in the field, but the rest of us have spent our lives making life-and-death decisions. And I promise you that there's not one of us who doesn't regret occasionally making the wrong choice."

Gabe stepped around Jack and advanced on Ethan with menacing purpose. Ethan finally caught on to the fact that he was in deep shit and backed away from Gabe until he hit the wall.

Gabe's voice was low, but each word was clear. "I assembled this team for reasons that you'll never know or hope to understand. It's not your place to say or question *anything* I decide to do. Everyone here starts on a clean slate. And if you have a problem with that, then you're free to leave and go through debriefing. Have I made myself clear?"

Grace winced and looked at Jack. Being debriefed was a nice way of saying that Ethan would be drugged and brainwashed until he couldn't remember who Gabe was or anything they'd been working on. She'd heard they'd tried to do that to Gabe when he resigned from the CIA and that they could never break him. Gabe was lucky he hadn't been taken out by an inside source.

Ethan stared down Gabe, trying to get his temper under control. "Yes, sir," he said between gritted teeth.

Gabe nodded and backed away, avoiding her gaze as he headed toward the conference room. "Now let's get some work done," he called over his shoulder. "Because we'll all end up dead if we don't catch this bastard."

CHAPTER FOUR

Tension vibrated in fine waves from everyone in the room, and Gabe sighed. Grace sat there stoically, pretending it didn't matter what Ethan thought about her when he knew damned well that somewhere deep inside of her it did. Jack sat beside her like a guard dog ready to defend her honor. And Ethan sat sullenly on the far side of the table. By the time Logan walked in and gave him an arched look in question at the atmosphere, all Gabe wanted was a drink and maybe a good fight.

Logan took a seat next to Ethan, and Gabe slid thick black folders to each of them.

"All of this information is in your packet in greater detail, but I'll hit the high points." Gabe took his seat at the head of the table and flipped open his folder. "Before World War II, the United States began research on a biochemical weapon called The Passover Project. It started much like its counterpart—The Manhattan Project—as an experiment for annihilation. But it was never meant for mass destruction like The Manhattan Project was with the atomic bomb. The Passover Project was meant as an assassination tool designed for one specific target. Of course, the target at the time was Hitler. All The Passover Project needed to become viable was a single strand of DNA—a piece of hair or skin cells to add to the basic formula—and the weapon would turn live. In theory, once it was launched, it could seek out its DNA match from a crowd of hundreds of thousands of people and eliminate the target once contact was made.

"Holy shit," Jack said under his breath.

"To say the least," Gabe said. "The core formula could be modified for any specific target by changing the DNA."

"I've never heard of The Passover Project before," Ethan said. "I've never even seen it mentioned in any Pentagon or CIA files."

Gabe nodded and stood up to move around the room. He never liked being in one place very long. It made him restless.

"It never came to fruition," he said. "The Passover Project began production in 1939 in an underground laboratory in Nevada. The whole purpose for experiments like The Passover and Manhattan Projects was that intelligence indicated that the Nazis were already working on similar weapons. At that point, it was just a race to see who could finish first.

"Clearance was so restricted on The Passover Project that there were only four scientists on the original development team. Dr. Josef Schmidt, a biochemistry professor from Stanford, was the project's creator and lead scientist."

"And what happened to Dr. Schmidt?" Grace asked cynically. "Knowing our government the way I do, they wouldn't let a man with that kind of knowledge live very long."

"The lab, the research, and the weapon's developer were all destroyed in an explosion before it could do what it had been created for. The lab wreckage was carefully searched, and all traces of The Passover Project were removed and taken to the Pentagon. It was hushed up and swept under the rug. Not even Roosevelt knew of its existence."

"Whoever was responsible for the explosives did a piss-poor job," Logan said, his English accent barely noticeable. "If it had been my job, my first priority would have been to make sure there was nothing to sift out of the rubble."

"Well for our sakes, I'm glad you didn't handle the demolition." Gabe went back to the table and took out the photographs he'd shown Grace on the plane. "As you can tell from the pictures, someone is trying to resurrect The Passover Project."

"Just to play devil's advocate, why would you make that leap?" Grace asked. "It does look like something bigger than an assassination attempt on one person happened in all of these photos. These places have been completely obliterated."

"You're right. But I had a little help in connecting the dots. Former Deputy Director of the CIA Frank Bennett sent me this information eighteen hours before his death. He made copies of everything that was left from the 1943 explosion site, and he included the current photos of the destruction done to these different locations. All he said in his note was that he trusted I would take care of this and find who was responsible."

"I heard Bennett's death was ruled a suicide," Ethan said. "And I'll look to be sure, but I believe that's the final ruling in Frank Bennett's CIA file. Rumor was that he was being forced to retire because of a drinking problem, and he just couldn't handle being let go. His whole life was the agency."

Ethan shifted uncomfortably in his chair as Gabe's eyes narrowed to thin blue slits and addressed the rumor in question. "Bennett was found hanged in his office, and a suicide note was left on his desk in his handwriting. The medical examiner said it was an open-and-shut case, but everyone in this room knows how easy it is to fake a suicide and forge a note. It's a basic tactic learned early on. Not to mention that Frank would be the last person I know who'd kill himself. I was the closest friend he had, and if anyone at the CIA had bothered to check before they started the rumors that he had a drinking problem, they'd know that Frank Bennett had never touched a drop of alcohol in his life because his father was an alcoholic and beat the shit out of him and his mom as often as he could. Frank Bennett was murdered."

Gabe stuck his hands in his pockets and leaned against the bookshelf. Bennett's death was still a bitter pill to swallow. The man had been like a father to him—more than his own father had ever been. There was no way in hell Frank had killed himself. Frank was dead because of The Passover Project.

"So if Frank didn't kill himself, who did?" Ethan asked.

"I don't know, but I know the documents in these folders are the reason he's dead. Frank did all the beginning legwork for us. A portion of the formula base was found in the wreckage of the lab. It seems pretty obvious by the testing pattern in these photos that someone is trying to recreate the formula. They haven't hit on the right combination just yet, but it's only a matter of time. All I know is that we have to stop whoever it is. If we find out who's behind recreating The Passover Project, then we'll find Frank's killer.

"They've got a pretty big hunting ground to choose from for these experiments," Jack said. "We can't keep eyes on every small, unknown tribe around the world. Hell, we both know there are tribes in the jungle that aren't even documented. They have languages we've never heard spoken."

"We'll start with the scientists behind the testing. The list of those capable of recreating something like this can't be long. But we have to hurry. The next step in any scientific experiment is moving to the next level—raising the bar higher. We don't want them to start testing in major cities around the world."

"If the knowledge of The Passover Project has been sitting in the CIA vaults for half a century, then it has to be someone high up who's behind it all," Grace said. "Especially factoring in Frank's death. Only someone who had high-level security clearance would know what Frank had access to."

"That's not necessarily true," Ethan said. "I hacked into top-level CIA security when I was a sophomore in high school. Nothing electronic is fail-safe. I'm guessing the only reason I've never heard of The Passover Project is that everything is still in hard copy. Breaking and entering that doesn't involve a computer isn't my style. So you're looking for someone who has access to the vault and enough money to pay off the guards, or someone that could break into Langley and sneak past the guards without being noticed. The only person I know who could do that is you, Ghost."

Ethan had his feet propped up on the corner of the table and was drumming his fingers restlessly on the arm of his chair. He seemed to be back in an affable mood, their earlier tension already forgotten. Gabe didn't remember what it felt like to be that young or carefree. And he hoped above all else that Ethan grew up soon. He'd really hate to have to kill him.

Gabe sighed. "There's always someone younger and better coming up behind you, kid. You'll learn that someday. As far as suspects to Frank's murder, no one is popping to the surface. I'm hoping you'll have more luck in that regard once you start digging a little deeper."

"So what's the mission?" Jack asked.

Gabe gave his friend a hard smile. "This is where things get fun. Bennett had done quite a bit of research on Josef Schmidt. It turns out Schmidt was a Nazi sympathizer and had plans to turn the weapon over to Hitler when it was completed."

"How do we know he didn't succeed?" Ethan asked.

"I've been digging through the German government files. Their technology is outdated, and their data is disorganized."

Ethan's eyebrows rose in surprise. "Did they know you were searching? Surely you know you leave a fingerprint every time you mess with technology. A good hacker could trace it back to here and find us." Ethan mumbled something under his breath about safeguards and amateurs.

Jack laughed at Ethan's naivety. "There's a reason why they call him the Ghost. Stick around kid, and you may learn something."

Ethan scowled at being called a kid. "It wouldn't hurt for me to double-check and make sure. No offense, but as much as any of you could kick my ass, none of you are as good as I am with computers."

"I know my way around computers, Ethan, but go ahead and take a look if it will make you feel better," Gabe said. "You're going to be going through all their files again anyway."

"Did you find anything useful?" Logan asked.

"You could say that. When the German equivalent of the CIA—MAD—was created in the 1950s, they took control of everything seized during Hitler's reign— artwork, journals, correspondence, family photos, everything. Most of the journals have been transferred to computer, and I found a very interesting reference to Josef Schmidt."

Gabe walked back to the table and sat down in his chair. A dull ache was starting to form at the back of his neck, and his eyes burned and felt gritty with lack of sleep.

"It seems Hitler met with Schmidt twice. He writes about his frustration with Schmidt because the man's demands for payment kept growing. Each time he met with Hitler, Schmidt gave him a portion of the formula. They were scheduled to meet one last time before the explosion destroyed Schmidt's lab, and Hitler planned to execute him so he couldn't sell the formula elsewhere. But Hitler only ended up with two-thirds of the formula."

"Did he write them down?" Grace asked.

"No. He painted them."

Grace sighed quietly, but even that small sound had Gabe looking at her sharply. Her green eyes were bright with anticipation, and her spine was straight. He could practically see the energy running across her skin. He leaned forward and set his arms on the table to cover the erection that had been plaguing him for the last twenty-four hours.

"That's right," she said. "Hitler was an amateur artist. He was never good enough to get accepted into the Royal Academy."

"No, but after his death his paintings were sold for millions."

"Oh, man," said Ethan. "That is wicked awesome. Where are they? Do we get to steal them?"

Gabe wanted to laugh at Ethan's enthusiasm but kept his mouth firm. God, had he ever been that young and eager? Maybe. When had the rose-colored glasses come off? After his first kill? After his twentieth?

"One of them is in the Tehran Museum," Gabe answered. "The second was bought by a private collector from a Sotheby's auction. The purchaser is hidden behind anonymous bidders and a couple of private corporations. I don't have a name yet."

"So let me get this straight," Jack said. "We're going to Iran to break into their national museum so we can destroy a painting created by the most hated man in the world?"

"That pretty much sums it up."

Gabe's gaze never strayed from Grace, and he could see the slight stiffening of her shoulders as she realized what this could mean for them. Tussad spent a lot of time in Iran. They could kill two birds with one stone. And then maybe, just maybe, once they'd taken their revenge, they could start to put their lives back together.

"Everyone get a good night's sleep," he said. "We'll start recon in the morning at 0800."

***

Jack stayed behind in the conference room when everyone else left. He'd known Gabe too long and knew in his gut that something else was going on. Gabe and Grace had always set fire to each other, and it looked like things hadn't changed much. But very few people knew Gabe's true identity, and even fewer knew he'd once had a wife and family. The two of them needed to cool it in a hurry if they didn't want Ethan and Logan to speculate.

"What the hell is going on, Gabe?"

"Isn't it obvious?"

"The part about you having the hots for your wife is *real* obvious. At least to me. I've never had a meeting before where my commanding officer sported a boner the whole time."

"Fuck you."

"I'll pass. Besides, your sex life isn't what I'm referring to, though it's damned entertaining. There's something else going on, and I want to know what it is. You two are planning something."

"Shit." Gabe closed his eyes and massaged his neck. "Have I ever told you having you for a friend is a pain in the ass?"

"Daily," Jack said.

"I don't know what the hell I'm doing. Some ideas are better in theory than reality. I need to get out of here. Let's go get a beer."

Jack unfolded his long body from the chair and followed his friend outside. The night was warm and the humidity thick. Fog rolled low across the London streets and crept into alleyways. The steady drizzle of the afternoon fell faster in darkness, and the wet soaked right through to the skin. The black lampposts that lined Chapel Street glowed a soft yellow, and umbrellas of red and black covered the heads of those walking home from work along the dismal grey streets.

Neither of them noticed as passersby veered far out of their way. They looked exactly like what they were—dangerous.

The Lamp and Light was dimly lit and sparsely populated. It wasn't one of the nicer establishments in Westminster, so the tourist crowd was always small. If you wanted booze and privacy, then The Lamp and Light was the place to go.

Jack noticed the blonde working the bar right away. He looked her over slowly from head to toe, appreciating what the leather halter top did for her breasts. He caught her eye, winked, and held up two fingers. He followed Gabe to a round corner booth and sat across from his friend.

The bartender brought the drinks herself—hips swaying in tight black jeans and the edge of a tattoo peaking from her midriff. Yum, he loved tattoos. She set the bottles on the table and laid a folded napkin in front of Jack with a number written on it in black marker.

"Christ, can't you go anywhere without attracting women?" Gabe asked. "It's damned embarrassing the way they throw themselves at you."

"I'm just sowing my oats till the right woman comes along. They'd throw themselves at you too if you didn't look so damned scary all the time. Haven't you ever heard of a razor? Maybe getting a haircut?"

"I don't want them to throw themselves at me. I'm not interested."

"Are you telling me you haven't had sex since Grace left you?"

"Excuse me for not being a man-whore like you. I happen to think marriage means something."

"You might oughta tell your wife that, you know, since she divorced you and all. Speaking of Grace—"

"Were we?"

"Tell me what's going on. Why'd you bring her in?"

Gabe took a long drink of beer, his gaze constantly moving, looking for threats that weren't there. "Because I was afraid the rumors might be true. I thought bringing her back into a legitimate game might—I don't know—make her not so hell-bent on the path of self-destruction. She's not that person. I have to at least try."

Love was a ridiculous thing, Jack thought. For something that, in his mind, didn't even exist to have the power to make a man like Gabe Brennan vulnerable when the worst terrorists in the world had been trying and failing for the last sixteen years.

"You can't choose the timetable for a person to heal after trauma. Have you stopped thinking with your dick long enough to consider she might not be ready for this?"

"Yeah, I have. We can't do this job without her. There's not a marine sniper or an agent anywhere in the world who's as good at the long shots as she is."

"I agree with you. But you're leaving something out." Jack signaled for another beer and waited Gabe out patiently.

"She only agreed to come with me if I promised to help her take out Kamir Tussad."

Jack took an unfortunate swallow of beer just before Gabe dropped that bombshell, and the bitter liquid lodged in his throat. He coughed until he caught his breath and then said, "You've got to be fucking kidding me. Are you both so desperate to die?"

"It was only a matter of time. If I could have gotten to him before now, I would have taken him out, but the man knows how to disappear. I have contacts who still keep me informed of his movements."

"Gabe," Jack said, shaking his head.

"You don't understand."

"I do, my friend. There's never a more powerful motivator than revenge. But sometimes it's hard to see the outcome from the red haze clouding your vision."

"He ripped my life to shreds with one bullet, Jack. I lost my daughter and my wife because of him. I lost everything. Grace has just given me the excuse to do what I've been dreaming about. And I can do it easier with her than without her."

Jack closed his eyes and damned all friendships to hell. That's what happened when people started mattering. The checks and balances system never got even.

"Count me in," he said. "You're going to need me. I've been across damned near every square mile of Iran with my SEALs."

"Thanks. I'll owe you."

"They don't take paybacks in hell." Jack scooted out of the booth. "You want some advice?"

"Not particularly."

"Go make love to your wife. Watching the two of you makes me feel like a voyeur."

"Yeah, except that my wife hates my guts and blames me for the death of our child. And she has every right."

"To borrow one of your favorite sayings, fuck that. Now if you'll excuse me, I'm going to go get laid before you send me to my death. I suggest you do the same."

CHAPTER FIVE

Sleep eluded Grace.

It had been a long time since she'd slept a full night through. Her mind never seemed to be able to rest. If it wasn't nightmares, it was memories. And she'd take the nightmares any day. She hadn't been that lucky tonight.

She woke up in her bed, her flesh clammy and her mind disoriented. The weight of Maddie's limp body against her own and the stickiness of blood as it soaked both of them was vivid in her mind—as if she were truly reliving the event.

She rubbed her hands over her dry, cold face. She wasn't able to cry anymore. She wasn't sure she'd really cried for two years. But it wasn't the lack of tears that worried her. It was her hands. They shook violently. And she was useless without the steadiness of her hands.

This was all Gabe's fault. It had to be. There had to be

someone to blame, and he was the only person available. He was the only one who could make her face a past she so desperately needed to bury.

How could she have been so stupid as to end up with someone like him? Frank Bennett had introduced them her first year on the job. She'd been so young—barely twenty-one—and Gabe had been her first lover. And her first commander on an assignment, which was never a good combination. But it had been fireworks from the first moment they'd touched, and somehow, they'd managed to keep their relationship a secret from everyone except Frank. That man never missed anything.

They'd lived on adrenaline and sex—one feeding the other until she was sure they'd burn each other out. But they hadn't. They'd lasted seven years and had a daughter before she realized living on adrenaline and risking your life for your country on a daily basis wasn't a good foundation for a family.

They'd never planned to have children, knowing the risks of what they did and how they lived were too dangerous, but fate had stepped in, and Maddie had been conceived on their fourth wedding anniversary while they'd been under lockdown after finishing a mission that hadn't turned out exactly as they'd wanted. They'd both been in shock after finding out she was pregnant, but there'd never been any question of not keeping the baby. They'd just promised each other that adjustments would have to be made.

They'd built a home in the country that no one knew about, and they'd raised their daughter there. And they'd been happy. For a time. Gabe would go undercover for weeks, and she'd go on her own jobs all over the world, and Maddie hardly ever got to spend time with both of them together. They never talked about their work. But they always came back to each other and loved each other fiercely until they were called away again.

And then Gabe had started to change. It wasn't a little change, but all at once. He closed in on himself, spending a lot of time alone and rarely speaking at all. He rolled away from her touch at night, and it was then she knew something was really wrong.

It wasn't until after Maddie died that she'd found out Gabe had spent twelve years building different covers and infiltrating some of the biggest terrorist organizations in the world. She thought he'd been in charge of the missions, handling other operatives and sending them out on assignments. She'd never known he *was* the mission.

Her child had died because Gabe had been one of the top men in Ahmad Sayad's organization—a man that made Osama Bin Laden look like an altar boy. Gabe and Kamir Tussad took care of Sayad's nefarious businesses while Sayad stayed hidden. Sayad was more of a figurehead than anything. It was really Tussad who called the shots. And it was Tussad who had found out Gabe was a plant. He'd destroyed them all as payment—Gabe, because his cover had been blown and he could no longer do his job with any organization—Grace, because he'd taken the one thing that had given her light.

Without Maddie, the darkness in her life crept in at her around the edges, eating at her soul. She could blame it on the CIA for making her kill. She believed in what she did. But after Maddie's death, the kills stopped having meaning.

They were just targets, not life. And she knew it was only a matter of time before the darkness overtook her completely. She could no longer function as she had been. She was empty inside, and seeing Gabe had only made her remember what she'd lost and could never have again. It didn't matter that she'd loved him. The husk of her body was no longer capable of such things.

Grace's hands finally stopped shaking, and she threw the thick down quilt that covered her aside. She tossed the T-shirt she'd slept in on the bed and pulled on a black sports bra and a pair of matching cotton shorts. She laced up her shoes, grabbed her key card and her Sig, and she escaped.

The clock in her kitchen said it was just shy of four, and she unlocked and opened her door that led into the hallway she and Gabe shared.

Silence.

She crept down the hall and rode the elevator to the fifth floor. Gabe hadn't been kidding when he'd said there was a full gym. She ran her fingers over the free weights, picked one up and tested it with slow curls. There were machines of every variety, and an entire wall of mirrors. But it was the large sparring ring and punching bags that caught her attention.

Perfect. She needed to beat the hell out of something.

She wrapped her hands with tape and found a pair of gloves that fit. The first punch of her fist against the bag sent vibrations up her arm and down to her toes. Her body came alive from the pain, and the punches came faster and the hits harder.

***

Gabe didn't know how long he stood at the edge of the room and watched her. She was like a fury—all hands and fists and feet. She looked like she was fighting for her life. Maybe she was.

She'd forgotten to braid her hair. It was pulled back in a loose tail and curled riotously down her spine. Sweat gleamed on her skin, and energy vibrated out of every pore. Her body was a beautiful machine, and toned muscles flexed and bunched with every hit to the bag.

Gabe felt the tightening in his lower body and anticipation coiled in his gut. He'd always wanted her, but seeing her again after so long turned the want into need. He knew as well as she did it would only be a matter of time before they had each other again.

He thought back to Jack's surprise that Gabe hadn't been with another woman since Grace left. He'd had women before Grace. Hell, he'd been no better than Jack. Having a different name in every country was exciting in more ways than one. He could be anybody, and there was a certain amount of excitement in sleeping with a woman who didn't know your real name or that you'd killed someone the hour before.

But everything changed after Grace. He knew there was no point being with another woman ever again. No one would ever feel as good wrapped around him while he thrust into her wet heat. No one else would come close to fulfilling him as she did.

Only she had that power over him.

Grace hit the bag hard enough that Gabe winced in sympathy. The band around her hair fell to the ground, and a waterfall of red spiraled down her back. There was no point in fighting it. He was already lost.

***

Grace stopped punching and pulled off her gloves, putting them back in the slot she'd gotten them from. She unwrapped the tape and tossed it into the trash bin before reaching down to grab her hair band. Her fingers tightened around the elastic and she realized she was no longer alone.

She turned and saw Gabe watching her out of hooded eyes. The bulge in his shorts made it impossible not to notice that he liked what he saw. Her body jumped in reaction—wanting to answer his call like a cat in heat. The electricity between them made the hair on her arms stand on end, and her nipples puckered under the black spandex of her sports bra.

"What do you say? You up for a little one on one?" He dared.

She wanted to say yes, but her mind was screaming no. "I don't think so. I've already been down here an hour. You're fresh. It hardly seems fair to me."

"Come on. I figure you want to get even with me for taking you down in Colombia. I'll even spot you a round. We'll go two out of three."

He pulled his shirt off and threw it on the ground before she could agree or disagree. God, he was beautiful. Scars and all. His body was lean, and she was distracted by the hard ridges of muscle on his chest and stomach. A thin layer of black hair curled across his chest and swirled down his stomach in a line, disappearing beneath his shorts. His shoulders were broad and his hips narrow. The two little muscular indentions just above his hip bones just begged to be bitten. She'd done it before, and he'd gone wild.

His body was a finely tuned instrument that could bring pleasure or pain in equal measures, and moisture pooled in her panties at the sight of him. He was already climbing into the ring, sure she'd follow after him. Cocky bastard.

"Agreed." She climbed in after him, the anticipation making her jumpy. Their fighting stances were different, but both effective. They circled each other, waiting for the perfect moment to strike.

"Come on, sweetheart. If I'd known you wanted to dance, I would have put some music on."

Grace swept her foot out, but he blocked it with his forearm. They kept circling, and Gabe's taunting smile was beginning to get on her nerves.

"When was the last time you were in the ring?" she asked. "You've been out of the action for a while now. I think you've slowed down with old age."

"Like hell."

He swung out, and she blocked the strike, but she felt the vibration of his powerful punch all the way up her arm. She was glad he'd pulled it.

"Besides, sometimes slower is better. You remember, don't you?"

How could she forget? Her body tingled with awareness even as her brain fought for sanity. He was fighting dirty.

"The silver hairs are new. It makes you look very distinguished." She swept her foot again, but this time followed it up with a punch to the solar plexus, and then she pushed her full weight against him to bring him to the floor. He put his arms around her to cushion the fall, but it was still like hitting a cement wall.

"Pin," she said.

"I don't have silver in my hair."

"I know." She jumped up and bounced on the balls of her feet. She knew he'd let her take him down. She could tell by the brace of his body as she hit against him. But he wasn't going to let her win again. He immediately charged at her and took her down to the mat, pulling his weight at the last minute so he didn't crush her.

"Pin," he whispered against her ear, causing her to shiver.

Sweat dripped from his hair down his face, and his body was hard against hers. She could feel his arousal, and her hips ached to push against him. Her nipples hardened, and awareness widened his pupils until only a thin ring of blue showed. He pushed off of her slowly and pulled her to her feet.

Her heart was in her throat, and the fierce need building inside of her made it hard to think. Just as he'd planned. She jumped up and sent a roundhouse to his head, but he swatted her foot aside and laughed. Their strikes at each other grew faster and harder. Their bodies closer together. Their breaths mingled, and their skin slickened with sweat, and every touch was like a flash of lightning straight to her core. She faked a punch, and he ducked, grabbing her around the waist. Their limbs tangled, and they fell together to the mat in a twisted mass of arms and legs.

They stared at each other, eyes wide, as they panted for breath. "Pin," Gabe said softly.

"Looks like you win the prize."

His erection was long and hard between her thighs, and she immediately adjusted her position so he pressed just where she wanted him to. Her fingers curled into his back, and she let out a moan full of pent-up desire and frustration as she arched against him.

"Christ, Grace."

She shivered as he ran his hands up her sides and pulled the sports bra over her head. His fingers were calloused and knew just where she liked to be touched. Her nipples stood erect, waiting for his mouth like ripe raspberries, and she threaded her fingers through his hair as he lowered his head and took what was offered. Every tug and pull of his suctioning mouth echoed in her pussy until she was soaking wet for him and writhing in need.

He licked and kissed his way across her torso, paying special attention to each breast before kissing his way up her neck to find her mouth.

"You taste good," he said.

"Please." The sounds coming from her throat were

desperate as he finally took her lips in a wet kiss—teeth and tongues sparring just as their bodies had. He was demanding her surrender, and she was afraid she'd give in.

The feel of him against her was like coming home. And it scared the hell out of her. She couldn't do this. He would open up all the wounds she'd spent the last two years cauterizing, and she couldn't let it happen. No matter what her body wanted. She stiffened as he stripped her shorts down her thighs and she felt his fingers probe at her moist center. He scraped against the swollen nub between her folds, and her body shuddered in ecstasy even as her mind screamed in denial. Her body was more than ready for him, but was mentally miles away.

Her breathing turned to desperate gasps as panic clawed at her. His cock was poised at her entrance, the plump head ready to penetrate, just as she gathered enough breath to speak.

"No, wait. Stop," she rasped.

Grace pushed against his chest, and he looked down at her, the glaze of lust in his eyes so heavy she thought he wouldn't be able to stop. But Gabe had always had an inordinate amount of self-control. He shook his head once to clear it and pushed away from her, rolling onto his back.

Grace rolled onto her side and curled into herself. Her lungs burned, and her skin was clammy with fear and unspent desire. Nausea made her close her eyes and count her breaths. She didn't know how long she'd been closed in on herself when Gabe's panicked voice finally got through.

"Grace, tell me what's wrong, baby."

He was stroking her hair, and it felt good. She brought her hands up to her face and found her cheeks wet with tears. What the hell was wrong with her? She was losing her mind. She looked around to reorient herself. Gabe's hair hung low on his forehead, and his eyes were full of concern. His chest was still bare, but he'd at least managed to put his shorts back on.

Grace pushed his hand away and sat up slowly. She was still naked, but she didn't care. She cleared her throat before she spoke.

"Sorry about that. I get panic attacks sometimes. It's no big deal."

"You scared ten fucking years off my life. It seemed like a pretty big deal to me."

"It's none of your business, Gabe. Leave it alone." She stood and gathered her clothes off the floor, stepping into her shorts and then pulling the sports bra over her head.

"If something's wrong with you, it's very much my business. Other than the obvious reasons, I also have a team to manage. I have a right to know everything down to the smallest detail about each of you."

"I can go back on our bargain any time, Gabe. Don't push me on this." She moved toward the elevator and escape.

"Grace."

The sound of his voice stopped her. It wasn't demanding or threatening, but understanding, and she couldn't deal with it right now.

"I lost her, too," he said. "I lost you both because you

ran away. You can't just bury the pain and pretend it doesn't exist. You need to talk to someone."

Grace shook her head as her eyes filled and tears threatened. But she remained in control, and her voice was steady when she spoke. "It's over between us, Gabe. Seeing you is a painful reminder of things I don't want to think about. I signed the divorce papers a long time ago, and I think it's best if everything between us from now on is business only."

Grace swiped her card at the elevator and left Gabe behind. For the second time.

CHAPTER SIX

Hazy morning light filled the interior of Ethan's bedroom, and he opened his eyes with both reluctance and anticipation. He put his feet on the floor and stretched, knocking over an empty coffee cup on his nightstand along with a smattering of papers. He swore and reached for his glasses, though they didn't clear the sleep from his eyes. He grabbed his pajama pants off the floor and stumbled into them before shuffling to the bathroom.

When he came out, the smell of coffee greeted him, and the last lingering dregs of sleep faded as he realized someone had breached his security. He grabbed the closest thing to him, which happened to be a shoe, and crept into the main room as adrenaline flooded his system. Fear lodged in his throat, making it difficult for him to swallow as he ran probabilities and the implications of what a breach would mean. The others had to be dead or captured.

His thoughts spiraled out of control with every step he took closer to danger. What had he done wrong? He should have been alerted the moment someone stepped foot in the hallway outside his apartment. He'd never had problems with his security before. No one had ever been able to breach it. Well, except for Gabe, but that was to be expected of the guy in charge.

"Are you planning on shoeing someone to death?" A cold voice asked from his right.

Ethan whirled around to find Grace leaning against his kitchen counter, a cup of steaming coffee in her hands. She was dressed in a threadbare grey T-shirt and worn jeans, and her hair was braided loosely down her back. At first glance, Ethan thought she looked closer to his own age, but her eyes held an experience and wisdom that most people never achieved. There was no doubt in his mind that she'd earned every inch of her reputation.

"How in the hell did you get in here?" Ethan asked.

He felt the flush of embarrassment working its way up his neck, and that only intensified his anger. His system had not only failed, but *she* had been the one to do it. He dropped the shoe and ran to the front door, tripping over the corner of his rug and barely catching himself on the corner of the couch before he face-planted on the tile. He ignored the sting to his pride, too curious to see what she'd done to the system he'd installed. He opened the panel in the wall, but everything was just as it should be. The wires were intact, and the red light was engaged, just as he'd left it the night before.

The muscles in his back tensed, and his palms were damp with sweat. He turned around slowly, wondering if he could make it out of the building before she got him. He'd seen the looks Gabe had been giving him lately. He knew the team didn't trust him completely. Didn't think he could handle the pressure or remain loyal to what they were doing. Well, screw them. He knew damned well where his loyalties lay, but he wasn't going to stop having fun just because everyone else was *old*. And it might be perverse, but he was having a good time seeing how far he could push Gabe before the man snapped completely.

"Relax, Ethan. I'm not here to kill you," Grace said.

"Well, that's a relief. Like you'd even tell me if you were." He wiped his sweaty palms on his pants and headed back to the kitchen.

"Look at it this way. If I were, you'd already be dead by now. Here, it looks like you could use some of this."

He took the coffee she offered him, his mind split between thinking he was going to die and wondering how she'd breached his system. Ethan drank from his cup deeply and winced at the bitterness that touched his tongue. The coffee tasted like it had been boiled a week and stirred with a leather boot.

"Never eat or drink anything someone you don't know or trust offers you. It could be poisoned. Spy School 101."

"Is that a joke?" He ran his tongue along his teeth and waited for something to happen, for the bitter taste of arsenic on his tongue or foam to start bubbling from his lips, but there was only the bitter remains of too-strong coffee.

"I never joke."

"My mistake." They stood in uncomfortable silence for

a few minutes—or at least he was uncomfortable. She had a way of looking at him that made him think she could see into his soul. It was a little disconcerting.

He grabbed some cereal from his cupboard and ate it dry out of the box. "What did I do wrong with the system? How did you get in?"

"It's a good system. You had a couple of secondary traps set up that I've never seen before, and I don't see anyone outside of this group getting past your security. It took me almost fifteen minutes to get in, and if I was on a mission I would've had to abort. If it makes you feel better, probably Gabe and I are the only two people in the world who could've gotten in. We used to practice B&E for fun. It keeps you sharp."

Ethan relaxed a little at her explanation, though he was already thinking of ways he could tighten the system. A couple of more secondary trips and maybe a body-temperature sensor would take care of it. She'd thrown down the gauntlet, and he was determined to best her.

"So you and Gabe have worked with each other a lot, huh?" he asked, curious to know more about the man who didn't seem to have a past. Whose records had been wiped so clean there wasn't a trace of him anywhere. And Ethan had certainly looked. Hell, he wasn't even sure if Gabe Brennan was his real name.

Her lips quirked in either a grimace or an attempt at a smile, he couldn't be sure which, but she didn't answer the question.

"Now that we've had our moment of bonding, you might want to change out of your jammies for our recon meeting. Jack lives to torture, and he'll be here in about thirty seconds."

Even as she said it there was a knock at the door.

"Punctual as always."

Ethan speared his fingers through his hair and went to do just that, not sure if he'd passed or failed whatever test she'd just given him. At least he was still alive.

***

"This is very cool," Jack said, circling the table of a 3-D hologram of the National Museum in Tehran. "Nice going, kid."

"We'll need at least two men on the inside," Grace said. "Two more on point, and then Wonderboy here can set up as home base."

"Three on the inside would be better," Ethan said. He changed screens so the interior of the museum glowed with blue lights. Splotches of red lit up where cameras were located, and green lines crisscrossed in the main showroom where infrared beams rotated on a timer.

"That's too many bodies," Grace argued. "Three gives the opportunity for someone to get left behind if things go to shit."

"Agreed," Jack said. "Two can do it. Where's the entry point?"

Ethan narrowed the hologram to a small section. "The roof. They've got skylights, but I've got something to get through the security there."

"What about guards?" Grace asked.

"That's where things get tricky. The guards are hired guns, no more than a couple dozen, and only a handful of those are official employees on record. The government is still pretty shaky with the new transition, and money is scarce, so they've hired out without asking a lot of questions to fill holes. There have been threats against some of their national treasures, so that's why security at the museum has been upped.

"There are a lot of factions who still oppose the Iranian government, and from the background checks I've done on some of the guards, they definitely fall into that camp. We could always try to pay the guards off. Several of them are barely scraping by."

"No. Too big of a chance that one of them will cave under pressure if questioned." Jack rubbed the back of his neck. "Let me make some calls. I have a few men I trust who are still in the area. We need to know exactly how many we might be facing in and outside the building. We've got a good start here."

Grace's laptop beeped from the living area, and she went to see what it had come up with. Ethan's apartment was set up much like hers. An open living space where there were no walls between the kitchen and dining room, and a private bed and bath off the kitchen. The only difference in their spaces was that Ethan had a large workroom filled with electronics and his 3-D Hologram machine, which he for some reason felt the need to christen Wanda. The furniture in Ethan's apartment was more masculine and modern than hers—sleek black leather and glass tables—and he definitely had more clutter. There was a basket of clean clothes on the floor, computer parts and gadgets on every available surface, and a video game console and wires scattered every direction.

She stepped around the mess and sat on the edge of the sofa, pulling the laptop closer to the edge of the coffee table. She'd been running probable scientists and doing research on them since she'd left Gabe in the gym the night before. There was no way she'd have been able to go back to sleep after that fun encounter. So work had been her only option. Ethan and Gabe weren't the only two who knew how to use a computer, though she wasn't afraid to admit that her skills came nowhere close to theirs.

"What's up, Red?" Jack called from the other room. "Anything exciting?"

"I think I've got a hit on a scientist who's a viable candidate for recreating The Passover Project. I did some research last night and ran some probabilities, and less than half a percent of all scientists at various universities and institutes around the world have the genius to even guess at a formula as complex as this. And the percentage shrinks even more when you narrow the scientific field. We're looking at four, maybe five men who can pull this off."

"So who's your top pick?" Jack asked.

"The deeper level background checks just finished, and it looks like a Dr. Allen Standridge quietly resigned from MIT three years ago after a couple of graduate students complained they saw him experimenting on human test subjects without the people's knowledge. It was never proven since it was their word against his, and Dr.

Standridge insisted the students were just holding a grudge because he'd rejected their theses. But it made the MIT board nervous enough to ask for his early retirement and resignation."

"And what's Dr. Standridge been up to for the past couple of years?" Jack asked.

"That's the million-dollar question. He's disappeared, or at least he's hidden himself well enough that my limited tracking abilities can't find him. I couldn't find a death certificate or an obituary. And his name's not attached to any new project. I figured I'd turn this over to Ethan. He'll be able to dig deeper."

Ethan followed Jack into the room, his glasses skewed on his face and his hair mussed. "Rad. I like spying on other people. You find out the damndest things. They're strange."

Jack snorted out a laugh, and Grace buried her face in the computer so Ethan wouldn't see her smile. God, everything about this mission felt odd to her. She'd cut herself off so completely for the last two years that being around anyone was a culture shock. Guilt ate at her. She shouldn't be smiling and enjoying the excitement of starting a new team mission while her daughter was buried in the ground back in Virginia. Not while her murder was still unavenged and the monster who had killed her was roaming free.

Her smile disappeared, and she watched Ethan pull a can of soda from the fridge and pop the top, oblivious to their amusement or anything else. She and Jack had been rotating the room, checking their positions in the windows and watching for anyone outside who happened to pass by the building more than once or seem too interested. They'd been doing the things they'd been trained to do to stay alive. But Ethan just existed in his own world. He'd make a terrible field agent, and she hoped to God they didn't get him killed. She had enough blood on her hands.

"What are you guys staring at?" Ethan asked, his drink to his lips. Grace looked at Jack and she could tell he'd just had the same thought. Ethan was either going to be a great help or a huge hindrance. Only time would tell.

A hard knock on the apartment door kept them from having to answer Ethan's question. Gabe came into the room, his iPad cradled under his arm and his phone in the other hand.

"We've got another infection site. It's the same MO," he said, placing his things on the coffee table before looking at Grace.

The tension in the room skyrocketed, and she broke his gaze, returning her attention to the computer screen. She heard Jack mumble something profane under his breath, and Ethan, as unworldly as he was, asked, "What's going on?"

Gabe headed into the kitchen and came back with a cup of coffee. He took a sip and grimaced, and Grace felt a small satisfaction at his pained look.

"Christ, Grace, do you always have to boil it to death?" Gabe went back into the kitchen and poured milk into the mug.

Jack broke the tension by picking up Gabe's iPad and scrolling through the pictures of the new infection site he had stored on it. "This site isn't wiped clean like the others. They didn't finish the job."

"No," Gabe said. "I've been monitoring the World Health Organization's communications since Bennett sent me that package a couple of weeks ago. I got a hit about five a.m. from a panicked caller in central Mexico that a small native tribe was showing signs of an unknown virus. There are more than a hundred dead, but they're at the seventy-two hour mark, and there are still survivors."

"Maybe it really is an isolated epidemic," Grace said.

"Maybe, except a witness came forward and said a white man had been asking for directions to the village. The WHO doctors at the site said they've never seen any type of virus like this one before. They said it's unheard of for a disease that takes affect so quickly and violently to stay contained within one tribe."

"So the question is, what's the nature of that particular tribe—that it only affected them and no one else?" Grace asked.

"Bingo," Gabe said with a nod. "The Ahnimado Tribe prides themselves on being pureblood. They're a tribe of less than a hundred people who all share the same genes. Marriages must take place within the family, and no outsiders are allowed in their village."

Grace took the iPad from Jack and looked at the pictures. "So if we assume whoever made this batch of The Passover Project used a specific Ahnimado's DNA as a test for the weapon, then we can also assume that they're getting closer to finding the formula. The Ahnimado have all fallen ill because they share common DNA linked to their pureblood lineage."

Gabe nodded and said, "The virus doesn't seem to be contagious, and the doctor said they didn't have much hope for the remaining survivors. It's as if they'd all been purposely wiped out."

"Did the witness give an ID of the man?" Jack asked.

"I've just put Logan on a plane to go find out. He's going to check out the site in person and see if there are any survivors who are able to speak." Gabe turned to Ethan. "Is there progress on the museum?"

"Jack has some ideas," Ethan said, shrugging. "I just build the incredible machines. Someone else does all the real work."

Jack rolled his eyes. "We've got the basics, but I'll feel better about it after I contact some people. The kid has the design of the structure right, and we could get in and out if that was all there was to it. It's the nonelectronic aspects that are going to give us the most trouble. Bullets beat machines any day."

"Let me know if you need any help," Gabe said, gathering his things and heading for the door. "Grace, I need to speak to you a moment."

Grace followed Gabe reluctantly into the hallway, aware that two curious stares followed them out. She closed the door behind her and leaned back against it, crossing her arms over her chest and mentally preparing for Gabe to bring up what happened between them earlier that morning.

"I have a contact who said Tussad is visiting his sister in Abadan."

Grace straightened from the wall, the news not what

she'd been expecting. "What? How long has he been there? How did you find out so fast? Dammit, I've paid contacts near there to let me know as soon as he steps foot on Iranian soil. Why the hell wasn't I contacted?"

"We both know that what you're paying your contacts can be beaten. It's why you agreed to this deal in the first place. My pockets are deeper than yours. Besides, I've had all your communications intercepted since you've been here."

"Goddammit, Gabe—"

"You work for me now, Grace. You agreed. No outside jobs. I gave you my word we'd get Tussad. I'm delivering."

"You can't cut me off from my contacts completely. I won't be here working for you forever."

"Maybe not, but we'll cross that bridge when we come to it." He waited her out while she fumed silently. There was no way he was going to let her go back to the life she'd been living the last two years. Not even the most hardened criminals lasted long in that kind of work.

"Fine. Tell me about Tussad."

"He's been in Abadan since early yesterday morning. It's up to you if you want to try and flush him out now or wait until later."

Gabe's face was unreadable as he waited for her to make a decision.

"Does your contact think he'll still be there by the time we can fly in?" she asked.

"According to my contact, Tussad is there for the

three-day birthday celebration of his mother. He'll be there at least another twenty-four hours."

Grace nodded and swiped her card in the elevator. "Then we don't have a moment to spare. I assume you have a weapons room in this monstrosity?"

"You could say that."

"Good. When do we leave?"

CHAPTER SEVEN

Washington, D.C.

William Sloane had just sat down to breakfast on his private terrace when his butler tapped gently on the door.

"Excuse me, sir. There's a Mr. Shawn Kimball at the door. He's quite insistent on seeing you, though he's not on your list of callers for the day. He said you'd want to hear what he has to say. Should I send him away?"

"I'll see him. Send him in, Peters."

"Very good, sir."

Peters backed out of the room, and Sloane slathered his English muffin with butter. He glanced at his watch and saw it was just after seven. He had meetings that started at eight, and he was already dressed in an expensively cut suit the color of charcoal. Ruby cufflinks glinted in the sun when he turned his wrists just right, and business documents sat neatly stacked at his elbow.

He was an affluent man, though a busy one, and nothing could ruffle the calm exterior and quiet determination that had made people give him the nickname of Bulldog over the years. He didn't take his attention from the meal or papers in front of him as soft-soled footsteps made their way closer. He chewed quietly and looked out at the blooming gardens he'd had built in the back of his Georgetown home.

"Come in, Kimball. Have a seat."

Sloane watched the large man out of the corner of his eye. Kimball reminded him of a hulking cat, ready to spring. Dark brown hair that always needed a cut and a body like a linebacker. But it was the coldness and pure evil in Kimball's muddy brown eyes that had caused Sloane to hire him. And the fact that the man had a unique brain hidden under the obvious brawn. He was a man easily underestimated.

Sloane frowned as Kimball helped himself to a cup of coffee and propped a booted foot on one of the dining chairs.

"I take it you didn't come to see me for breakfast," Sloane said, not bothering to let his irritation show.

"You told me to dig into everything Frank Bennett was involved in, retrace all of his steps over the last month. Have you changed your mind?"

Sloane still regretted that he hadn't found out about Frank Bennett digging around in classified files before Frank stumbled across The Passover Project. If Bennett had waited even twenty-four hours to snoop around, all of the files would have been gone. But Bennett *had* found them, and taken all the information back to his home. It would have only been a matter of time before Bennett found out who was behind The Passover Project's resurgence. Bennett had been a good man—a useful man. But Sloane didn't regret for a minute having Kimball take him out, especially once Bennett started asking the wrong questions.

"Not at all," Sloane said. "Did you find something?"

"Possibly. Bennett used the CIA courier service to have a package delivered to London. I don't know what was in it, but it was signed for by an Edgar Harris."

"What do you have on Harris?"

"Not a damned thing. On the surface Harris is a forty-four year old financial investor with a prosperous business, Worthington Financial Services, LLC, located on Chapel Street. He's divorced with no children. Pays his taxes. Makes twice yearly visits to another home in the south of France."

"What are you not telling me?"

"I had one of my men put the business under surveillance. The place is more secure than Fort Knox. It's a hell of a setup, and it made my Spidey senses tingle, so I've had my men following Harris to see what he's been up to. He flew in on his private plane from a location that was undisclosed, and I couldn't get hold of the pilot to try and persuade him to tell me the location. Most of Harris's employees are former military intelligence, so they're always on the lookout."

Kimball grabbed a muffin from the basket in the center

of the table and tossed it all into his mouth, scattering crumbs across the table and his shirt.

"Harris knew he was being tailed, and his driver lost my men, but I already had the address Bennett sent the package to, so I sent them on to do surveillance and watch the comings and goings. It turned out my Spidey senses were right. My men emailed me a couple of photos late last night."

Sloane took the photos from Kimball and stared at the two men leaving the financial firm. "Should I recognize them? Which one is Harris?"

"I don't know, but I ran their photos through the database and got a hit. Jack Donovan is the second man. He's a recently retired Navy SEAL commander. Served two tours in Afghanistan and was in charge of all the VBSS missions after 9/11. He's a damned war hero and has gotten every commendation imaginable. He's been a guest of the President twice. All of his classified files have been encrypted by someone outside the CIA. I have one of my men working on it."

"Interesting that he'd relocate to London. What's he doing there?"

"No clue. After he retired from the service, he fell off the grid. Traveled around a little, then seemed to decide on London. His mail is sent to a private post office box. But he has no physical address that I can find. His family lives in Texas, but he doesn't get home often, though he does keep in touch with email."

"Did Donovan know Frank Bennett?"

"Oh, yeah. The SEALs loaned Donovan out to the

CIA on several occasions. Frank Bennett was always the DDO—Deputy Director of Operations—of record. And from what I could find out, they were also personal friends."

"What about the second man?"

"No fucking clue. I can't find a likeness anywhere in any database. He doesn't exist."

"Not good," Sloane said. "He's got to be government of some kind to disappear like that. For now keep your sights on Jack Donovan. Maybe have your men detain him for questioning."

"How much do you care about keeping Donovan alive?"

"I don't want him dead. Yet. Just do what you have to do to get him to talk. I want to know what was in that package Frank Bennett sent. If it's what I think it is, then I've got a big problem."

"I'll keep digging on the mystery man. Eventually, someone will know who he is. I may have to go up pretty high on the food chain to do so."

Sloane knew what Kimball was asking. Higher up on the food chain could include heads of state and five-star generals. Kimball would only have to break one of them to get the answers he needed. And Sloane knew from experience that Kimball was very efficient at getting information.

"Do what you have to do," Sloane finally said. "I'll clear any paths for you if you need me to. There are a lot of people who owe me favors. They'll keep quiet and should cooperate."

Kimball nodded and left. Sloane took another sip of coffee and looked at the photos of Jack Donovan and his companion. Frank Bennett hadn't been a stupid man. He'd only send sensitive information to the person he trusted the most. Sloane just had to find out who that person was.

"Peters," he called out.

"Yes, sir?"

"Cancel all my meetings. I need to work from home this morning."

"Anything else, sir?"

"Get the President on the phone."

CHAPTER EIGHT

Kuwait

"My contact knows me as Amir Shahzad," Gabe said as he loaded a large black case in the back of the Jeep. He covered it with a tarp and got behind the wheel. Grace finished loading bottles of water under the seats and slid in beside him. Her hair was covered with a long black scarf—a *hijab*—and she wore a loose white shirt, khaki cargo pants, and lightweight boots that were made for traveling over sandy terrain.

"Do you trust him?"

"My contact? Absolutely not. He's a merchant in the city and is bought easily enough. Our arrangement has worked out so far, but he's a businessman."

Gabe slipped sunglasses over his dark brown eyes. Between the contacts and his beard, he was pretty damned uncomfortable. Like Grace, he wore desert-colored cargos and a white linen shirt. He was grateful for the loose black turban that hung over his head and protected him from the blistering sun that shone like a ball of flame in the cloudless blue sky. It was going to get a lot hotter before they got where they were going.

Gabe put the Jeep in drive and they left Kuwait with minimal fuss, heading across the border with the fake IDs that had served him well during his days with the CIA. "We'll be given shelter for the night once we arrive in Abadan, and then we'll leave to find Tussad once the city sleeps. They have imposed curfews because of the bombings, so we shouldn't have to wait too long."

"Won't your contact find it strange you're bringing a woman with him?"

"Not necessarily." Gabe felt her stare, but he kept his eyes on the treacherous road as they bumped their way over the mountains and closer to the city. They still had another four hours to travel by car before they reached the entrance to Abadan. If he was a weaker man, he would have blushed under her gaze. He knew that look better than anyone. And he knew it meant trouble.

"So he's used to you bringing women with you when you visit?" she asked, her voice calm even as her eyes spit green fire.

"It helped with my cover. It's been three years since I last saw him."

"You mean you were bringing strange women with you here while we were still married?"

"Dammit, I told you it was part of the cover. It's not like I slept with any of them. Believe me, I've never for one second forgotten that you are my wife."

"I *was* your wife," she said.

Gabe didn't bother to correct her. It probably wasn't a good time to mention he'd never signed the divorce papers. As soon as they'd been delivered, he'd promptly shredded them and gotten rip-roaringly drunk. It hadn't been one of his finer moments. But he was still married in the eyes of the law, and that's all that mattered.

The sun was quickly fading, and its heat pulsed in waves of bright orange off the sand, making the tiny grains shimmer like glass and the barren land before them waver like a picture going in and out of focus. They were fortunate the scorching days were tempered by cool nights, and that they'd brought plenty of water. The desert wasn't forgiving to those who weren't prepared.

The rest of the drive was made in silence as they traveled farther and farther into hostile territory—both of them had their pistols ready on their laps. When the transition from day to night passed, they both pulled on their night-vision gear, their attention never wavering from the numerous hiding places the mountains provided.

"I've got something," Grace said. "Two o' clock, about a hundred and fifty yards ahead."

"I see him. That could be Kareem. He's a little heavier than the last time I saw him, but the posture is right."

"I don't like this, Gabe. There are too many good places to hide in these mountains. We might as well have targets on our foreheads."

"Where would you go if you were going to pick us off?" Gabe asked.

Grace looked her options over and pointed to the left. "Up that steep ridge there. I'd have visibility of anyone coming or going through the pass."

"Keep your eyes in that direction. I'll keep watch in front. My contact has a submachine gun slung over his arm, and he's ready to use it."

"The merchant business must be rough. Tell me what my cover is."

"You're my American wife, of course." Before she could sputter out a refusal, he said, "Pretend like you can't understand what we're saying and hide your weapon. He won't expect you to have one."

She did as she was told for once, shoving the gun in her black duffel bag, but not before shooting him a vicious glare. "You're going to pay for this."

"I can't wait."

A stream of Kurdish came in their direction. "Is that you, my friend, Amir?"

Gabe answered him back in the same tongue. "It is, my friend Kareem. *Salaam alaykum.*"

He slowed the Jeep to a stop beside a plump man dressed in black slacks and an oversized olive-green canvas jacket. The man's hair was thin on top, but a thick beard peppered with gray covered his face. They clasped hands affectionately.

"How are you, Kareem?"

"Not well, my friend. Come. I will take you to my home and tell you all about it." Kareem ignored Grace as he climbed into the Jeep beside her and pushed her closer to Gabe.

Gabe followed the desert road several miles before there was any sign of civilization. The town was just a shadow of what he remembered it being. "What happened here?"

"Abadan is too close to the border. There were bombings more than a year ago, and most of the people fled inland. Some left the country altogether. My wife and youngest son were killed. The rebuilding is slow, and it is even slower to repopulate."

"I'm sorry for your loss, Kareem. Your wife was a faithful woman. Has your business suffered much?"

"Your words are kind, my friend. My business has suffered greatly, but I've managed to find my way."

Gabe drove slowly through the deserted streets as Kareem gave instructions to his home. Businesses and houses of pale colors with traditional flat roofs passed by. Trees were scarce and those with money seemed to be even more scarce, but he noticed as they pulled onto Kareem's street that the merchant was obviously doing very well for himself.

The wind was high, and dust swirled around them as Gabe parked the Jeep to the side of a house made of smooth white stone. It was two solid stories and had a balcony on the upper level. The downstairs windows were large and square, and covered with heavy drapes to protect from the sun. It was larger than most of the other houses on the street and had a row of palm trees flanking each side.

Gabe grabbed both his and Grace's belongings, and

they followed Kareem inside. A young girl of about fifteen opened the door before they reached it.

"This is my daughter, Sarala. She will show you to your room and provide you with food and drink. I'm sure you're famished after your journey. We will speak in the morning about why you've come."

"I'll look forward to it, but don't trouble yourself providing us with food and drink for the night. We can wait till morning." Gabe said.

"I insist, my friend."

"Then I give you my thanks."

Kareem nodded and disappeared down a long hallway, and Gabe ushered Grace up the stairs behind Kareem's daughter. She was small, and she kept her eyes lowered as she opened the bedroom door for them.

"Tell your father thank you for the offer, but my wife and I are really much too tired after our travels to eat tonight."

She nodded silently and closed the door behind her, leaving them alone. Gabe held his finger to his lips and warned Grace not to say anything. She nodded and unwrapped the scarf from around her head.

The room was lovely, decorated in shades of gold and cream and white. A large bed, covered by a white comforter threaded with gold, sat low to the ground, and two beautifully carved wooden chests flanked each side. The finely woven rug on the floor was the only color in the room—a jewel-toned red.

Gabe upended the backpack he carried on the bed

while Grace checked the room over. He stuffed extra magazines in the pockets of his cargo pants and tossed a couple to Grace so she could do the same. He put a backup piece in his ankle holster—a 9mm Ruger—and a seven-inch blade in a sheath that fit around his thigh. His double shoulder holster had two Sig Sauer SP2022s fully loaded and ready to go. He wrapped a circle of wire loosely around his hand and slipped it into his jacket pocket.

Grace was already outfitted with her own weapons and waiting for him in the bathroom. He turned on the shower and she turned on the sink. He drew her into his arms in an easy embrace and ignored the stiffening of her body.

"What's wrong?" she whispered against his neck.

He breathed in the scent of her hair and couldn't help his body's reaction. The adrenaline running through his veins only intensified it. "I've got a bad feeling. Something seemed off with Kareem. I want to go now and flush out Tussad."

"Do you know how to get to him?"

"Kareem said he's staying with his sister, but I don't believe it. I had Ethan check CIA records before we left, and it shows Tussad has a brother-in-law and a cousin who own property in Abadan. The brother-in-law has a wife and five children under one roof, so it isn't likely he'd be staying there. The cousin has been missing for the last eight months, but someone is still paying his bills. We'll start there and hope we get lucky."

"How far? Will we need the Jeep?"

"It's less than a mile down the road. We can run it."

She nodded and tried to pull out of his grasp, but he

didn't let her go. She looked up at him with wary eyes, and the feel of her against him was so right that he couldn't do anything but kiss her.

"For luck," he said, and lowered his mouth to hers.

He kissed her at each corner of her mouth first before tasting her full bottom lip with the tip of his tongue. Her breath hitched, and her mouth opened, and Gabe couldn't resist the temptation. Her lips were soft and moist, and he groaned as her tongue gently rubbed against his own. This wasn't the frantic mating of mouths from the night before. This was remembering. And savoring.

Gabe pulled away slowly, pleased to see the dazed look in her eyes. He leaned around her and reached to turn off the faucet, but his body pressed more into hers and she let out a small whimper. He wanted to whimper himself as she pressed back against him, but he held back from tempting himself even more.

She inhaled an unsteady breath before ducking under his arm to turn the shower off, and Gabe felt the loss of her warmth immediately. He went to the window and pushed back the heavy curtains that insulated the room against the hot afternoon sun and muttered a curse.

"What?" Grace whispered.

Gabe pointed to the window and the iron bars that covered it. They had no choice but to go out the front. He dropped the curtain and went to the door of their room to listen for movement in the hallway. His weapon was in his hand and he eyed Grace as she moved into an automatic position to cover his back. He unscrewed the doorknob so it fell off in his hand, and the door opened soundlessly. He caught the doorknob on the outside quickly before it fell to the wooden floor.

The hallway was deserted, and he moved like a ghost through the house and out the front door, Grace shadowing his every move.

"Do you think the bars are to keep us in or others out?" Grace asked as they took cover behind the house next door.

"I don't know, but we'll assume the worst." Gabe pulled out his GPS and looked at their position. He pointed to the west side of town and said, "We'll take cover every twenty feet just to be safe. If Tussad is there, we'll do whatever necessary to flush him out."

"And if he isn't?" Grace asked.

"Then we'll gather more intel and try again. I won't go back on my word, Grace."

She nodded, and he closed his eyes, letting the adrenaline rush through his body, and he opened his senses. The night was quiet, but that was to be expected of a town so sparsely populated. The air was cool, and it wouldn't be long before the excitement of the chase stopped warming their bodies and they were left shivering in the desert night.

They ran in short, silent sprints. The farther they ran, the less evidence there was of the well-kept, prosperous city of Abadan. This part of the city had been abandoned after the bombings. Homes and buildings were no more than ruins. Cars lay on their sides or crushed under large slabs of rock. A mosque was completely intact from the front, but as they ran around the side they saw the entire middle had been torn apart. And just as some of the buildings were completely destroyed and had no hope of repair, there were others that stood perfectly intact.

This was the part of the city people had decided to forget. They'd taken what was left of their belongings and moved to the other side, where they could pick up their lives and move on. It was the perfect place for someone like Tussad to lie low for a few days.

The GPS vibrated in Gabe's pocket, and he signaled to Grace to take the opposite side of the small white rock house. It was no more than a shack really. Barely standing a few inches over six feet, the roof was made of rushes tied together and packed with mud to keep out dust or rain. The hum of electricity was nonexistent. There was nothing anywhere to indicate any kind of life inhabited the premises.

Gabe signaled with his hands again to Grace, and she nodded with understanding. They'd go around opposite sides and meet at the back of the structure.

"There's no one here," she said disappointedly as they came back together.

"No," Gabe agreed. There were chinks missing in the mortar, and it hadn't been difficult to peek in and see no one was hiding inside. It was hardly more than one large open room. "Let's go inside and check it out."

He pulled the powerful flashlight from one of his pants pockets and waited until they were inside before turning on the light. Even then, he left it pointed at the ground so the beam couldn't be seen from the outside.

"Nothing but cobwebs," he said, moving his light

around the room.

The choked scream had him whirling around and searching for the threat with his weapon and the flashlight aimed and ready. When the beam hit Grace, he watched with complete surprise and horror as a woman who had a reputation for never losing her cool in a bad situation drained of all color and collapsed in a dead faint on the dirt floor.

He ran as fast as he could, but he couldn't make it to her in time to catch her. He dropped the flashlight, but held tight to his weapon as he felt for the pulse in her neck. It was fast and thready, and her color wasn't good. He felt up and down her limbs to make sure nothing was broken, but she was physically fine. He didn't know about mentally.

Gabe grabbed the flashlight and stood slowly, moving it in a sweeping arc on the side of the room Grace had been on. The light reflected off something on the table, and he moved closer so he could see.

His blood ran cold, and a fury he thought he'd buried came rushing to the surface as he looked at the scattered photographs on the table. They were all of him and Grace and Maddie. Taken just days before their lives had been destroyed.

His eyes rested on the largest photograph—one of his daughter's lifeless eyes as she bled in Grace's arms—and he promised himself that Tussad would die a terrible, painful death.

CHAPTER NINE

London

"I've got him," Ethan said, a big grin on his face. "Dr. Allen Wilbur Standridge. His house was purchased by The Darwin Corporation, which has no owner or CEO as far as I can tell. But the dumbass loves to order online, and he uses his real name every time, though the credit card he uses also trace back to Darwin."

"Arrogance," Jack said. "He's got someone protecting him. What else have you got on him?"

"Other than he gets his groceries delivered twice weekly and all the porn he buys has a distinct BDSM feel, not much of anything. He stays to himself. Doesn't associate with anyone by the look of things."

"Where is he?"

"Watch screen one." Ethan hit a few keys on his

keyboard, and information filled up on one of the wall-sized screens he had set up in his apartment. "He's got a house in Boston in the Back Bay area, but most of his phone and computer records trace to a building in Cambridge. Probably a lab of some type from what I can tell from satellite imaging."

"Who owns the building?" Jack asked.

"No clue. The paper trail is buried deeper than Jimmy Hoffa, but I'll figure it out."

"Good work, kid. I'll let Gabe know."

"Where the hell did he and Grace take off to?" Ethan asked. "One minute I'm messing with the museum schematics and the next Gabe has me by the balls, demanding I look up a bunch of information on some guy I've never heard of. We're kind of in the middle of something important here. You'd think they'd want to stick around."

"Relax, kid. You know Gabe's the kind of guy who always has a bunch of different irons in the fire. They should both be finished up with their side mission and be headed to Boston within a day or so. Don't worry about Gabe and Grace. They know what they're doing."

"Which is apparently each other from what I can tell. Don't you think it's a bad idea for agents to get involved with each other?"

Before Ethan could blink, Jack had his chair turned around so they faced each other. Jack didn't look happy.

"Son, you're going to want to watch making stupid assumptions before Gabe gets wind of it. I can count on one finger the number of people who've poked into

Gabe's business and lived to tell the tale."

Jack pushed away and grabbed his windbreaker from the back of a chair. He pulled it on so it covered his gun. "Text me if you hear from Logan. I want to know what he's found out."

"He'll probably call you directly anyway. I seem to be somewhat superfluous in this organization."

"That's the spirit, kid. Always look on the bright side."

"Wait, where are you going?" Ethan asked. "How come I'm always the one who has to stay and do all the work?"

"Where I'm going is no place for kids like you. We'll have the birds and the bees talk once you're a little older."

"Dammit, Jack, can you ever be serious?" Ethan asked.

"Where the hell is the fun in that? Life's too short to be serious." He saluted on his way out the door. "Don't do anything I wouldn't do."

CHAPTER TEN

Iran

"Come on, baby, snap out of it," Gabe said, holding her in his arms and shaking her gently. "We've got to get out of here."

He shook her again, and Grace's eyes snapped open. They were wild and unfocused, and she began struggling against him, fighting to get free of whatever nightmare she was trapped in. Tears streamed down her face, and Gabe's heart shattered at her pain. She opened her mouth to scream, and he clamped his hand across it to muffle the sound. He winced as she bit down and broke the skin.

What the hell had she been living with the last two years? Guilt ate at him because he knew whatever she'd gone through, she'd gone through it alone. It didn't matter that the isolation was her choice. He should have been there for her.

"Grace, snap out of it!" He slapped her lightly across the cheek twice before her eyes started to clear and she focused in on his face.

"What happened? Where are we?"

"I need you to pull it together. I don't want to have to carry you out of Iran. We'll both end up dead."

He could tell his no-nonsense approach was starting to sink in, and she was beginning to think like an agent again. She pushed out of his arms, dried her face with her sleeve, and wiped her damp palms on her pants.

"I apologize," she said stiffly. "You didn't follow SOP. You should have left me."

He didn't bother to argue with her. Instead, he grabbed her hand and pulled her out of the darkened hut. "We need to get to the Jeep and get back across the border. Tussad was obviously expecting us. I don't want to wait around for an ambush."

They sprinted back to Kareem's, not taking as much time for cover, and when they finally reached the big white house, they approached cautiously. Every light was on, and the front door was left wide open.

"Looks like business was harder on Kareem than he let on. Tussad must have lined his pockets well."

"What do you want to do?" Grace had pulled herself together with remarkable, and worrying, speed. She was cold to the touch, and her pale face showed no signs of anything other than rigid determination.

"Stay here. I'll be right back."

Gabe let go of her hand and checked out the perimeter

of the house before going through the front door and checking out the interior. He slipped back out and headed towards the Jeep. He put it in neutral and pushed it to the back of the house, out of the direct sight of anyone coming down the street. He ran back around to the opposite side and found Grace exactly where he'd left her.

"It's deserted. Kareem and his family are gone."

"If this was even his house to begin with," Grace said.

"Let's get locked and loaded inside. I have a feeling we're going to need all of our resources. If Kareem has already reported back to Tussad, then we probably only have a few minutes to get a head start."

Gabe went to the Jeep and took the big tarp off the back end while Grace kept watch. He hefted the large black trunk, and Grace followed him inside. She bolted the front door behind them while he went to secure the back of the house.

"Grace, look at me." When she did her green eyes were defiant and angry. "Don't bullshit me. I need to know if you can hang. I'll think of another way out if you don't think you can."

Grace didn't immediately tell him she was okay as he thought she would. She was starting to scare the hell out of him, and he knew better than anyone that the middle of a mission was the last place for emotions. She visibly gathered her resolve and didn't break eye contact. Her strength was something he'd always admired most about her.

"I can hang. You won't need to carry me out of here."

She popped the latches on the trunk and opened the

lid. The M40A5 lay in pieces and was separated by different compartments, the dull black well polished and oiled. She put it together quickly, her hands intimately knowledgeable as they caressed each part.

Gabe reached inside the bottom of the case for the small cylinders Logan had made for him. He placed them carefully in his bag, and Grace was just closing the trunk lid when the slam of car doors sounded from outside.

"Down, down!" Gabe yelled, pulling Grace with him to the ground and rolling with her across the floor as the windows seemed to implode around them all at once. Shards of glass reigned down on them, and the staccato burst of machine-gun fire deafened his ears. Dust and debris floated heavy in the air, and sight was almost impossible.

"We've got to get upstairs." He rolled them both in that direction until he hit the base of the stairs with his back. "You go first. Stay low."

She scuttled up the steps, and Gabe followed just behind her, hovering over her back with his body. He turned back in time to see a canister thrown through the window and burst into flames. Another came through a side window, and the fire breathed life into the arid room with a whoosh.

"Shit. Faster!"

They ran into the room they'd been assigned earlier, and Gabe closed the door behind them. He tore down the curtains and pushed up the window, so only the iron bars kept them from freedom. It was attached to the stone with rusted screws.

Grace was already stripping the beds while he dug through his bag until he found a small screwdriver. He heard the sink running, and Grace came back into the room with a soaking wet comforter that she shoved in the crack of the bedroom door.

Gabe jiggled the bars and then started the laborious task of detaching them from the rock. The screws had been in place a long time and didn't want to budge, and he had to use all his strength to force them to move. Sweat poured from his temples, and he looked at the door, gauging how much time they had. Smoke was already seeping past the wet bedspread and creeping into the room.

Grace had ripped the white bed sheets into thirds and held them in her teeth as she braided them together tightly. The smoke thickened and made her almost impossible to see.

"Got it," Gabe said, and immediately went into a coughing fit. Even with the screws out, the bars didn't let go of the wall. He pushed them with his feet until they released and crashed to the ground. Grace tossed the braided sheets over the windowsill and anchored it around the heavy bedpost.

"Will it hold us?" Gabe asked.

"Long enough. You go first. I'll fire cover shots."

Gabe propelled himself over the ledge and scaled down the wall while Grace shot rounds from her Sig into the smoke-filled night. The only good thing about the smoke was that it was just as hard for the enemy to see as it was for them.

He moved quickly and ignored the chinks of plaster that exploded close enough to his face to slash at his cheeks. He dropped to the ground and laid down a quick *pop, pop, pop* of fire so Grace could climb down after him.

The smoke covered them as they piled into the Jeep and hunkered down low in the seats while Gabe started the engine. He floored the gas pedal and they jerked forward, gravel and sand spitting under the tires.

Grace grabbed a water bottle from under the seat and poured it over her face to clear the grit and grime from her eyes before passing it to Gabe so he could do the same. He put his gun in his lap and had just taken hold of the bottle when the wheel jerked under his hands and the right side of the Jeep seemed to explode underneath them.

CHAPTER ELEVEN

Grace grabbed onto the seat with one hand and her rifle with the other as her teeth knocked together. The back tire exploded in a puff of smoke and rubber, and Grace was afraid for a moment that the Jeep was going to flip over.

"Be my eyes. What do you see?" Gabe yelled over the noise. She tried not to notice how hard he was having to fight the wheel to keep them right side up.

She looked through the night-vision and infrared scope on her rifle and pinpointed the targets. "A white van. I can't tell how many passengers, but at least three, probably more. The guy in the passenger seat has a machine gun. I can't see any other weapons. They're too busy scrambling to catch up with us. The second vehicle is an old military jeep, and it's flanking the van's left side with two more men. Looks like both are carrying subs."

"We won't be able to make it to the mountain pass with this much damage to the car. Can you take them?"

"Yeah, I can take them. Just try to keep it steady."

"Make sure you leave one of the cars drivable."

Grace pressed her back against the dashboard and her feet against the back of her seat to brace herself. The Jeep rolled unevenly, and she made allowances in the give of her body to counteract the missing tire. She put everything out of her mind but the job and sighted through her scope. God, she loved the feel of a rifle in her hands.

The targets glowed red and would be slightly blurry to the average eye, but she saw each man clearly. She pulled the trigger gently and felt the familiar kick of her weapon as the bullet left the barrel. The windshield of the white van crumpled as the glass fell like a waterfall, and the driver slumped over the wheel. It swerved back and forth uncontrollably until the driver's side door opened and a body rolled out. A new driver took his place, and Grace put the scope back to her face.

Bursts of machine gun fire came from her right, and she saw the other jeep gaining momentum on them out of her peripheral. Her shots stayed steady as she kept firing into the white van, and she trusted Gabe to take care of the other vehicle. She fired five more shots, and the van slowed down, finally rolling to a stop, all its occupants dead.

She turned her attention toward the jeep. Time moved in slow motion as she set her sights on the man in the passenger side just as he did the same to her. They stared at each other through their scopes. Cold fear rushed through her, but she knew the risks. All that mattered was the shot, and that hers hit the target first. She pulled the trigger just as Gabe swerved hard to the left, jerking her across the seat and into his lap. Their windshield exploded, and the sharp sting of glass cut her face and neck.

"Stay down!" Gabe yelled.

She couldn't see what he was doing, so she turned her head and looked up. He steered the wheel with his knee while he grappled with one of the tiny cylinders he had stashed away. It was a plastic tube filled with clear liquid, but when he snapped the cylinder in the middle, the chemicals mixed and began glowing an eerie yellow. Gabe tossed it over his shoulder, and it landed just in front of the other jeep before it exploded. The front of the jeep flipped end over end before landing in a fiery heap.

Grace sat up quickly and looked through her scope at the wreckage as Gabe circled around.

"We're clear," she said. "They're both dead."

Gabe stopped their badly damaged vehicle, and they both jumped out, grabbing everything they'd need. They worked in tandem, pulling the bodies out of the van so they fell to the sand. If no one came for the bodies soon, the desert would claim them. The wind had picked up, and it was impossible to avoid the invasion of grit as it burned eyes and buried itself inside clothing.

Grace felt a smile on her face, and she looked over at Gabe. His black hair hung down in his eyes, and there was a slice on his cheekbone dripping blood. But he had the same exhilarated grin on his own face.

They were alive, and they'd kicked ass.

***

The lights of Kuwait were a welcome sight to see. Gabe spoke briefly to his pilot once they were safely boarded, and then the doors closed behind them, and he and Grace were left alone—energy running like an electrical current over their bodies and their adrenaline pumping hot.

Gabe knew the look in her eyes. If he didn't do something to piss her off in the next two seconds, they were both going to be naked and writhing on the floor. And as much as he wanted her naked, he wanted more to know what had happened to her back at Tussad's house. And more importantly, he wanted to know if it happened often.

"Grace, I…" He didn't get the chance to finish. She plastered herself to the front of his body, and he went rock hard in an instant. He'd always had that reaction to her. She grabbed his head and brought her mouth to his, hitching her legs around his waist so he had no choice but to catch her or topple both of them to the ground.

Her mouth was hot and wet, and her tongue teased him, stroking in and out of his mouth in a parody of what she wanted. Gabe rocked against her and swallowed her moan as he hit her most sensitive spot. Dizzy with lust, he stumbled against the table, knocking something to the floor with a crash.

"Inside me," Grace panted. "I want you inside me."

The desperation in her voice pulled him back from the haze, and he choked on a curse as her nimble fingers found their way below his belt.

"Wait, Grace."

"No. I can't. I need you now."

Despite the storm raging inside of him and the whispers that told him to take and conquer what was rightfully his, he gentled his hold on her. He stroked his fingers tenderly across her cheek and nuzzled against her neck. And then he did the hardest thing he'd ever done before. He unwrapped her legs from around his waist and took a step back. And then another.

"We need to talk," he finally said.

Irritation and hurt briefly flitted across her face before she hid it behind a coy smile. "There's plenty of time to talk later." She pulled the ragged T-shirt she wore up so just a hint of her stomach showed. The shirt rose higher and higher, exposing flesh with torturous slowness, until she finally pulled it over her head, leaving her in nothing but the black bra she wore.

"You can't tell me you don't want me," she said. "Your body never has been able to lie as well as the rest of you."

"I'll always want you. There's never been any question of that. But I'm not going to be a substitute for whatever the hell is going on with you. I want to know what happened back there. I thought you were dead."

The color drained from her face. "My health isn't any of your damned business." She pulled the shirt back on, inside out.

"Has it happened before? Have you seen a doctor?"

Grace laughed bitterly and moved past him, with short, agitated strides. She grabbed a bottle of water out of the fridge and drank deep. "A doctor can't fix me, Gabe. I'm fucked up. Broken. And there's nothing that can put me back together again."

"Cut yourself a break, Grace. We lost a child. It's going to take some time." He tried to go to her. To comfort her. And himself. But she jerked out of his arms.

"Really, Gabe? *We* lost a child. There was barely a *we* before she died, much less after. Did you even care?" she yelled. "I needed you. But your job was always more fucking important than your family. You didn't even come to her funeral."

"I couldn't, goddammit, and you know it. Bennett put me in isolation so fast after my cover was blown that I didn't even get a chance to see her. Do you think I didn't want to hold her again? To touch her face one last time?" He rubbed his burning eyes and then ran his fingers through his hair roughly. "Do you think I didn't try to fight my way through the agents who had me under lock and key?"

"How the hell should I know, Gabe? All I know is that you weren't there, and if you'd paid more attention to what was going on in your other life, then she'd still be alive. You've always been good at keeping your thoughts to yourself. This is the most emotion I've seen from you in all the years I've known you."

Her words cut fast and deep, and his heart was bleeding. Gabe punched his fist through the door leading into the bedroom. "Is that enough emotion for you?" He walked toward her, a predator stalking his prey, but she didn't back away. "There's not a day that goes by that I don't wish that Tussad had killed me instead. I know she's dead because of me. And I know you'll never forgive me, but I wasn't the only one who wasn't there, Grace. I needed you, too."

She turned her head so she wouldn't have to maintain eye contact, but he took her chin and forced her to look at him—to see the pain that raged deep inside of him and know that it wasn't hers alone to bear.

"I needed you too," he repeated. "But when things died down and they released me, you were already gone. The first thing I did was visit her grave. The second was to come find you. But you'd already left the country and sold yourself to the highest bidder like a…"

He welcomed the sting from her hand as she slapped him hard across the cheek, and he grabbed her wrist as she tried to follow through with a punch to the stomach.

"Enough," he said as they struggled against each other.

"Nothing you can say or do will ever be enough. As far as I'm concerned, you're as dead to me as she is."

"Damn you, then. Damn us both."

All he wanted was for the pain to go away. At least for a little while.

Gabe pressed her back against the sidewall of the plane, his body hard and hungry for hers. Her eyes went wide, but she didn't push him away. Their racing breaths mingled, and his heart pounded desperately in his chest as his mouth crashed down on hers.

It wasn't a kiss filled with tenderness or affection. It was a kiss full of pain and longing—a desperate attempt to fill the aching emptiness that consumed them both and to claim what had once been his.

Grace bit his lip, and the metallic taste of blood filled

his mouth. She ran her hands under his shirt and across the hard planes of muscle, and he gripped her hips and pressed her against his straining cock, grinding against her sweet spot until she whimpered into his mouth. They'd both be sore tomorrow.

Their breathing was harsh, and Gabe lifted her shirt over her head, ripping it in his haste. He inhaled the muskiness of her scent. Her arousal was potent—the sweetest aphrodisiac, calling to his animal nature. He trailed his lips down her neck and laved his tongue across the groove of her collarbone. He flicked open the front clasp of her bra with two fingers, and her breasts spilled free. They were small, but they filled his hands completely and swelled under his attention.

She pulled off his shirt and raked her nails across his chest and abdomen, and he shuddered at her touch. Her hands trembled in excitement as she worked at the buttons of his pants and found him large and heavy in her palm.

"Mmmm," she purred as she stroked him, spreading the liquid that seeped from the tip of his cock over his plump head.

Gabe turned his attention to the pert nipples that stood up and begged for his attention. She'd always been sensitive there. He bit down gently, and she went crazy with desire, her hips arching and her moans turning into demands.

"Inside me," she panted.

He watched her from under his lashes, continuing his assault on her nipples with his teeth and then soothing the sting immediately with the flat of his tongue. Her face was flushed with desire, and her hand continued to stroke him to the point that he hand to concentrate not to come. He wanted to be deep inside of her when he orgasmed.

"Fuck me, Gabe. I can't wait any longer."

Grace kicked off her boots, and he tugged at her pants. She lifted up so he could strip them down her legs, and he tossed them to the floor. Her fingers were relentless as they worked him back and forth, and he knew he wouldn't last much longer if she kept it up. He bound her wrists with one hand and kept them imprisoned above her head, and he plunged his fingers into the wet heat of her pussy. She immediately tightened around him, spasming as she came with a gush of liquid cream into his hand.

"Christ."

"Let my hands go. I need to touch you."

He did as she asked, and her nails trailed down his chest and stomach until she held him in her hands.

"Now, now," she chanted as she guided his cock inside her.

Gabe closed his eyes as he pushed into her. She was tight, and the spasms from her last orgasm pulled him deeper inside. He gritted his teeth at the agony of prolonging the inevitable, but he wanted to give her more before he found his own fulfillment. He grasped her hips and hitched her higher so the angle would allow him to hit the spot that always made her scream. He ignored the scrape of her fingernails down his back and took her mouth in a savage kiss as he felt the last dregs of his control fade away.

He slammed into her to the hilt and swallowed her

cries of pleasure, thrusting again and again even as she tightened around him once more. Heat gathered at the base of his spine, and his balls tightened against his body. He felt her contract against him with a new wave of liquid heat, squeezing his cock to the point where pleasure almost turned into pain. She screamed her release into his mouth, and he swallowed every sound before thrusting into her one last time and filling her with his come.

Their breaths came in rapid pants, and they sagged against each other in exhaustion—two warriors at the losing end of a fight.

They'd both found fulfillment, but neither of them had found satisfaction.

CHAPTER TWELVE

London

The bartender's name was Lucinda. Or maybe it was Lorraine. Jack couldn't quite remember which, but she'd been a welcome distraction for the last couple of nights. She'd also been creative as hell in bed, which he appreciated in a woman.

It was close to 4 a.m., and his cock was already beginning to stir again. The woman was insatiable.

"Yeah, sugar. You get on top this time. You've worn me out."

She laughed, low and husky, and his blood ran a little faster. She straddled his hips and he was just about to get his own little piece of heaven on Earth when his phone buzzed on the nightstand beside him.

"Shit," Jack said.

"Just ignore it, baby." She pushed down on him so just the tip of his cock was inside, and he groaned in frustration.

"I can't, sugar. But give me a few minutes and we'll start right back where we left off."

She huffed out a sigh and shoved herself off him, grabbing her robe as she stalked out of the room and slammed the door behind her.

"This better be good," Jack said as he answered the phone.

"Better than good," Logan said. "I found out some very interesting things while visiting Mexico. Things that I can't share over an open phone line."

"Any trouble?"

"No more than usual, though I ran into a couple of goons who didn't care for my questions."

"You always did have trouble keeping your mouth shut. How soon can you get back to London?"

"I'm about to fly out of Mexico City. I'll be there by midafternoon."

"See you then." Jack disconnected and went to search out Leanne. He'd never met a woman he couldn't talk out of her mad, and he was in the mood to finish what they'd started.

***

Gabe felt like he'd been run over by a truck. He and Grace

were standing upright against the wall, their bodies still joined and the sweat cooling on their skin. She shivered as chill bumps covered her skin.

"You're cold." He didn't recognize the sound of his voice. It was raspy—lethargic—and then he cursed himself for speaking at all as she stiffened in his arms.

He pulled out of her slowly and watched her face as their bodies separated. She closed her eyes and covered her breasts with her arms. Gabe fell back into the chair, his legs weak and his mind muddled. An apology was on the tip of his tongue just as his phone chimed a series of beeps.

"I have to get that. It's Ethan."

Grace passed him his phone and said, "I'm going to take a shower and get some sleep." Her voice was steady, but he could feel the emotion vibrating just under the surface.

He let the phone continue to beep as he watched her. "Grace, I…"

"Don't apologize, Gabe. We both know we would have ended up here eventually."

"We still have things unsettled between us."

"Answer the phone, Gabe. You've always been able to have my body. I accept that. But my mind is my own. Nothing will ever be settled between us." She walked out of the room—gloriously naked—the impression of his fingers already showing up on her skin as pale blue bruises.

"What?" Gabe growled into the phone.

"Is this a bad time?" Ethan asked.

"No more than usual. What's going on?"

"Standridge is in Boston. I figured you'd like to take an impromptu trip to pay him a little visit."

"Yeah, we'll take care of it." Gabe rubbed his eyes with his thumb and first finger and thought of sleep.

"I'll send his address and a map to your phone."

"Thanks. Has Logan checked in with you guys?"

"Not with me, but he might have called Jack."

Gabe raised his brows at the way Ethan said Jack's name. "Is there a problem with Jack?"

"Everything's great. He's screwing himself across London last I checked."

Gabe laughed at Ethan's obvious disgruntlement. "He doesn't mean anything by it. It's just the way he is. You'll get used to him."

"Yeah, like a hole in the head. Let me know what happens with Standridge. Are you going to try and bring him back with you?"

"We'll play it by ear."

"How's the mercenary? Has she had any more lucrative offers while you've been gone?"

"Lay off, Ethan. She's doing what she's supposed to." He knew he sounded harsher than he should have, and Ethan was a smart enough guy to pick up on it. The silence on the other end of the line told him Ethan understood he'd gone too far.

"I apologize, sir." Gabe rolled his eyes at the formal title and the sullen attitude. "If you'll excuse me, I'm expected online for a *Call of Duty* tournament. Unless you have more orders for me. Sir."

The line went dead, and Gabe was left alone with his thoughts.

"Shit." Alone with his thoughts was the last place he wanted to be. He put his clothes back on and went to talk to the pilot. It looked like they were headed to Boston.

***

Jack whistled tunelessly as he made his way through the dark streets of Westminster. His body was relaxed and his muscles thoroughly stretched. That woman could fuck like a thoroughbred and had the stamina to match. But it was time to cut her loose. In his mind, after a couple of nights together, a woman started to think in terms of relationships. And he didn't do relationships. At least not anymore. He'd learned his lesson. And he'd be damned if he repeated his mistakes.

Unlike Gabe and Grace. He shook his head as he thought of his friends. They were both just begging for more heartache, and by the looks of Grace, he didn't think she could take too much more. Jack had told Gabe they were being too obvious about their involvement, and damned if Ethan hadn't already picked up on it. It would be best for everyone if Gabe and Grace could put their problems on hold until after the mission was over, but Jack knew them too well. He just hoped they were both still standing once the dust cleared.

He breathed in the night air. His thoughts were clear

and his eyes alert. Sex didn't muddle his brain—it made everything come into sharp focus. So he noticed immediately when he picked up the two tails. They weren't trying to be subtle. They were big bruisers, but he'd faced down bigger.

He kept his pace steady, and his eyes saw everything. He was only a couple of blocks from headquarters, and he had to assume the Worthington Financial cover had been compromised.

One of the men split off, and Jack assumed he was going to try to loop around and take him from the front. Jack kept his hands loose at his sides and almost welcomed the fight. It had been a long time since he'd gotten into a good brawl. His fists ached for the contact.

He turned off the main street into a narrow alleyway. The smell of rotten garbage was overwhelming, and rats scurried from dumpster to dumpster, looking for food. Jack leaned back against a brick wall and waited patiently.

The two men didn't disappoint him. They blocked his escape, one on each end of the alley, and moved toward him. They were scruffy and sported black leather jackets. The one on his left was just shy of six feet, but was thickly muscled. He had a tattoo that snaked up his neck and scrolled around his eye. The other guy was taller and leaner. He had dirty-blond hair tied back in a tail and carried a crowbar like he knew how to use it.

"What can I do for you boys?" Jack asked with a lazy smile. He made sure his posture was relaxed but kept his feet spread for balance. "I don't think we've had the pleasure of meeting before."

"We're going to ask you a couple of questions, mate," Tattoo said. "If we don't like the answers, then you're going to suffer." Brass knuckles gleamed in the streetlight, and he flexed his meaty fingers. His accent was thick enough that some of his words were unintelligible, but Jack got the gist.

"Well, you're certainly welcome to ask. When you're done, I'd like to ask you guys some questions too."

The guy with the ponytail came up on him fast. The crowbar grazed his ribs just before Jack grabbed the guy's wrist and squeezed. He felt the bone give beneath his fingers, and the guy sucked in a silent scream. The crowbar fell to the ground with a clatter.

Tattoo rushed him from the opposite side, and a fist in the gut with those brass knuckles stole Jack's breath. The flash of silver had him dodging on instinct, and a wicked blade cut into the flesh of his arm instead of burying itself straight into his heart.

"This was my favorite shirt, asshole." He gave two short jabs to the guy who'd stabbed him, bringing him to his knees. Jack snapped his neck with a quick twist of his hands and watched the guy slump into the garbage where he belonged.

Jack put his foot on the neck of the other guy and grabbed his broken wrist. His eyes were pain filled, and his breath came in shallow pants. "Now, I'm going to ask you a couple of questions, mate, and you're going to answer me. Do we understand each other?"

The guy nodded, and his eyes glazed over as Jack squeezed his wrist. "Yeah, man. But I swear I don't know anything."

"Wrong answer." Jack squeezed a little harder, and the man squealed. "Who hired you?"

"He'll kill me."

"I'm going to kill you a lot slower if you don't answer, so you might as well tell me."

"His name's Kimball. He's American."

"Description."

"I don't know."

Jack squeezed again, and the man blacked out for a few minutes. He slapped him across the face until the man came to, and Jack waited until his eyes gained focus before asking again.

"Please, man. I need a doctor."

"You're about to need an undertaker. Give me a description of Kimball."

"Big guy. About your size. Military. Or at least he looks that way. Scary son of a bitch."

"How does he pay you?"

"Electronic transfer."

"Good boy. You're finally starting to learn." Jack tapped his cheek a couple more times as the guy started to drift off. "You can pass out in a minute. Tell me what information you were supposed to get from me."

"We were supposed to find out about the package some bloke sent to the place you're living."

Chills ran down Jack's spine. Whoever was behind The

Passover Project had a longer reach than he'd thought. "And what if I didn't tell you?"

"Then we were supposed to knock you out and take you with us. If we couldn't get the information out of you, then Kimball thought he could."

"I bet he did." Jack stood up. A grey, hazy light was starting to peak over the city, and he knew it wouldn't be long before traffic started to pick up.

"Did he want to know only about me, or did he mention other names?"

"He said something about an Edgar Harris, but you were our priority."

"What's your name?"

"Brian Kirby."

"Today's your lucky day, Kirby. Go back to Mr. Kimball and tell him that if he wants to tangle with me, then he needs to have the guts to do it himself. Tell him I'll be waiting for him."

Jack stepped over the dead guy and headed out of the alley. One of his damned ribs was cracked, and he'd need stitches in his arm, but the important thing was he had information to give to Ethan to put in that amazing computer of his. Brian Kirby had just given him part of the pieces to the puzzle.

The good news was they were making someone out there really nervous. People who were nervous made big mistakes. And people who made big mistakes ended up dead.

CHAPTER THIRTEEN

Gabe waited until the water went off and Grace was out of the sight before going to take his own shower. Her words pounded through him over and over again until all he could hear was the accusing tone of her voice in his mind.

Had he been too involved in agency work to pay attention to what was happening with his family? He knew he'd started to shut down that last year of their marriage. Living a double life had taken its toll on him. Life among terrorists and human beings of the lowest life form was a cruel and terrible existence, and the only bright spot in his life had been Grace and Maddie. And he hadn't wanted them to be touched by the other life he was having to live.

Despite it all, he and Grace had somehow made their marriage work. Or at least he thought they had. When one of them was away on assignment, the other was always at home with Maddie. But his time with Tussad, and what the CIA wanted Gabe to do within Sayad's organization, had made him pull away from the goodness that waited for him at home. He had a duty to his country. That had been drilled into him from an early age, and he was glad to do it. Proud to do it. But he'd had a duty to Grace as well—the most basic being to love, honor, and cherish. Somewhere along the way he'd failed miserably.

And when Maddie had died and Grace had left, he'd closed in on himself. Grace spoke the truth when she blamed him. He blamed himself. If he hadn't been working with Tussad, then Maddie would still be alive. He couldn't even blame the CIA for giving him the job—he'd been eager to take it, eager to see the terrorist finally brought to justice.

But things had gone terribly wrong, and he and Grace had each wallowed in their own fear and anguish and guilt until something else formed—something unhealthy and consuming. It had obviously affected Grace differently than it had affected him, and he needed to do whatever it took to fix it. She was hurting. And she wasn't healthy. If she wanted him out of her life after she was better, then so be it. But he owed it to her to help with the healing. He owed it to both of them because he needed to heal too.

He ducked his head under the hot spray and let the water soothe his sore muscles. He thought of Grace and how she'd felt around him, and his body automatically hardened. She'd felt better than he'd remembered. And he couldn't help but wonder if she'd found comfort and solace with another man over the last two years. Jealousy consumed him, and he closed his eyes and blanked his mind against the faceless man he saw in his imagination. He needed to get a grip.

Gabe turned off the water with an agitated flick of the wrist and wrapped a towel around his waist. He brushed his teeth but was too tired to bother with shaving. The beard would have to stay a little longer. When he opened the door into the bedroom area, he saw Grace lying on her side, facing away from him. She was burrowed under the covers, so only the flame of her hair showed against the white of the sheets.

He dropped the towel and slid in next to her, pulling her against him so their naked bodies spooned together. He buried his face in the scent of her hair and drifted off to sleep.

***

Grace woke up slowly—and somewhere familiar. The heat of flesh was wrapped around her in a comfortable cocoon, and she sighed with contentment before realization struck her and her muscles tensed.

"Relax," Gabe whispered in her ear. His breath was hot across her neck, and his hand splayed possessively over her stomach.

She let out a slow breath and didn't fight against his hold. It felt too good. "I'm not strong enough for this anymore, Gabe."

"For what?"

"For anything. The job. You."

"You're the strongest person I've ever known, Grace. But everyone needs a little help now and then."

"Not you. You've never seemed to need help with anything." Or from anyone, she added silently.

"Not true." He pulled her closer and burrowed into her softness. Grace wondered if anyone else knew that the most dangerous man in the world liked to snuggle. Her heart pounded in her chest, and something inside her felt so full she thought she'd burst from it. She wanted to tell him the rest of it. What else had happened after Maddie's death and their estrangement, but she didn't have the courage. She didn't want his pity. And she didn't want to see how the news affected him.

"Touch me, Gabe" she begged. "Make me feel. It's been so long since I felt anything but cold."

Gabe dropped his head against her and groaned. His fingers tightened against her stomach, and his erection stirred against her ass.

"Not fair, Grace. I'm trying to be good here."

"Just once more. Please, Gabe. Make me warm."

He ran light kisses over her shoulders and in the hollow of her neck. She turned over onto her back so he loomed over her, and she wrapped her arms around him, bringing him closer. She smoothed his unruly hair back from his forehead and looked deep into the blue of his eyes.

"I want this," she said, lowering her hand until she grasped his hard cock. "And you want this too."

Grace lifted up and took his mouth in a hot kiss that promised a fast and furious coupling. She gripped his shoulders hard and scissored her legs to get him into the position she craved, but he softened the kisses, making each one slow and steady, nibbling his way across her body, and driving her absolutely crazy.

"What are you doing? I want it faster. I need you inside me now."

"And I want it slower. Believe me, we'll both get to the same place eventually." He whispered the words against her skin, causing her to shiver.

Grace shook her head in denial. He was going too slowly. Giving her too much time to think. She needed him hot and hard and fast, and she moved under him frantically, trying to bend him to her will. She squeezed his hardness in her hand and began pumping him up and down.

"I don't think so," Gabe said, grabbing her hand and anchoring it with his own. "If you do that, this will be over much too fast."

"That's the idea." She didn't recognize the throaty purr when she spoke. He was doing this all wrong. He kissed his way to her lips, his mouth soft and moist against her. The kiss was sweet—loving—as he stroked the inside of her mouth with his tongue. He didn't give her room to evade, to shield herself from everything it meant. She lost herself in the kiss, the room spinning around her in delirium as she didn't know which way was up, only that Gabe was her anchor in the storm.

He moved from her mouth and trailed wet kisses lower, stopping to savor the taste of each nipple. Circling the stiffened peaks with his tongue and sucking gently, making her cry out as each suckle pulled at something low in her womb. He kissed his way even lower, leaving a wet trail.

"Stop it, Gabe. This isn't what I want." She pushed against his head, but he wouldn't be deterred.

"Just stop thinking and enjoy." He swirled his tongue in the dip of her belly button and then lower into the moist curls between her thighs.

"I've always loved the way you tasted," he said, inhaling the scent of her arousal. "Sweet, like honey. God, you're so wet and ready for me."

His mouth clamped over her clit and she couldn't help the moan that tore from her throat. He was relentless, and his tongue flicked across the nub unmercifully until she was screaming with pleasure. She buried her fingers in his hair and rode the wave that pushed her over the edge.

She fell back limply on the bed, her body slicked with a light sheen of sweat. Her heart thudded in her chest, and colors danced behind her closed eyes. She shivered again as she felt the flat of his tongue licking her slowly like a cat with a bowl of cream. The heat started to build again.

"I can't take any more," she pleaded.

"Liar." He grabbed her ass with both hands and lifted her to his mouth like a starving man at a banquet table, and he devoured her until she was begging for mercy. Her climax slammed through her, and it was still going strong as he moved over her and pushed inside the pulsing walls of her pussy.

"Fuck, you're tight."

Grace was incapable of speech. She'd been making love to this man for almost a decade, and she'd never felt anything like what was happening to her now. Her body was no longer her own, just as she knew Gabe's body no longer belonged to him. They were truly melded—mind, body and spirit.

He grabbed her hips and changed the angle, thrusting deep so the tip of his cock hit against her womb. An orgasm rolled through her again, and her legs tightened around him, holding him closer. He thrust against her one last time before she felt him swell and release his seed inside of her.

She didn't remember falling asleep.

***

Grace didn't know how long she slept or what time it was. She just knew that when she woke, she was still in Gabe's arms. It felt good to be there, but she didn't deserve anything good in her life, so she moved out of his grasp as punishment to herself.

He ignored her movement and pulled her back against him, rubbing her head gently and tangling their legs together.

"It was my fault." She could barely get the words past her dry throat as she broke the silence between them.

"What?" Gabe asked, leaning over her so he could see her face.

Her eyes were dry. She didn't think there were any more tears left in her.

"Maddie's death was my fault. I should have known we were being watched. It was my job to know. But we went to the park that day anyway. I wanted to spend some more time with her because I'd been given a job in South America, and I was supposed to leave the next day. Whoever took the shot was good. I didn't hear the report until she was already down, and by then it was too late."

Gabe stroked her back, and she slowed her breathing, trying to get the images from that day out of her mind. "I kept waiting for my turn. I kept hoping for it as I held her. But the second shot never came, and I knew that living was going to be its own kind of death. Everything I'd been trained for failed me that day. I never even noticed them."

"Believe me, Grace. Tussad can afford to hire the best. You can't blame yourself for this. Sometimes bad things just happen, and you can't question why. I liked it a lot better when you were putting the blame on my shoulders."

She tried to smile, but her face seemed frozen. "I wanted to blame you. You were the most convenient target. But it wasn't your fault. I understand the burden you carry with your job, Gabe. I didn't want to understand at that time, but someone has to do it. And no one's better at it than you are."

"If Tussad hadn't found out I was undercover, none of this would have happened."

"I've stopped trying to play the 'What if' game. Nothing will bring her back. I don't know if I can finish this job with you. I'm no good anymore. My instincts are off, and Ethan was right. I'm no better than a mercenary, though I do have my standards as to who I'll work for."

"I know that. I've been keeping track of you the last couple of years."

"I needed the money the side jobs brought. I couldn't

afford to pay my contacts to keep track of Tussad. He moves so frequently, and I had to make sure I'd be told whenever he surfaced. But every lead I've gotten has been a dead end."

"I know, baby. I understand why you've made the choices you have. You don't have anything to justify to anyone."

"But I'm not the same person I was, Gabe. You saw what happened back in Iran. I never know when it's going to happen. Anything can set it off—a group of schoolchildren walking down the street, a family having a picnic. Making it through a job without losing focus is rare. I know it's dangerous, but I can't seem to find the strength to care."

She longed to tell him what had finally sent her over the edge, and the words were almost on the tip of her tongue before he spoke.

"Do you know the reason I really left the agency?"

Grace turned partially over onto her back so she could face him. Her nipples rubbed against the soft mat of his chest hair, and she found the familiarity of it bittersweet.

"Why?" she asked.

"Because I stopped caring. I started taking ops that were no more than suicide missions. I had to have that element of danger that made me think, *this will be the one that finally kills me*. It was the only way I could feel alive."

"And now?"

"Forming The Collective has kept me busy. I've worked eighteen-hour days for the past year so I wouldn't have to remind myself that I should be dead. To remind myself that I can't kill Tussad if I'm six feet under."

"You have to promise me something, Gabe." Grace could tell by the stiffening of Gabe's body and the hard look that came into his eyes that he already knew what she was going to say.

"No, I won't do it. We go in together and we come out together. Those are the rules."

"No, Gabe. This is what the rest of my life is meant for. I know it with certainty. I will gladly trade my life for Tussad's. You have to promise me that when it's time to take him out, that I go it alone. If I don't make it, you have to swear you won't jeopardize your own life by trying to get me out. What you do is too important to risk yourself."

"Shut up, Grace. I'm not even going to have this discussion. I'd never send anyone on my team on a suicide mission." Gabe sat up on the side of the bed and ran his fingers through his hair. "We're all worth too much, not just me. I swear to you we'll find a way to get to Tussad. It might take some time, but we'll get him. You've got to trust me on this."

Gabe couldn't mask the hurt in his eyes as she hesitated in her response. She didn't mean to hurt him. Didn't want to hurt him. But she wasn't sure she was capable of trust anymore after everything she'd been through.

He blew out an impatient breath and got out of bed, rummaging through the closet for clean clothes. Her breath caught at the beauty of his naked body.

"You were asleep before I got to tell you before," he said. "We're headed to Boston. Ethan tracked Dr.

Standridge there." Gabe pulled on underwear, fresh cargo pants, and another black T-shirt while she stared at him in silence. "You're going to have to put your acting skills to the test once we get there. Wear the green silk dress. Standridge won't know what hit him."

Gabe buckled his high-tech watch around his left wrist and looked at the time. Grace wished she knew the right words to say. What she could do to do to make things right.

"Gabe," she said, her voice barely a whisper. "I thought you'd understand."

He shook his head. "The only thing I understand is that I love you and I don't want you dead. We have a couple more hours till we land. Try to get some more sleep."

He closed the bedroom door behind him quietly, and Grace winced at the amount of control he used to make sure it shut quietly. There was no way in hell she'd be getting any more sleep. Restless thoughts invaded her mind, and for the first time in two years, her goals were being altered. She couldn't afford to let Gabe make her wish for things that weren't possible. She had a score to settle, and nothing would stand in her way. Not even Gabe.

CHAPTER FOURTEEN

"Where the hell am I supposed to put my gun in this dress?" Grace asked her reflection in the full-length mirror that hung on the back of the bathroom door. She looked at her Sig and then back at the miniscule dress in irritation.

The green silk plunged in the front and the back. It fit like a second skin, and it barely covered all the parts that needed to be covered. It emphasized all the curves she'd thought she'd lost over the last couple of years, and it made her breasts look spectacular. She was pretty sure that wearing this dress on the street would be illegal in some states.

She slipped into a pair of black stilettos that were going to make her feet scream with agony by the end of the night, and she finally settled on dropping her Sig into an oversized black handbag.

"I've got a problem here, Gabe," she called out.

He'd occupied himself by keeping as far away from her as possible for the remainder of the flight. They'd each needed a little space after what had happened between them. She hadn't been able to go back to sleep as he'd suggested, though. She'd lain in bed with her eyes open, her mind a symphony of memories overdubbed by Gabe's words.

It didn't take her long to come to the realization that leaning on Gabe and trusting him again was asking for more heartache. He would always see the final outcome of any mission in his head first—decide on the right course to take and act on it—before any of the rest of the team had a chance to catch up. It was a gift he'd always possessed. If Gabe said a mission would be successful, then it would be. Plain and simple. He could blend in anywhere, a chameleon for every climate and any country.

Gabe had promised her that Tussad would be taken down. But he'd promised her things before. He'd promised he'd love her and their daughter forever and protect them both. There were some promises that were just impossible to keep.

The quick knock on the door gave her enough time to blank any emotions from her face.

"What's the…" Gabe didn't finish his sentence, and the look on his face was enough to make the woman in her purr with pride. He circled his finger, and she obligingly turned around.

"Jesus Christ, woman. I can't let you go out in public like that." He took a step toward her with his hands reaching out to her before he caught himself. "I've seen every inch of your body, and I had no idea you had curves like that."

"I'm just following orders, sir. You told me to wear the green silk. But I do have a small problem as to where I should put my weapons. This dress is so tight that I can't even wear underwear, much less a thigh holster."

Gabe's eyes darkened with desire, and he started toward her with predatory steps. Her heart pounded in her chest, and her nipples were sensitive against the silk as they hardened. She stood her ground as he closed in on her and moaned as his calloused hands touched her thigh just where flesh and fabric met.

He skimmed his fingers over her hips, across the dip of her stomach, and along the mounds of her breasts before tangling his fingers in her braid, all the while never breaking eye contact with her. God, he had such beautiful eyes—streaks of silver shot through deep blue. She was powerless to look away.

"You should wear it down." He tugged at the end of the braid and ran his fingers through it until it hung in curls over her shoulders. He rubbed the ends between his fingers. "It's like fire, but cool to the touch."

She waited for the animal she saw inside of him to take control, for him to press her back against the wall and take her with all the want and desire that vibrated off his body. But just as his lips skimmed across hers, no more than a taste, the shutters came down over his eyes, and his face was a hard mask of determination.

The job came first. Just like always.

"This is going to be up close and personal," he said. "We need Standridge alive enough to talk for a while.

We've got to destroy his research and test formulas. Just get us inside his home, and we'll decide where to go from there."

"He can't be left alive, Gabe."

"I know. But I figure after one look at you in that dress, he'll drop dead of a heart attack."

"That would be the easiest way. Blood stains are hell to get out of silk."

***

Grace had never been drunk in her life. She'd never liked the idea of being completely out of control. But she'd seen her fair share of fools stumbling around, so she figured she could act the part sufficiently enough.

She gathered her bag and the half-full champagne bottle close and rang the doorbell at Allen Standridge's Back Bay home. It was a couple of minutes before she heard the shuffle of feet and felt his gaze as he looked at her through the peephole. She took a quick slug of champagne, wobbled unevenly on her heels, and rang the doorbell several times again.

The door opened slowly, and Grace got her first look at Dr. Allen Standridge. He was no prize, that was for damn sure, but she played her part to perfection.

"Ollie, baby," she crooned, throwing her arms around his considerable bulk. She swallowed the gag at his stench and turned it into a hiccup instead. "Thanks for inviting me. It's so nice to finally meet you. Awesome house. Do you have a pool?"

Grace left him at the door with his mouth hanging open and stumbled inside. The place was cluttered with papers and empty coffee cups. Clothes hung haphazardly over the furniture, and empty potato chip bags were stuffed into the pocket on the side of his recliner.

"Where is everybody? This isn't much of a party."

"Wh…who's Ollie?" Standridge finally stuttered out. "I think you've got the wrong house, lady."

"Nope, I wrote it down. Where'd I put it?" She smiled drunkenly and clunked her bag down on the table, where she could get to her gun easily, and then fished down the front of her dress for the tiny scrap of paper hidden there. Standridge swallowed audibly as her fingers dipped inside her cleavage. God, men were so easy.

"Here it is." Grace waved the little piece of paper under his nose and intentionally dropped it to the ground. "Oops! Let me get that, honey." She grabbed hold of his arm and slithered down to the floor to pick it up. She'd be damned if she was going to bend over and let her ass hang out.

She did her best to entice him without having to touch him too much. Gabe was going to owe her big for this. Standridge's hands shook as he took the paper from her. He couldn't take his eyes off her cleavage and was barely able to unfold it.

He glanced at the paper. "Hmm, this is the right address." He licked his lips nervously. "But as you can see, I'm not having a party tonight."

"Awww." The whine in her voice was starting to grate

on her nerves. She ran her fingers up over his shoulder and mussed his hair. "My friends must have written it down wrong. But I have a better idea."

"You do?"

"You look like a fun guy, Ollie."

"A…Allen. My name's Allen," he said in a rush of Frito breath that made her want to recoil.

"Allen is a very sexy name." She grabbed him by both arms and led him into the house, trying not to trip over her feet in the ridiculous shoes. "What do you say we have our own party? Just the two of us?"

She took another swig from the champagne bottle and then handed it to him. His eyes were glazed with lust, and he was hers to do with as she pleased.

"Just the two of us?" he parroted. "Is this a joke? Did Kimball put you up to this?"

"Now, Allen, you're going to hurt my feelings." She pouted prettily and pushed him back into one of his dining room chairs. It was made of sturdy oak and had armrests. It was exactly what she needed. "Do I look like a joke to you?"

He landed with an oomph, and his face was practically buried in her cleavage. "N…no. No joke. Our own party."

"Do you know what my favorite game is to play at a party?" Grace asked, reaching for her bag and digging around inside. She pulled out a black scarf slowly and ran it across Standridge's overheated flesh. He was panting like a racehorse, and Grace figured she'd better tone it down a bit before he really did keel over from a heart attack. He was incapable of speech at this point. Sweat beaded on his upper lip, and his face was flushed an unhealthy shade of red.

"Have you ever been tied up, Allen?"

He shook his head no and watched, eyes mesmerized, as she tied his wrist to the arm of the chair. She took another scarf out of her bag and did the same to his other wrist.

"Do you know how hot it makes me to have someone completely at my mercy?" His breath turned into a wheeze as she knelt at his feet and tied each ankle to the chair leg. She stood up and took one final scarf from her bag. "What about you, Allen? How hot does it make you to know that I can do whatever I want to you?"

Grace trailed the scarf over his shoulder as she walked behind him. Her mouth grimaced in irritation as she pulled the scarf over his eyes and noticed his fat head almost made tying it impossible.

"I c—c—c...can't see." The panic was ripe in his voice, but Grace knew he couldn't break the bonds.

"No, you can't," she whispered against his ear. "But everything you feel will be enhanced. Just relax, Allen. You're in good hands. Are you ready to get started?"

"Yesss."

Grace kicked her shoes off and went to the kitchen door where Gabe waited. He rolled his eyes at her as he slipped past her and made his way over to Allen Standridge.

"Hello? Hello?" Standridge called out. "Are you still

here?"

Gabe kicked out his foot and pushed the chair over. All three hundred pounds of Allen Standridge went straight back and landed like a ton of bricks on the kitchen floor. The air went out of him with a *whoof,* and he lay so still Grace was afraid he might be dead after all.

"Rise and shine, Sleeping Beauty," Gabe said, pulling off the blindfold and smacking him a couple of times on the cheek. "Let's have a conversation."

"My back. I think my back is broken." Tears streaked his face, and Grace shook her head at the pitiful sight he made. She grabbed her Sig from her bag and dug around inside for the silencer. She screwed it on slowly and went to stand on the other side of the weeping man.

"Come on, Dr. Standridge. Let's be a big boy about this," Gabe said.

"Who are you?" He looked back and forth between Gabe and Grace, obviously confused.

"Seriously? Are you really so dumb as to think a woman like her would want you? Damn, and I thought you were supposed to be brilliant."

"I don't have any money. You can look. Take whatever you want."

"I will, thanks. Let's talk about The Passover Project."

Standridge's eyes grew big and round in their sockets. The scent of fear wafted from his skin along with the urine that ran down his leg and soaked his clothes.

"I don't know what you're talking about." Standridge closed his eyes, and Grace couldn't tell what prayer he was muttering under his breath.

Gabe let his fist fly into Standridge's stomach with a meaty thwap, and Standridge's crying turned to all-out sobbing. Gabe grabbed the doctor's face and held it still between his hands.

"Open your eyes and look at me," Gabe ordered. Standridge didn't have any choice but to obey. "You're not a nice man, Dr. Standridge. And if you don't tell me what I want to know, then I'm going to kill you. The world will be a better place without you. So let's try this again. I'm going to ask questions, and you're going to answer."

"No, I won't talk. I'm dead either way."

"You're right. Looks like you're pretty smart after all. So let's cut the bullshit. Are The Passover Project files here or at your lab?"

Standridge stayed silent, and Grace's estimation of the man went up a notch. Gabe was a scary son of a bitch.

"You can either die easy or die hard. The choice is up to you." Gabe grabbed the chair by each arm and lifted it back into a sitting position. Grace appreciated the sight of muscles and the impressive show of strength. Gabe pulled the spare 9mm Ruger from his ankle holster and checked the clip. He pulled a silencer out of his jacket pocket and screwed it on. Grace moved to stand behind Gabe so she was out of the blood spatter range.

"You've got a lot of extra fat on you, Dr. Standridge. There are plenty of places I can shoot that won't come near any major organs. You ever been shot?"

Standridge shook his head no, his eyes wide as he stared down the barrel of the gun.

"It hurts like a bitch. Like liquid fire is flowing in your blood and your flesh is being stabbed with a hot iron poker."

Standridge's pasty complexion paled even further.

"Where are the files?"

Dr. Standridge took a shaky breath and swallowed. "Most of them are at the lab. I bring what I need home with me every evening."

"Good. That wasn't so hard, was it? Where do you put them once you get here?"

"Everything I have is on my desk. Just take it and leave."

Gabe barely took the time to aim as he pulled the trigger. The smell of cordite and a blood-curdling scream filled the air. Blood welled from a tiny hole in Standridge's right calf.

"Don't lie to me, Doctor. I'm not a fool. There's no way you'd take the chance of anyone discovering what you were working on. I'll bet as soon as my associate rang your doorbell you put all of your top secret papers in a safe. Tell me where it is, or you'll have a matching bullet in your other leg."

Standridge leaned to the side of the chair as far as he could and vomited on the floor. His head hung down on his chest for several minutes before he answered.

"There's a safe behind the mirror over the fireplace."

Grace moved quickly and lifted the mirror from the wall. A thick metal door, no bigger than a foot long and wide, sat behind it.

"What's the combination?" she asked.

"Even if you steal all of my research, you won't be able to recreate The Passover Project," Standridge said. "There's not another scientist in the world who has the genius to restore it to its original form. If the price is right, I'll finish it for you."

The wheedling sound of his voice was getting on Grace's nerves. She was an assassin, for God's sake. She'd killed some of the most terrible people in the world. But here she was, stuck with a man who was a combination of Boris Karloff and Baby Huey. It was degrading.

"Nice try, doc," Grace said. "You know as well as I do that you're not the only one who is capable of recreating the formula. The list is short, but it still exists."

"And we might have forgotten to mention something at first acquaintance," Gabe said. "We're not stealing anything from you. We're the good guys. The Passover Project isn't leaving this room. If you think for a second that your life is worth more than the safety of the rest of the world, then you're completely out of your mind."

"What's the combination?" Grace asked again, looking at Standridge. "This is your chance to do something right for once." Rivulets of sweat beaded across his face and snaked into the crevices on his jowls and neck.

Standridge was quiet too long, and Gabe raised the Ruger and pointed it at his other leg.

"No, don't!" Standridge screamed. "I'll tell you. I'll tell you." Gabe put the gun down and waited. "S...seventeen to the left. Three to the right. Six to the left. Twenty-eight to the right."

The safe door opened on well-oiled hinges. "Looks like we have a winner," Grace said, flipping though the thick stack of papers inside. "There's a lot of cash in here, doc. What were you planning to do with all that money?"

He didn't answer, and Grace didn't press him for one. She shoved the papers back inside the safe and left the door open as she went back to her bag. She jiggled the box of matches to make sure Standridge was watching and swiped the match head against the rough surface on the box. Sulfur and smoke permeated the air, and she flicked it onto the stack of papers and cash and watched as the flame took hold.

"No! Are you insane? Do you even know what The Passover Project is capable of?"

"Oh, we know," Grace said. "It's why we're here."

"He's all yours," Gabe said.

Grace barely spared a glance at Gabe as he pulled the charges out of her bag and dispersed them throughout the house. Her eyes were all for Standridge.

She picked up her Sig, the cold steel comfortable in her hand. "You know, Allen. It never would have worked out between us." She pulled the trigger and put a bullet right between Allen Standridge's eyes.

"Let's ride," Gabe said.

Grace looked at her shoes on the floor and decided to leave them there. They deserved to be reduced to ashes. She grabbed her bag and followed Gabe out the back door to the black Audi he had hidden down the block. They got inside the car and were just pulling away from the curb when the force from the explosion shook the ground beneath them.

Neither of them looked back.

CHAPTER FIFTEEN

Grace pulled a black duffel bag from the backseat into her lap and took out a change of clothes. She unbuttoned the halter from behind her neck and peeled the dress down her body.

"Good thing there's no oncoming traffic. I'd hate for some middle-aged stockbroker to run off the road at the sight of your breasts."

Grace snorted out a laugh as she pulled on black cargo pants. "I hate to break it to you, but breasts like mine are a dime a dozen."

"Not true. They're the finest breasts I've ever seen." He reached over and cupped one in his palm before she could slip the black T-shirt over her head.

Her breath caught as the heat from his hands sent shivers up her spine, but she shifted out of his grasp and turned her attention to putting on her boots.

"Did Ethan send you the blueprints for Standridge's lab?"

A battalion of fire trucks and police cars passed by them in a blur of blue and red flashing lights. Grace watched them in her side-view mirror while she braided her hair.

"Yeah. The security system isn't registered with any particular company, so I'll have to see what we're dealing with once we get there. We should have plenty of time to get things done. It'll take awhile for the authorities to go through all the legal channels and see that the company that owns Standridge's house also owns the building where his lab is."

Gabe took a smooth right off Harvard Street onto Trowbridge and looked for a decent place to park the car. Things would be a little trickier in this neighborhood. The buildings were closer together, and more people roamed the streets since it was so close to the college.

He was in luck. An apartment complex sat to one side of Standridge's building, and a pizza place sat on the other. Both of the parking lots were packed with cars. Gabe pulled his car into the apartment building complex and parked in the last row. The dense groupings of trees that could be found on every street divided the lots and provided ample cover.

"How do you want to approach?" Grace asked.

"I don't suppose I could get you to stay here and cover me, could I? I'll be in and out in ten minutes."

"Like hell, Gabe. Don't try to keep me out of the loop. I'm fine and I'm functioning."

He gave her a long, studying look, but she made sure her emotions were tucked deeply away. "Fine. Let's go." He grabbed a windbreaker from the backseat and pulled it on so his weapons didn't show, and she caught the second one he tossed in her direction. She pulled her black toboggan on to cover her hair and tucked away the stray wisps. Gabe grabbed his backpack and walked in the opposite direction of Standridge's building.

She followed him into the trees and behind the apartment complex, where a narrow alley housed dumpsters and empty boxes. It dipped lower in the middle for drainage and was cracked and uneven in several places. They stopped when they reached the back entrance to the lab.

"Do you think the cameras have live feed?" Grace asked.

"We'll find out about two minutes after we breach the front door. It looks like a key-code security system. The windows are sensored, and there's probably a trip wire and a secondary system once you get past the key code."

"It's a pity Standridge didn't have Ethan design his system. I very rarely find a challenge nowadays. It took me fifteen full minutes to get into his apartment the other morning."

She could see Gabe's teeth gleam in the light. "It took me eight. Though he never knew I was inside. Do you want to do the honors?" Gabe asked, holding out his hand as if to say "Ladies first."

"As much as I hate to admit it, you're faster. Be my guest."

The back entrance was surrounded by a black, wrought iron fence, and Gabe had his pick in the lock and the gate swinging open in a little over two seconds. He strode up to the back door like he owned the place, and Grace kept her position at the gate so she could keep watch up and down the alley.

Gabe had the door unbolted and the cover off the keypad by the time she looked back. She shook her head in pure appreciation. He could have made a hell of a living on the other side of the law. He held a screwdriver between his teeth, and his fingers were sure and steady as he cut wires and disarmed the system.

Grace left the gate open and went to join him inside the building. She pulled out her weapon and kept quiet as Gabe dealt with the secondary system. The cameras panned and scanned, and if someone was watching on the other end, things were going to get interesting real soon. If the cameras recorded straight to video, then it would all be destroyed anyway, and they'd get away free and clear. It was a chance they'd have to take either way.

"Done," Gabe said. He hadn't even broken a sweat.

Grace looked at her watch. "Four minutes start to finish. Not too shabby."

He gave her a smile that made her pulse jump and then headed further into the building. A series of see-through cubicles ran the length of the space, and she assumed they were different testing areas. Each one had a separate entry door with its own security system. The cubicles were sealed across the top, keeping whatever was going on inside completely contained.

"Damn," Grace said. "This is going to make things more difficult."

"Maybe not. Logan gave me something new he's just developed. It would go faster if we could get into each room and start a separate charge, but it'll work just fine with one point of acceleration."

Gabe looked quickly into each room and chose the one that was obviously Standridge's main research room. Mathematic formulas were written along the clear walls, and maps were spread across every surface. He bypassed the security and opened the door.

"All of these rooms are connected to one electrical circuit," Gabe said, squatting down next to the baseboard and unscrewing the plate that covered the electrical outlet.

"How does the bomb work?"

Gabe sliced plastic coverings and exposed the raw wires and then pulled out a tiny glass vial.

"Logan wouldn't tell me what the hell was in it when I asked, but the basic concept is that once the liquid touches the wires it travels through the entire electrical circuit. It works like an acid and a combustive at the same time, the heat getting so intense that it melts everything surrounding the wires. Once the wires reach a certain temperature, they spontaneously combust, which causes small explosions at each major circuit point."

"How long from start to finish?"

"Anywhere from five to ten minutes is what Logan said." Gabe carefully pulled the dropper from the glass vial and placed one drop on the exposed wires.

"Well, that's rather anticlimactic, don't you think?"

"There's nothing like the satisfaction of a big boom," he agreed.

Several car doors slammed from the street side.

"We may get a big boom one way or another." Grace checked her clip and then moved back to the alley entrance. She ducked behind the doorframe just as the wood splintered above her head.

Gabe took position on the other side, and Grace hunkered low against the wall. Something that smelled like burning plastic reached her nostrils just as a barrage of shots was fired into the open door. Gabe held up a small mirror, shielding the glare with his hands so the enemies couldn't pinpoint their exact location.

"I see three," he whispered. "Ten, two, and three o'clock. All slightly downhill from our position." The door at the front of the building rattled as someone tried to get inside and trap them from the other direction.

"Got it." Grace scooted down so she lay flat on her stomach. She waited until another shot was fired and she could tell exactly where he was standing and what angle she needed to fire. "Gotcha." She leaned out slightly and fired. All she heard was a groan in response.

"Hurry," Gabe said.

Smoke started to fill the room, and she was glad she was down on the floor. Breathing was almost impossible as it was. More shots were fired at them, and she quickly leaned out and fired back in quick succession.

They were already up and running by the time the third

body dropped to the ground. Gabe grabbed her hand and pulled her with him down the alley. Shots fired behind them as they dodged and weaved between dumpsters and trees. Gabe started the Audi with the keyless remote, and they both dived into the car. He already had the pedal pressed down and the car speeding through the parking lot by the time she got the door closed.

"Holy shit. Did you see what happened to that building? It practically melted around us."

"Logan gets a raise," Gabe said. He joined the traffic along Cambridge Street and blended in perfectly with the other cars. There was no sign of anyone behind them.

"Though I'm not too fond of the smell." Grace sniffed her clothes and grimaced. "Melted building isn't exactly my perfume of choice."

"I'll flip you for the first shower."

"I've got a better idea. Why don't we just share?"

"Why don't we?"

Grace laughed as Gabe sped the rest of the way back to the airport.

***

William Sloane leaned his head back against the leather chair that sat behind his desk and groaned at the feel of the wet mouth around his cock. He didn't know the girl's name. Didn't particularly care. She'd be paid for her time and her silence, and if she was good enough, he'd ask her back.

He held her head in a firm grip under his fingers and squeezed tighter as she whimpered with the pain. The sounds of her discomfort brought him closer to the edge, and he thrust against her mouth.

"Suck harder, you stupid bitch."

He felt the release boil in his balls and groaned as he pumped come down her throat. God knows he needed it after the week he'd had, and it had been ten years since his wife had given him a decent hard-on.

He pushed the girl back, and she fell to her hands, gasping for breath at his brutal assault. He pulled an envelope filled with money off his desk and threw it on the ground beside her. His private line rang, and he took the time to zip himself up and straighten his clothes before he answered.

"Be here tomorrow," he told the girl as she righted her own clothes. "Same time."

He answered the phone, hoping whoever was on the other end had good news for him.

"Hello," he said.

"Mr. Sloane, this is Darius Cole at the communications center. I've just sent out a team to the property you own on Trowbridge in Boston. You told me to keep a special eye on it, and sure enough, a couple of folks showed up there about fifteen minutes ago."

Sloane grabbed the whore's wrist before she could leave his office, and she squealed as he squeezed hard.

"What happened? Why didn't you call me immediately?" he asked.

"I'm sorry to say, sir, that two subjects bypassed security and entered the building. I sent our security teams out first, assuming they could handle the problem. Video shows a male and female—not yet identified—set off some type of device, and the building has been completely destroyed. They also managed to kill three of the team I sent out."

"I see," Sloane said. His voice was soft and deadly, and the strength of his rage caused his hands to shake.

"Tell Standridge I'm on my way to the site, and I expect him to be there to meet me." Sloane moved to hang up the phone, but his man on the other end stopped him.

"That's the other news I'm sorry to give you, sir. The police and fire rescue were called to the property you secured for him in Back Bay this evening. It seems that an explosion destroyed the home, and Standridge was purported to still be inside at the time. They'll search for his remains once the fire cools, but it doesn't look hopeful."

Sloane hung up the phone on his man's apology, his anger so all consuming he was afraid he might have blacked out for a few moments. His heart thumped wildly in his chest, and he threw the phone across the room, finding satisfaction in the sound as it crashed against the wall.

The girl cringed and tried to move away from him, but she just brought his attention to focus directly on her. He backhanded her across the cheek and then did it again before she had time to fall to the ground.

"Get up, bitch." Her lip was split and bled, and her eye was already swelling shut. "I said, 'get up.'"

He pulled her up by the neck and threw her against the desk, not caring as she landed hard against the objects that littered its surface. Terror filled her eyes as he clawed at her clothing. She was a whore—a receptacle for the rage that had to escape.

She screamed as he thrust into her hard, and he hit her again just to shut her up. Blackness filled his vision as he pounded away, and his hands squeezed tight around her throat until she stopped fighting back. He stiffened and came inside her, and he didn't even notice she was dead until he pulled out and fell back into his chair.

His breath heaved, and his pulse slowly returned to normal. He straightened his clothes and picked up the phone to call his butler.

"Peters, I have a mess that needs to be cleaned up in the office. Please see to it immediately."

William Sloane grabbed the keys to his car and slipped out the back door, leaving the dead whore to his butler. He was going to look at the surveillance tapes and find whoever was trying to thwart his plans. And when he found out who they were, he was going to hunt them down like dogs and kill them slowly.

CHAPTER SIXTEEN

"Well, you two look…rested." Jack had his feet propped up on the conference room table and his hands folded over his stomach. He'd been waiting for Gabe to walk through the door ever since he'd gotten the call that their plane had landed at Heathrow.

"I didn't know you missed me so much," Gabe said. "Your adoration is making me a little uncomfortable."

"Up yours. Your ugly face is the last thing I want to see." He turned to Grace and gave her a wicked smile. "Hello, beautiful. Did you miss me?"

"I could hardly think of anything else. What happened to your arm?"

Jack sighed and let his feet hit the floor. The sore ribs were a nuisance, and he did his best to ignore them. "I ran into a couple of friends while you guys were off globetrotting."

"Oh, yeah?" Gabe asked. "Anyone we know?"

"Not in the flesh. I was able to get a name out of one

159

of them. I've had Ethan doing a little background check for me, and I think you'll be interested in seeing what we've found."

"Let's go then. I'll put my stuff away and meet you at Ethan's."

"I'll take it," Grace said, grabbing the black bag he carried. "I've got to take mine anyway. See you in a few minutes."

Jack waited until she got on the elevator before he spoke. "Things seem a little easier between the two of you. I'm glad to see you scratched your itch. It's not so obvious now."

"I wouldn't say things are easier between us," Gabe said. "We're still feeling our way. There are a lot of things we have to work through."

They waited for the elevator to come back down and got on, hitting the button for the third floor, where Ethan's apartment was.

"Just be patient, my friend. At least she still loves you." Jack knew better than anyone what it felt like to love and have that love thrown back unwanted. If Grace still loved Gabe, then Gabe was sure to come out on top.

"I want you to keep an eye on Grace," Gabe said. "I'm worried about her. Really worried."

"What's going on?"

"I don't know. But I don't want to be waist deep in shit while we're in Iran and have to worry about her too. Just stay close to her if I'm not around. She might need you."

"Is it her health? Her personality has changed a bit.

She's harder than she was, and not as easy to laugh. She's not hiding her feelings as well as she once did, either, but I haven't noticed anything alarming."

"She's holding on by a thread. She's got a lot of guilt inside. And I have a feeling she hasn't really given herself the chance to grieve."

"We can't take her on a mission like that, Gabe. You, of all people, know it as well as I do. She'll be a liability to all of us."

"She needs to go, and I need to have her there. All I'm asking is that you keep an eye on her."

Jack shook his head as the elevator doors opened and they stepped out. "I hope you're not making a mistake, my friend. But I've got your back."

"You guys have good timing," Ethan called out as they walked through his door. "Here's our man."

Ethan sat behind a black, U-shaped console that dominated the middle of the room. Every part of Ethan's computer system was built into the console, and as Jack got closer, he could see what looked like five or six separate screens underneath the clear surface of the desktop. Ethan's fingers flitted across the surface of the desk with ridiculous speed, so he looked like some sort of mad scientist, moving and shifting pieces of information from one location to the other with just a touch of his finger.

The first wall screen displayed an image of a man Jack didn't know, but he recognized the type. He was tall and broad shouldered. Lots of muscle. His hair was buzzed short in the picture, and his eyes were muddy brown and mean. He looked like a SEAL at first glance, and the thought gave Jack a bit of unease that one of his brothers could be involved in this.

"Definitely has a military background by the looks of him."

"You'd be right," Ethan said. "Shawn Kimball was USMC Force Recon with two tours of duty under his belt before he retired. Sniper specialty. He was then recruited by Uncle Sam."

"You're shitting me," Gabe said. "He was CIA?"

"It's buried deep, but it's there. He didn't do as good of a job at wiping his records as you did."

Jack whacked Ethan on the back of the head for admitting to Gabe that he'd been trying to poke through his classified files. The kid definitely suffered from foot-in-mouth disease.

Ethan rubbed the back of his head. "Sorry," he said to Gabe. "I was curious."

"Right. So where is Kimball now?"

"That's the million-dollar question. Actually, it's the twenty-million-dollar question. Kimball went rogue in the middle of a mission to intercept millions of dollars worth of museum-quality jewels from the Russian Federation while on their way to China. No one's seen Kimball or the jewels since. But I found his Swiss bank account and another in the Caymans that both have tidy sums in them."

"So we can assume that Kimball is now for hire," Jack said. "A man who has those kinds of talents is dangerous out on his own."

"Who's paying his bills now?" Gabe asked. "Any luck with that?"

"Kind of." Ethan fingers tapped another pattern across the desktop and another screen came up on the wall. "The Munich Exchange has made several deposits in his Swiss account. On the surface it looks like a Wall Street brokerage firm. They have dealings worldwide and offices in just about every major trading center. No CEO of record, though. The Munich Exchange is owned by the Darwin Corporation, which is owned by Führer International. I can't find a common name or a figurehead that pieces all of them together. But when you put all three of these companies into the computer, this is what comes up."

Jack let out a long, low whistle. Someone had an intense fascination with Hitler. A surge of adrenaline hit his bloodstream and got his heart pumping. That was a cocky mistake for their enemy to make. They were close to finding the bastard. He could feel it.

Gabe leaned around Ethan and began scrolling through the information with a practiced hand. "Ethan, I want a full background check on every scientist involved with the original Passover Project. I want to know everything about them, down to what kind of toothpaste they used and every relative they had, no matter how distant."

Ethan blew out a breath and scrubbed his hands through his hair. "Just so you know, that's a massive undertaking. Even for me. It could take weeks to put all of it together."

"Then you'd better get started. Pull Kimball back up."

Ethan did as he was told, and Jack watched Gabe, wondering what his friend saw that none of the rest of them did. Gabe had a mind like a computer and could put pieces of the puzzle together better than anyone he knew.

"Something about him—" Gabe broke off, shaking his head. "If we've ever met, he was obviously in deep cover. Who was Kimball's handler at the CIA?" Gabe asked.

"Let's see." Ethan's finger flew across the desk as he hacked his way into CIA files. He whistled tunelessly under his breath as he worked, and the computer screen filled with jumbled numbers and letters before it cleared into an understandable language.

Kimball, Shawn F. popped up on the screen, and Ethan tapped it with his finger, scrolling quickly through the information.

"It looks like Assistant Deputy Director Derrick Kyle with Weapons Intelligence."

"Pull up Kyle's file."

Ethan worked more magic, and Derrick Kyle's bio popped up on the big screen with a full-color photo.

"Now that's a face I do know," Gabe said. "He's changed the shape of his face and hairline, but the eye shape is the same. Frank Bennett told me there was another plant in Tussad's organization. I didn't know who he was, but I suspected it was a man named Umar Salleh, also known as Derrick Kyle. He'd been undercover a couple of years already before I joined the op, but he gave himself away with little things. I wasn't there six months before I had him pegged for an agent."

"Tussad. That's the guy you asked me about earlier. I

did some research while you and Grace were gone. He's one badass motherfucker." Ethan's brain caught up with the words that were coming out of his mouth, and his eyes widened. "Holy shit, you worked undercover for Kamir Tussad? And now you're actively searching for him? You're going to get us all killed."

"Focus, Ethan," Jack said, smacking him on the back of the head again. "One cluster fuck at a time."

Ethan scowled and rubbed the back of his head. "Someday, Jack, you're going to be sorry you ever messed with me."

"I'm shaking, kid. It looks like you weren't the only one who figured Kyle out, Gabe. He was shipped back to the U.S. in teeny-tiny pieces. Tussad practically gift wrapped the box before mailing it to Langley."

"He was killed just before—" Gabe shook his head, clearing the thoughts that bombarded him. Ethan stared at him with curiosity, and Jack put his hand on Gabe's shoulder, either in warning or comfort.

"Someone sold Kyle out," Gabe finally said. "The way this all connects is making my skin crawl. I'm right in the middle of this whole mess. I'd like to have a talk with Shawn Kimball."

"Who did Kyle's body get shipped to at Langley?" Jack asked.

Ethan scrolled down a little further in the file. "Man, the news just keeps getting better. Frank Bennett. Bennett was Kyle's immediate boss at the time he was sent undercover."

Gabe heard the elevator and knew Grace was about to

join them. "Take the file of Derrick Kyle down. Put it away. Now."

***

Grace knew something was up the minute she stepped off the elevator. None of the three men in the room even glanced at her, but she could feel the tension in the air surrounding Ethan. He wasn't as good at masking his feelings as Jack and Gabe were. She wanted to laugh as she saw Jack look at Ethan and shake his head.

She caught Gabe's eye, but he didn't glance away. He'd tell her whatever news he'd discovered when he was ready and not a minute before.

"Looks like I missed the party."

She heard footsteps in the hallway, and her hand went to the weapon at her hip as she stepped to the side of the door. Logan came in and gave her an arched look when he saw where her hand was, but he stayed silent. Grace's curiosity piqued every time she saw him. There was something about him that was different. She wanted to know how he got the scars that puckered across the back of his neck and seemed to go down even further, but she wouldn't ask Gabe, and she knew he wouldn't volunteer the information about another of his agents.

He wore a long-sleeved gray T-shirt and worn jeans. Grace noticed he always wore long sleeves, leading her to believe that the scars were all over his body. His hair was pulled back in a leather thong and his face had two days' worth of stubble.

"So how was Mexico?" Gabe asked.

"Interesting." Logan sat back in one of the comfortable leather chairs and stretched out his legs. "The entire tribe was dead by the time I left." Logan's accent was thick with exhaustion and anger.

"But not by the time you got there?" Gabe persisted.

"No. Whatever the hell is in that formula is a sodding terrible way to die. It liquifies every organ. Slowly. I was there for eight fucking hours, and all I could hear was the screams of the dying, begging to be put out of their misery. The WHO doctors who were trying to keep the site contained couldn't even go into the tents without casting up their stomachs."

"Were any of them able to tell you anything?"

"Jesus, Gabe, they were all dying," Ethan said angrily. "How could you even have him question them? 'Rest in peace' should mean something."

Gabe ignored Ethan and kept his gaze steady on Logan. He could read the grief in Logan's eyes. The job had been a hard one, but it had been necessary.

"The man our initial witness had seen turned out to be a missionary, so it was a dead end there. But everyone I questioned, at least those who were able to talk, said they all heard the same thing. A loud hissing sound and then the vibrations from the aftershock as the missile hit its target. They didn't recall anything else unusual about the day until they all started getting sick."

"Did you find the shell casing for the missile?"

A slight twitch at the corner of Logan's mouth was the

only way to tell he was smiling. "I brought it back with me. From what I could tell, and the location where I found the casing, it looks like it was released from the south. That's guerilla territory. Any of those pilots could've been bought and done the deed. Most of them are used to running drugs and guns, so they wouldn't have blinked at firing a missile over a peaceful village. The formula was released as an aerosol, and obviously found the DNA it was searching for. I found the casing buried in the sand almost a thousand yards away."

"Good work, Logan." Gabe went to stand in front of the wall screens where Ethan had information set up.

"You guys are a piece of work," Ethan said, pushing back from his console. He ran his fingers through his shaggy hair, his face colored with anger and frustration. "It's like you're all robots. Don't you have any feelings? Sympathy? I should not be the fucking voice of reason in this room."

Gabe turned to face him and sighed tiredly. "We are who we are, Ethan. There is not one person in this room, one tribe, or even one goddamned country more important than the whole. None of us have any illusions as to what we do. We're fighting a war that 99.9 percent of the population doesn't even know exists. They're happy and clueless in their homes and with their jobs. We will all do what it takes for the big picture. If that means the torture of a captive or questioning an innocent who is dying a terrible death, then that's what we'll do. It's time to grow up or get out."

Ethan's breath grew ragged, and Gabe could tell the boy wanted nothing more than to plant his fist right in

Gabe's face. "Fuck," Ethan said, scrubbing his hands over his eyes. "You should at least be sorry."

"We're all sorry, but it doesn't change the fact that the job has to be done."

"So what now?" Jack asked, pulling the attention away from Ethan and onto himself.

"The mass killing should be halted for a while now that Allen Standridge is dead," Gabe said. "It's going to take some time for whoever is behind this to line up a new scientist and get a viable test product. We've got two goals to achieve. The first is to get the rest of the formula that's still out there in Hitler's paintings and destroy them. The second is to flush out this man."

Gabe turned and faced the picture and dossier of Shawn Kimball that popped up on the screen. "Kimball's working for whoever is behind The Passover Project. He's former military, and he's got CIA connections. I also have a feeling that this is the man who killed Frank Bennett. If he did, then he had the opportunity to search the personal files Frank kept at home. He might know more about some of us than I'm comfortable with."

Grace narrowed her eyes at Gabe as if trying to read between the lines. There was something deeper here than Kimball knowing about their private lives.

"How are we going to flush him out?" Ethan asked. "He obviously knows where we are since he's sending thugs after Jack."

"We won't have to. He'll come to us. He's got us under surveillance. We're going to have to get rid of most of his team before we can leave for Tehran and destroy the painting, but we'll leave one of them alive to deliver a message."

"We'll be ready for him," Jack said. "I've got a little something of my own to deliver to Mr. Kimball." He rubbed at his sore ribs.

Ethan's anger hadn't dissipated, but he'd gotten control over it for the most part. Gabe knew he was asking a lot of the kid, but they'd all been young when they'd started, and they'd each had to make certain adjustments to be comfortable with the kind of people they'd become. The job wasn't for everyone, and he still wasn't sure Ethan would be able to cut it.

"So, great. We're going to save the world and kill or torture everyone who deserves it. Just one question. How the hell are we all supposed to get into Iran? There's no way we're going to get in unnoticed with all the security checkpoints they have."

Gabe decided to let Jack handle this one since he was already laughing at the kid's naivety.

"Well, son, since you'll be staying here, I don't think you'll have to worry about it overmuch," Jack said. "Leave the hard part to the big boys."

"The hell I'm not going," he said, launching himself at Jack and getting a quick punch in before Jack could block him.

Jack's eyes narrowed, and he shoved Ethan back on the couch with barely any effort, dabbing at his split lip. "Don't touch me again, kid," Jack growled. "It's the only warning you'll get. If you want to be an adult, it's time to start acting like one. We're a team. And you can't get past your own pride and immaturity to see that there are four other people whose lives count on the trust of each other, and they're all waiting on you to grow up."

Ethan deflated a little and said, "You need my eyes inside the museum. What if something goes wrong?"

"Ethan," he said. "It's safer for all of us with you here. Getting electronic equipment into the country is always tricky. You can do everything you need to do from the comfort of this room." He kept going before Ethan had a chance to argue. "The rest of us have covers already built and the paperwork we need to get into the country without a hassle. It's time you started trusting the rest of us to do our jobs because we are all trusting you to be our eyes and ears once we're in. What do you say, Ethan? How about being one of the team?"

Ethan stared at him a long time, and Gabe wasn't sure what answer the kid would give. He had a complicated brain and a whole lot of baggage.

"Do I get to have a gun?" Ethan asked.

"Why don't we work up to that?" Gabe said. "I'm sure Jack would love to give you some lessons."

Jack grimaced, and the others laughed as the tension was finally broken.

"Let's get to work," Gabe said.

CHAPTER SEVENTEEN

"Stop looking at me like that," Grace said. "This isn't a date. We're hunting."

"I'll take whatever I can get at this point." Gabe grabbed her hand and twined his fingers with hers. "Have I ever told you I like feeling the callous on your trigger finger? It's a hell of a turn on."

"I'm sure a therapist would have a field day with that."

"We both know exactly what we are Grace. There's never been any room for remorse in our line of work. Sympathy and compassion, yes. But not remorse. Someone's got to do the dirty work. And only the best survive. We're the best. I'd think it's perfectly normal for people like us to find a certain skill set to be attractive to the opposite sex."

"Your psychology minor is showing."

"Wait till I get you on my couch."

She laughed before she could help it. The sound was rusty, and a part of her wanted to feel guilty. She shouldn't feel joy. Should she?

They strolled casually through the streets of Westminster—a couple holding hands, both armed to the teeth. It was midafternoon, and the sun was shining bright overhead, burning off the perpetual gloominess of gray clouds that kept threatening to fill the sky. There'd be more rain once the sun went down. They had one goal only for their outing—to flush out Kimball's men and give them a message to give to their leader.

"What do you think?" Gabe asked.

"I spotted one on the roof of the building across the street. He's probably working as part of a two- or three-man team on a rotation schedule. They could've rented the top floor of the entire building. It's what I would do."

"Did you get that, Ethan?" Gabe asked.

"Loud and clear. I'm already checking."

They were testing out the equipment they'd use once they were in Iran. Ethan had developed a wireless listening device that used satellite technology so the listener could hear conversations thousands of miles away. The device fit entirely inside the ear, so it was completely out of sight. They could turn the device on and off with a touch of a button on the watches they all wore. Gabe was still amazed at how clear the sound quality was. It was like Ethan was in the same room with them.

"She's right. Top floor was rented out two weeks ago by the Darwin Corporation. The day after the package from Frank Bennett arrived here."

"Jack, my guess is that Kimball's other team is down at the end of the round-a-bout, since we're on a dead-end street. He'd be able to follow our tracks for longer from that end."

"I'm already down here and have spotted them. It's a two-man team."

"Let one of them live. Give him the message that I want to meet with Kimball."

"You got it, boss."

Grace touched the tiny switch on her watch and turned off her mic. She grabbed Gabe's hand and did the same to his.

"You might as well tell me what you're hiding about Kimball, Gabe. You're trying to protect me from something."

They walked through an alley and came out on the street behind their headquarters. Gabe tugged on her hand and pulled her close.

"What makes you think I'm hiding anything about Kimball?"

"I can read you like a book. I know every expression on your face. I might not know exactly what the circumstances are, but I know when something is wrong. I've always known," she said, referring to their past. "You don't have to protect me. I can take whatever it is."

He drew her closer until their bodies bumped together, and he took her face gently between his hands. Grace's breath caught at the look in his eyes—a mixture of longing and want and need. And love.

"You still love me," he said softly.

She didn't have the power to deny him. His gaze captivated her, and her eyes fluttered closed as he brought his mouth to hers and whispered the softest kiss across her lips. He pulled back, a look of regret that he couldn't finish what he started in his eyes, and he ran his hand affectionately down the length of her braid before releasing her completely.

"I'll tell you about Kimball when we get back to our room. I promise."

"Our room?" Grace asked with a raised brow.

"You don't think you're sleeping alone tonight, do you?"

"No, I suppose not." Grace took her Sig from her shoulder holster and checked the clip. "You take point, and I'll be clean up."

"I never argue with a lady."

They both turned their ear pieces back on and checked in with Ethan before seeing to their task. The building was modern, a gray-bricked structure of five stories that was used for various businesses but was for the most part unoccupied. Gabe made quick work of the back door lock, and they slipped inside quietly. They took the stairs instead of the elevator to the top floor, their footsteps silent on the concrete steps.

They spoke to each other with their eyes and hand signals only as they reached the door for the top floor. They knew there was a man on the roof, but they weren't a hundred percent sure how many others they'd find. From what Jack had said about the men who attacked him, they were professional thugs, not professional killers. There was a world of difference between the two.

They went in hard and fast, Grace taking the low stance while Gabe took the high. There was no one in the long, narrow hallway. The walls were painted a stark white that was so bright it hurt the eyes, and the carpet was industrial-strength burgundy. The overhead lights were fluorescent, and the one at the far end flickered on and off.

They hurried down the hallway, guns pointed at the floor, and flanked the lone door that divided the long walkway. Gabe knocked, and they listened as feet shuffled across the room and came to a stop in front of the door. The very distinct sound of someone chambering a round in a shotgun echoed from inside the room.

Gabe didn't wait. He fired twice through the door and once into the deadbolt and kicked it open. Grace moved in fast, stepping over the body, and a man by the window reached for his gun on the table just as she took her shot. They hurried through the room, pocketing the men's cell phones and searching for anything else that might lead them to Kimball. There was a laptop on the couch they'd send Ethan over to collect later.

"Everybody okay over there?" Ethan asked.

"We're good. Heading to the roof," Gabe said.

The rest of the floor was clear, so they headed back into the hallway and to the stairwell that led to the roof. Grace opened the heavy gray door and went through quickly and quietly. She knew where the man had his equipment set up, and the door faced away from his line of sight.

He was right where she thought he'd be, looking through the scope on his camera, looking for them. There wasn't a weapon in sight. They'd decided shots fired on a roof in the middle of London wasn't a great idea, so Grace motioned to Gabe, and he snuck up behind the man like a bandit, snapping his neck cleanly with a twist of his hands.

"Clear," he called out to Jack through the mic.

Gabe picked up all the surveillance equipment and left Grace with her hands free for her weapon in case they met anyone else on the way down.

They reached street level when they heard Jack through their earpieces. "Clear on my end," he said. "My new friend is already on his way to give Kimball our message."

"Good. You and Logan are staggered to leave for Iran within the next twelve hours under your new identities. Grace and I will stagger our leave with yours in the next sixteen hours. We'll meet you at the rendezvous point at three p.m." Gabe clicked his earpiece off before Jack or Ethan could comment. "Let's go."

Grace laughed as Gabe grabbed hold of her hand, and they traced their steps back the way they came. "You're in an odd mood."

"We're about to start the most important mission of our careers, and I'm about to make love to a beautiful woman. That's pretty much all I've ever wanted out of life."

"Oh, really? So any beautiful woman would do?"

Gabe kissed her deeply, and when he broke away, they were both gasping for breath. "Only you, Grace."

***

Gabe was acting different. Grace couldn't put her finger on when it started exactly, but she had to get things back under her control. She wasn't ready to face what would happen if she ever did lose control, and as good as it felt to be with Gabe again, she wasn't really ready to face that either.

The grief boiled inside her, threatening to spill over the edges with every passing day. She'd been able to keep it under control since Maddie's death because she had a goal to focus on. She could grieve after Tussad was dead.

But Gabe's unspoken compassion and his need to share the burden with her made her want to break down before the right time—before her plan was complete. She couldn't let him get past her defenses like that. As long as she called the shots during whatever was going on between them—she didn't want to call it a relationship—then things would be okay.

He'd been right when he'd said she still loved him. She always had, and she knew she'd never be able to stop, no matter how much time or distance was between them. But just because two people loved each other didn't mean they needed to be together. Sometimes the pain outweighed the love.

She and Gabe met Jack on the street on their way back to headquarters. He took one look at them and shook his head. "I'm going to get a beer. You two have fun." He veered off in the opposite direction, and they checked in with the security gate and made their way through the front door.

They kept a respectable distance between them once they were inside the safety of the building, not knowing if anyone was watching. Tension vibrated between them, and Grace ached to get her hands on him. They waited patiently for the elevator, not making eye contact as the doors opened. By the time they made it to the sixth floor, her heart was pounding so hard she was sure Gabe could hear it.

"My place. I have something for you." Grace grabbed his hand and led him to the door of her apartment. She hadn't stepped foot inside his private rooms since she'd been here. She didn't want to see how he'd been living since they'd parted ways. She didn't want to notice if he still left the cap off the toothpaste or if he still kept his bread in the refrigerator.

"Chicken," he said. "What happened to *our place*?"

"Why can't our place be my place?"

He shook his head but followed her into the room. There was nothing personal lying around. It looked exactly the same as it had when she'd first stepped through the door. She never kept pictures or mementos of her former life with her.

"Let's talk about Kimball," Gabe said.

Grace looked down at her watch. "We only have a limited amount of hours until we have to get back to work, and you want to talk about Kimball now?"

Gabe's eyes narrowed in suspicion. "What's going on here, Grace?"

"I always thought you were so smart. Can't you tell when someone's trying to seduce you?"

"Well, it's been awhile. I'm a little rusty."

"Maybe I can jog your memory." She took him by the hand and pulled him toward the bedroom.

"I don't know," he said. "You might have to try really hard."

The smile Gabe gave her sent shivers down her spine. His eyes challenged her to do her best, and she decided then and there that Gabe wouldn't know what hit him.

"I'll make you a deal," she said.

"Oh, yeah? What's that?"

She pushed him so he stood in front of one of the four posts on the bed. She ran her fingers over the rigid muscles of his stomach and chest and felt the power rush through her as he shuddered under her touch. She pulled off his T-shirt and dropped it on the floor at his feet.

"Have I ever told you how much I love your body?"

"It's been awhile." His voice was husky, and she could see the pulse pounding in his throat.

"If you promise to stay right here and not move, I'll do that thing you like."

"I'd be crazy to turn down a deal like that."

"But you can't move. No matter what. If you do, I'll have to stop."

"What, you think I can't keep my end of the bargain? I've been tortured by worse than the likes of you, sweetheart."

"I guess we'll find out. Do we have a deal?" She circled her fingernail over his hard nipple, and he sucked in a breath.

"We have a deal. Do your worst."

Grace took his hands and lifted them up over his head, wrapping his fingers around the post at his back. "Leave your hands there. Remember, you promised not to move."

She skimmed her fingers back down his chest until they rested over the button of his jeans. He quirked a brow at her in a dare, and she unsnapped the button, keeping her gaze steady on his. She pushed the jeans and his underwear down to his feet.

"Step out." Her voice was low and husky, and the sight of his obvious arousal enhanced her own. She wanted to move faster, but she held herself back, determined to make him crazy by the time she was done with him. It was time he got a taste of his own medicine.

Grace left him there, naked, aroused, and bound only by his word, as she made the preparations she wanted. She gathered candles and placed them throughout the room. When she lit them, a glow filled the area with soft light.

The first rumble of thunder echoed outside, and she couldn't help but smile. She'd always done her best work in the rain.

"I hope you're planning to come back over here soon," Gabe said. His hands were exactly where she'd left them, stretched above his head, gripping the post so his muscles strained.

"Eventually." Grace took her time unbraiding her hair. She knew how the sight of it had always turned him on. It tumbled around her shoulders and down her back, and she ran her fingers through it. His eyes were hot as they followed her every move.

She went back toward him but stopped about ten feet away. "You know I'm going to drive you crazy."

"You've been doing that the better part of ten years. Give it your best shot."

She smiled at the challenge and lifted her shirt slowly over her head. Her breasts strained against the confinement of her bra, but she waited to take it off. She unbuttoned her pants and wiggled out of them so she was left standing in the emerald green bra and panties she'd found in her drawer. She'd known without asking that he'd picked them out himself. He loved it when she wore green.

"Christ, you're beautiful."

"Did you pick out underwear for all your agents or just me?"

"I had a special interest in your underwear."

"I never thanked you."

"No, you didn't. I'm not sure I want you to keep it. Maybe you should take it off."

"Maybe I should."

Grace skimmed her hands over her thighs and closed her eyes, feeling the change of textures between her skin and the lace. She followed the dip and swell of her curves, her own breath hitching in anticipation at what was to come. Her nipples were sensitive against the fabric of her bra.

Grace opened her eyes and looked straight at Gabe as

she unhooked the front clip and her breasts spilled out of the cups. She let the scrap of lace fall to the ground, and reveled in the wild need that came into Gabe's eyes. His hands squeezed the post, and his arm muscles bulged and strained until she thought he might snap it off completely.

She didn't remove the panties, but cupped the weight of her breasts in each hand, tweaking her nipples between her fingers and feeling the tug and pull of desire deep inside of her.

"You're killing me, Grace. Don't make me beg."

She kept her gaze steady on his as she moved one of her hands down her torso and dipped her fingers inside her panties. The curls that covered her desire were moist, and her fingers slipped through the delicate folds. She couldn't help but moan as her fingers hit the sensitive bud of her clitoris.

Gabe's erection looked painful. It stood rigid against his stomach, the head engorged with blood and the tip seeping precum. His sac was tight against his body, and the muscles in his thighs quivered.

She stopped her teasing and moved closer to him, the sway of her hips answering the call of his desire. She kissed him gently, despite the need consuming her. She wanted to devour her conquest, to take no prisoners. The storm raging outside matched the one taking place in her body. But self-control was key, and she had self-control in spades.

She ran her finger, still damp with her juices, over his bottom lip, and he immediately took it into his mouth, swirling his tongue around the tip and savoring her taste.

"Don't get greedy. I told you not to move." He released her finger and promised retribution with his eyes. She couldn't wait.

She kissed her way down his chest, lowering herself to her knees in front of him. She breathed in the scent of his arousal and nuzzled her cheek against his rigid length.

"It's been awhile since I've done this."

"It's probably like riding a bike. You never really forget how."

Grace laughed against him and looked up into his eyes. Sweat dampened his skin with the restraint he used to hold himself still, but his gaze was steady as he stared back at her. She didn't look away as she took him in her hand and kissed away the moisture at his tip. Her lips were salty as she ran her tongue over them.

His taste and texture were familiar, as was the growl he made in the back of his throat when her tongue hit the sensitive spot on the underside of his cock. Her throat opened as she took him farther and farther down, and she kept the pump of her hand steady.

He spread his legs apart for better balance, and she cupped his balls in her other hand, massaging the area just behind with her fingers.

"Shit, Grace. I'm going to come. Stop." He lowered his hands and took hold of her head, and she immediately stopped what she was doing.

"No one said you could move your hands. You made a deal. If you break it now, the whole thing's off. We can play cards for the next few hours."

"When this is over, I'm going to make you beg for mercy."

"I'm counting on it. Now get your hands back where they belong."

He did what he was told, and Grace took him back in her mouth, redoubling her efforts to get him back where he'd been. He strained against her, trying to hold back his release, but she was relentless. She took him deep, swirling her tongue around him while keeping the steady pump of her hand going.

"Last chance, Grace. I'm going to come."

She purred while her mouth was wrapped around him, and the vibrations sent him over the edge. He shouted out, and she drank every drop of him down like wine. She licked her lips and slithered back up his body, her own need for release even more potent since she'd experienced his.

His hands were still above him, but his head hung down, and his breath rasped in and out of his lungs. Sweat covered his skin. Grace kissed him deeply, her tongue sliding sinuously against his, and she felt him stir against her. She ran her hands over his shoulders and up his arms, unwrapping them from the post and pulling them around her so he held her close.

"Mmm, I guess you fulfilled your part of the deal after all."

"A deal's a deal. Now it's my turn."

"I was hoping you'd say that."

Before she knew what was happening, he had her

wrists held captive behind her back and her torso bent over the side of the bed. The texture of the bedspread was rough against her sensitive nipples, and she could feel the moisture pooling between her legs and running down her thighs.

He didn't give her warning as he plunged into her wet heat. He filled her completely, and the position made him feel even larger. He leaned over her, her arms held prisoner between them, and she screamed as the head of his cock hit the furthest point inside her. Her inner walls clamped around him, and her climax tore through her, wrecking her body and leaving her nothing more than a shattered shell of a woman.

Too many sensations bombarded her system. The coolness of the sheets beneath her. The heat of Gabe on top of her. The candlelight flickered behind her closed eyelids, and the smell of wax and sex permeated the air. He released her arms and moved her so she lay fully on the bed. He grabbed the bed pillows and wedged them beneath her, spreading her legs wider and changing the angle of penetration again.

"I can't, Gabe. No more."

"Yes, you can." He kissed his way up her spine and nipped at the base of her neck. "Do you have any idea how good you feel around me?"

All she could do was moan in response. He'd stopped moving, and she wiggled against him in anticipation as the heat started to build inside her once again. He moved his hand beneath her and cupped her mound, holding in the pulsing heat that quivered there. His hand skimmed down her back, leaving chills along her skin, and his finger circled the puckered star of her anus.

"Oh, God, Gabe." Sensations spiraled through her like lightning. "Please."

"Please what?"

"Move inside me. Just fuck me. I'm begging."

He pulled out of her slowly until only the very tip of his cock was still inside her. He dipped his finger lower and gathered her juices before bringing it back up to her rear passage. He sank his finger in slowly just as he pushed his cock back inside of her to the hilt. His fingers kept busy in front and behind, building the pressure and matching his thrusts in intensity, and sensitive nerve endings she never knew existed had her pushing back against him, eager for more. He was relentless in his goal, giving her no choice but to feel the myriad of pleasures he was providing.

It only took a few thrusts before the heat gathered in her pussy and spiraled outward. She buried her face in the covers and screamed as she flooded his cock with her come. He thrust one last time and moaned into her hair before he collapsed on top of her.

***

"We've got to learn to pace ourselves," Gabe said a while later. "I can't feel my feet."

Grace smiled and burrowed closer into his side. "Tell me about Kimball while you're recovering."

Gabe stiffened slightly at the sound of Kimball's name—the hazy, postcoital bliss short-lived. Being with

Grace made it easy to forget the other things in his life. He took a minute before he answered her, just enjoying having her pliant in his arms.

"You saw the dossier on Kimball. He was former CIA, but he's connected to us. To me at least." Gabe combed her hair with his fingers. "His handler was a man named Derrick Kyle, and Kyle worked undercover for Tussad."

Grace froze in his arms at the mention of Tussad's name. "You're kidding me?" She sat up beside him, the sheet covering her lap but leaving her breasts bare to his gaze.

"Oh, it gets better. Derrick Kyle's direct boss during the duration of his time in Tussad's organization was Frank Bennett. But someone leaked Kyle's identity to Tussad, and he was sent back to the US in a tiny box."

"You think Shawn Kimball knew about Kyle's involvement in Tussad's organization? You think he was the leak?"

"It's all pieces to the puzzle, Grace. I'll know for sure once I talk to Kimball."

She pushed back the covers and got out of bed, pacing around the room in agitation. She was a sight to see, red hair flaming behind her, skin as pale as milk in the candlelight. He shook his head in disbelief as his cock started to show signs of life beneath the sheets.

"You know what this means, don't you?" she muttered under her breath. "Of course you do. You've already assessed every possible scenario in that brain of yours." She crawled back into bed. "Kimball could know everything about you."

"I know. I'll cross that bridge when I come to it."

"I want to see everything that you had Ethan hide from me earlier." She looked at the clock on the nightstand and winced. "We've got to be up soon anyway."

"I figured you might. I've got it all on my laptop."

"I'll make some coffee. I'm going to need the pick-me-up."

"Christ, no. Let me do it."

"You know, a less confident woman would take offense to that," she yelled at his back. He chuckled once and then realized he hadn't felt this content in a long time. Life was good. He couldn't help the sense of dread that curled up his spine. Nothing good could last forever.

***

"I want to know who the hell these people are," William Sloane yelled at the man who sat across from him. He'd finally found something, or in this case, someone, who could shake his unflappable composure. He didn't like the feeling at all.

He'd been in Boston for two days trying to clean up the mess that had been left for him. He needed a new scientist badly. He also needed a new head of his control center since he'd blown the man's brains out and left them scattered across the wall of surveillance monitors. There should have been no reason for two operatives to be able to break into his lab and get away scot-free. The next person in charge of seeing to the security of his properties had best do a better job.

It had taken him hours to get through to Kimball and order him to Boston. He wanted a report from him in person. For the amount of money he'd been transferring into Kimball's account, it was the least the man could do for him.

To his annoyance, Kimball looked unconcerned at Sloane's tirade, and an amused quirk sat on his lips.

"Something funny, Kimball?" Sloane asked.

"Nope. But you have to expect an undertaking of these proportions to have the occasional setback."

"If you'd done your job and gotten hold of Jack Donovan, then we might not be in this position."

"Perhaps, but getting hold of someone like Jack Donovan is like pissing in the wind. They're trained to have their guards up all the time. They've taken out all my men that I had on them for surveillance. All except one, and he can barely stutter out a coherent sentence without pissing his pants in fear of Jack Donovan. They're trying to make contact with me. I'm thinking about letting them."

"So they can kill you too?"

"Don't underestimate me, Mr. Sloane. I've played in the same game as they have. And I've got a few tricks up my sleeve yet."

"My patience is running thin, Kimball. And I've got to be in Zurich in sixteen hours to speak to a new scientist. Your job is to find out what Jack Donovan and these others are up to. We captured another of them on the surveillance camera from the laboratory before it was destroyed. Take a look."

Sloane hit a button on the remote and a screen lowered from the ceiling. The lights went out with the touch of another button, and surveillance video started playing.

"I'll be damned," Kimball whispered. "Pause it."

Sloane did as he was told and watched as Kimball got up and moved closer to the screen.

"That looks a little like the same man from the surveillance photo you brought me the other day, though there are enough differences to make me wonder," Sloane said. "You told me you didn't recognize him."

"I didn't. And I still don't."

"Then it's the woman you recognize?"

"Yeah. Shit, I knew I should have killed her too. A gamble on my part to leave her alive, but I enjoyed her torment."

"Who is she?"

"Her name's Grace Meredith. She's inconsequential to you. Only a pawn in a complicated game. But if she's involved in this operation, then that means her husband is too. Probably the man with her at the laboratory break in. I think we found the owner of Worthington Financial."

"Stop fucking with me and tell me who he is!"

"His name is Gabriel Brennan, and this agenda of yours just became a lot more complicated. My price is going up, and you'd better hope to God he doesn't find you before we find him."

CHAPTER EIGHTEEN

Iran

Grace could never figure out what exactly Gabe did to make himself unrecognizable to those who knew him. His face was different, more square, his jaw packed with cotton to change the line. His hairline receded slightly and came to a sharp widow's peak at the center of his forehead, but the color was still as black as night, though strands of silver were interwoven. The lifts in his shoes gave him an extra couple of inches, and padding in his jacket gave bulk to his already muscular frame.

But the physical differences weren't what made the man. It was his mannerisms—his walk, the tilt of his head, the slight twitch of his fingers against his thigh. Gabe was Luc Piccoult, and even though the terrorist had been dead for close to eight years, the rest of the world and Piccoult's organization thought he was still very much still alive, only in hiding for the past few years. Gabe brought Piccoult back to life when necessary.

And it was definitely necessary.

Gabe took her by the elbow and led her into the lobby of the Azadi Grand Hotel, which happened to be a straight shot down the road to the museum. It's the reason he'd chosen to use Luc Piccoult's identity. Piccoult never stayed anywhere but the penthouse suite of the Azadi, and it afforded them the privacy they needed as well as putting them in a prime location.

Grace caught a glimpse of herself in the floor-to-ceiling mirrors that walled the lobby, and she decided she liked being Stella Gautier. She liked it a lot. Her flame-red hair was covered by a sleek black wig that was cut so it curved just at her jaw line. Her eyes were almost as black as her hair, and her breasts were a good cup size bigger. She wore an expensive black suit and sky-high heels. Her lips were red and full and her expression mildly bored. But no one in the lobby could ignore the size of the diamond nestled at the hollow of her throat. It was just ostentatious enough to show everyone her station in life. It wasn't the kind of jewelry a man gave to his wife, but Stella Gautier made out very well as the mistress to a very powerful man.

"I can't begin to interpret the look that just came across your face," Gabe whispered in her ear.

"I'll tell you later." Her smile was coy as she stepped out of his embrace. "It involves the wig."

The purr of pleasure in his chest was low enough that only she heard it, and she put a little extra swing in her hips as she went to window-shop at the jewelry store the hotel provided for their more exclusive guests.

"Monsieur Piccoult." The hotel manager greeted Gabe familiarly in stilted French. "We are honored to have you back at the Azadi. The penthouse suite is ready for the arrival of you and your…guest."

The manager's eyes swept over Grace with unhidden desire, and he whispered something to Gabe that had him laughing and slipping a sizable tip into the man's hand. Gabe looked at her with complete possession and jerked his head so she'd know to follow him. Her eyes spit black fire at the unspoken command, but she did as she was bidden. It was all part of playing the game.

Gabe dominated the center of the elevator, checking his watch every few seconds, while Grace scrolled through messages on her phone from people she'd never heard of. There was never a way to know who was watching or listening, so they both stayed silent until the doors opened on the top level. Gabe's hand was warm and sure against the small of her back as he led her to the large double doors at the end of a long, elegant hallway.

Her shoes sunk into the plush patterned carpet of blues and grays while she made quick work of noticing where the cameras were located. Ethan would have to tamper with them so no one would notice them coming and going, but it wouldn't be difficult for someone with his level of skill.

They stepped inside the penthouse suite, and Grace immediately felt the hairs prickle on the back of her neck. She reached for the small Beretta she had at her back just as Gabe pulled out his Ruger.

"It's about damned time," Jack said from one of the smaller bedrooms. "You're two hours late."

His transformation was remarkable. His skin had been darkened, and his hair was thick and dark. Brown contacts covered his green eyes, and he wore an expensive suit. A diamond ring glittered on his pinky. Just another business man who'd get easily lost in a crowd. Nothing remarkable about his features.

"Jesus, Jack," Grace said. "What are you doing in here?"

"I got worried when you missed rendezvous time."

"We ran into a little maintenance trouble with the plane."

"Uh-huh," Jack said disbelievingly. "Maybe next time you guys could keep a clock by the bed while you're getting reacquainted."

"Fuck you," Gabe said as Grace laughed.

"Not unless Grace agrees to join in. Otherwise it would just be awkward."

Gabe's smile was razor sharp as he opened his mouth to respond to Jack, but a soft knock interrupted them.

"Bedroom," Gabe whispered to Jack. "It's our luggage."

Jack went into the spare bedroom and closed the door just as Gabe let the bellboy in. Grace wandered around the room, ignoring the opulence surrounding her as if it were subpar and instead checked out the balconies and the best vantage point of the museum.

It was a modern building of angles and glass, and it sat

at a diagonal a little over five hundred yards away. All sides could be seen except for the back. It would be up to Ethan to be the eyes on her blind side and watch Jack and Gabe's backs until they were safely on the roof.

"What do you think?" Gabe asked when they were alone once again.

"I think it's risky," she said. "If things go to shit and I have to take a shot, we'll have to get out fast and quiet. And with as many guards as there are, the chances of me having to bail one of you out increases. We're practically trapped up here, and any investigator worth his salt will know this is where the shot was fired from."

"Then Jack and I will have to make sure you don't need to fire any shots. Just be our eyes."

"Speaking of eyes," Jack said, "Ethan has us all tapped into his screens at headquarters."

Gabe tapped his watch, and Ethan's voice came through clearly from his earpiece. "Checking in, Dragon. Do you read?"

"Loud and clear, Ghost. Grim Reaper and Renegade checked in earlier," Ethan answered, referring to Logan and Jack. "I'm only waiting to hear from Kill Shot."

"I assume that's me?" Grace asked, rolling her eyes. "I guess I should be grateful it's not Pussy Galore."

Jack burst into laughter, and Gabe's eyes crinkled at the corners as his shoulders shook. She flicked the switch on her watch and said, "Checking in, Dragon. How's the security at the hotel?"

"Why is everyone laughing? What's going on?" He

asked.

"Jack's fly was unzipped." Grace answered.

"I'm sorry, who am I speaking with?" Ethan said deadpan. "I don't recall you having a sense of humor."

The smile left Grace's face, and she averted her gaze from Gabe's as their laughter died. Something tightened in her chest, and she realized she was holding her breath. She could feel the person she'd once been hammering away at the woman she was now. There had been a time when she'd had a sense of humor—when she'd been the one on the team who always had a sarcastic word or a quick quip. The thing that made her feel the worst was she was just realizing how much she missed being a part of something like this over the past couple of years. Being part of a team—a family. But there was something inside of her that felt ashamed that she could so easily go back to the person she'd been when her life was only tatters of what it had once been.

"Security, Dragon. Tell me what we're dealing with." Her voice was cold this time, and she could hear his sigh over the line.

"It wasn't hard to tap into the main computers at the hotel. They use a satellite system, so I slipped in undetected and can monitor and control as you need. I can override the elevators and phone systems if needed. The hotel is covered unless you get ambushed inside your room. Gabe wouldn't let me set up visual in your suite."

"I can't imagine why, you perv," Jack said.

"I would stop looking the minute I saw she was taking her clothes off. I swear," Ethan said soberly.

"Jesus," Grace said. "Someone tell me again why we're working with a teenager."

"I'm an adult. I'm eighteen."

Jack groaned, and Gabe looked like he wanted to start drinking heavily. "Dragon" he said. "You're pushing it."

"It's not like you can replace me," Ethan mumbled under his breath.

Gabe's fists were clenched tightly, and his voice sounded like he'd swallowed shards of glass when he growled out, "Dragon."

"Sorry. Like I said, the hotel is covered. It's the museum we need to worry about. I can't tap into their feed. They're using a military-grade security system, but the sensors I gave you should render it penetrable."

"What do you mean '*should* render it penetrable'?" Gabe asked.

"It's not like I have the opportunity to practice on many military-grade systems. But it will work. I'm almost sure of it. Just place the sensors I gave you in the correct locations. Technology will take care of the rest."

"We hope," Jack muttered.

Ethan had created a camera so small it fit on a clear sticker no bigger than the tip of a woman's pinky finger. It was almost invisible and virtually undetectable, so they'd have a clear shot of every dark corner and niche inside and outside the museum, as well as every guard. Once the sensors were in place, Ethan would activate the device, and the electronic frequency would give him the ability to tap into the control room and manipulate everything from the temperature to the monitors watched by security.

"Kill Shot will run through the spot checks in case we run into trouble," Gabe said. "She'll be able to alert us if anything unusual is going on around the perimeter of the museum. Grim Reaper will be our eyes inside, and Dragon will monitor the security while we get the painting."

"It doesn't seem like Renegade is very important to this mission," Ethan said. "I don't know, Ghost, it seems on a mission like this that everyone should be pulling their weight. Maybe you should cut him loose."

"I'm too fucking old for this," Gabe muttered and turned to Jack. "I'm going to give him to Logan when we get back to headquarters. He has more patience than Job, and he probably won't kill the kid."

"Bollocks to that," Logan said through the earpiece. He was walking all the exit paths from the city to the cars they had stashed for a quick getaway to make sure no unexpected construction had popped up to block their escape. "They'll never find all of the pieces once I get through with him."

"You guys are a laugh a minute," Ethan said.

"Enough," Gabe commanded. "It's go time. Everyone stay connected and report in as if this were tonight. I want to know everyone's line of sight at all times."

"Roger that," Logan said.

Gabe nodded and left the suite. As Luc Piccoult, Gabe had an enormous influence over a lot of very important people in Iran. Piccoult also happened to have a collection of bronze statues from the Renaissance period that the curator of the Tehran National Museum had been salivating over for several years. Gabe had set up a meeting with the curator so he'd have the opportunity to place the sensors throughout the museum while promising the man a loan of his bronzes for display. Everyone would be happy. Except the curator when he found one of his paintings had gone missing.

Grace went to unpack her weapon. Her hands were sure and steady as her fingers glided over the cold metal. With every piece she put together it was as if she were becoming more whole. No matter what was going on in her personal life, she always had this she could count on. She didn't load the rifle for this practice run.

"What's your ETA, Ghost?" she asked.

"Fifteen minutes on foot."

She went into the bedroom and closed the door behind her, stripping off the expensive suit and pulling on khaki cargos and a long-sleeved T-shirt of the same color. Thick socks and boots came next, and she slapped a hat over the wig to keep her hair out of her face.

When she came out of the room, Jack was sitting at the dining table with two laptops open in front of him. He'd be able to see the inside of the museum once Gabe got all the sensors in place.

"Lookin' good, sweetheart," he said, giving her a wink.

"Nice," Ethan said. "I'm sure your SEALs loved to be called sweetheart when you were on missions."

Grace winked back and pulled a pair of eye protectors from her gun case. She put the strap of the rifle across her body so it lay across her back, and she opened the balcony door of the suite. A hot wind slapped at her face and clothes. The balcony was large, and the railing around the outside was more than chest high and made of solid stone. But at each corner the architects had ignored safety and gone for artistry instead. Wrought iron bars spiraled out of the smooth concrete floor and tapered into a jumble of twisted metal that resembled something faintly feminine and erotic.

Sand swirled across the floor in lazy patterns, and she got down on hands and knees, adjusting her position until she lay flat on the ground. She pulled her rifle around and set it up so it was propped on the tiny stand that would keep it stable if the wind shifted, though she was protected fairly well by the high balcony walls.

"Approaching the first checkpoint," Gabe said softly.

"Grim Reaper in position and placing outside sensors," Logan said. The outside sensors would only be placed on the side of the museum that Grace was blinded to. They didn't have enough cameras to monitor the entire perimeter, so her eyes would have to be good enough.

"Hot damn," Jack said. "Will you look at that? They actually work."

"Of course they work," Ethan said, offended. "You stick to being the brawn, Renegade. I'll be the brains."

"Of course, we still don't know if they'll override the system. We could have the Iranian Revolutionary Guard surround us in minutes if they don't. I've been in an Iranian prison. It isn't fun, and I'd prefer not to go back."

"They'll work," Ethan growled.

"I've got you in my sights, Ghost," Grace said, using her scope to pick Gabe out of the busy pedestrian traffic in front of the museum. She panned around the building, looking for threats or unknowns that might pop up. "It sure is nice of them to have all those big windows everywhere. Christ, I can basically see right through the whole place. Everyone is a sitting duck."

"Geez, bloodthirsty are you? Too bad you're not here to kill anyone," Ethan said.

"The biggest challenge for you guys isn't going to be getting in and out," Grace said. "It's going to be keeping to the shadows so some Good Samaritan walking down the street doesn't see you and turn you in. It's literally a glass house."

"I've gotten in and out of worse places," Jack said.

"It looks like luck is going to be on your side," Ethan said. "The National Weather Service has just sent out an alert for an approaching sandstorm. It's not a large one, but it should do the trick."

"Ghost just placed the first sensor inside the entryway. I've got a clear picture coming through on my screen."

"I see him," Grace said. "The curator has terrible taste in clothes. That's the most hideous tie I've ever seen. I'll give you fifty bucks, Ghost, if you tell him so." Laughter filled her earpiece and she saw Gabe's lips tighten at the corners.

"All of my sensors are in place," Logan said. "Am I clear to head back?"

"Just a minute," Ethan said. "Let me make sure I've got a good visual here." Silence reigned for a few minutes as Ethan messed with the electronic end of things. "Okay, we're good to go. I've got a complete visual of the back of the museum. Line of sight ends about a hundred feet out."

"You're clear to come back, Grim Reaper. You haven't picked up any unusual traffic." Grace adjusted her view and panned around Logan, his right hand in the pocket of his business suit and a briefcase in his other as he joined the pedestrians on the sidewalk.

"Ghost is on the third floor now," Jack reported. "We've got a visual of the control room doors and the painting. It's an ugly bastard. I can see why Hitler turned to tyranny."

"Here we go," Ethan said. "Ghost just placed the last sensor. You'll see the visuals on your screen, Renegade, as soon as I tap into their system. Circuits are going live now."

Grace watched Gabe and the curator both look up at the ceiling as the lights inside the museum flickered. But no guards came running out of the control room yelling that they'd been breached, so she let out the breath she'd been holding.

"And we're in," Ethan said smugly. "Told you they'd work. All monitors are up—stairwells, elevators, bathrooms, the employee lounge, and all areas of the museum, including the restricted areas, are visible. Mission accomplished."

Grace panned through the crowd of faces outside the museum looking for threats. Something was making her uneasy, but she couldn't put her finger on it. But the feeling was gone the moment she saw the gleam of black curls in the reflection of her scope. The girl's scarf had blown around her shoulders, and a blue bow was tied in her hair. She rested her head on her mother's shoulder and tapped chubby fingers to an internal tune against the woman's back. The curve of the little girl's cheek was so familiar that pain rushed down Grace's spine and her muscles seized.

"No," she moaned, her mouth going dry and her heart leaping in her chest with hope—just a glimmer of hope that it might really be Maddie. She didn't hear the change of her breathing or the animal cries of pain that escaped from her throat.

The little girl turned her head, and Grace saw black eyes instead of Gabe's clear blue, and her world crashed around her once again. Her hands shook, and her rifle clattered to the concrete. She pulled her legs up and hugged her knees as she tried to get control. She closed her eyes, and images bombarded her mind, piercing her soul with the accuracy of a well-aimed knife. The darkness slithered across her body like thick tar and clung to her without remorse as it suffocated her thoughts and hopes and dreams.

No, no, no she screamed over and over in her mind. It wasn't her daughter down there hugging another woman—a woman that didn't know what true emptiness felt like. Maddie was gone. Gone forever. Grace's body felt battered as rage and pain fought to find something solid to anchor itself to. She wanted to scream—to lash out—to fight, but she knew she had to keep it all inside. It was her pain, her loss, and she didn't want to share it with anyone.

"Shit, snap out of it, Grace."

Jack's voice sounded as if it were coming from underwater—distorted and slow—the urgency her subconscious knew should be there diluted by something greater. Her body was floating, and she thought, *finally…this is finally the end.*

Reality slapped her in the face with a cold hand, and she sputtered and spit as frigid water rained down on her face from the showerhead and soaked her to the skin.

Her mind was a jumble of memories, and Jack's face became clear as the blackness started to fade. His mouth was a thin line, and she could see the worry in his eyes. She could also see the anger. She'd compromised them all— put the entire team in danger—even though they were only doing a routine run-through. But Jack had every right to be mad because she'd known this could happen going into the mission, and she hadn't shared it with the team.

"What the *fuck* is going on?" she heard Ethan yell.

She rolled to her hands and knees and pushed up slowly, her muscles stiff and protesting. Strings of red hair hung down her face. She'd lost the wig somewhere. Her teeth chattered, and the cold wracked her body in spasms.

"I'm in the lobby," Gabe said in her ear. "I want everyone offline by the time I get upstairs. We'll have a team briefing in a half hour. Everyone meet in the suite. No arguments. And Ethan, if I find out you've patched through to listen in, there won't be a box small enough for what's left of your body to go back to your mother. Understood?"

"Loud and clear. Dragon is out."

"Grim Reaper out."

Grace hauled herself out of the tub and took the towel Jack offered her. She didn't look at herself in the mirror as she dried her face and hair. Her breathing was ragged, and only sheer force of will kept her legs steady beneath her.

"Grace," Jack said.

"I can't Jack. Not yet. I'm sorry."

She heard him sigh and say, "Oh, baby," just before he pulled her into his arms. She was stiff against him because he wasn't Gabe, and she knew if she let him comfort her that she wouldn't be able to keep her emotions in check.

"I'm okay, Jack," she said, pushing away. "It's my fault. I got distracted. It won't happen again. I need to apologize to the team."

"Yeah, not telling us this could happen is your fault. And Gabe's." His voice was gentle as he handed her a thick robe to stop her shivers. "But whatever is causing this to happen isn't your fault. *Nothing* that happened is your fault. I don't have the words for you. I don't know what to say to help you. But I know you have to get control over this. Or it's going to kill you. And this world needs you, Grace. Whether you need it or not."

"Grace," Gabe said as he came into the bathroom in a rush.

He didn't have time to touch her or ask if she was alright before Jack shoved him into the bedroom. They went down with a heavy thud against the thick carpet, and she winced when Jack's fist connected with Gabe's ribs. The fight wouldn't last long. They never did. Jack was bigger and had more bulk, but she'd never seen Gabe come out on the losing end of a fight. The fact that he let Jack land a punch at all meant that he was feeling some guilt over not letting him know about her sooner.

"You told me to keep a fucking eye on her," Jack said. "You didn't tell me she might collapse and go into a trance during the middle of a fucking mission. Those are important details, my friend."

Gabe only grunted as he dodged Jack's fist.

Grace stripped out of her wet clothes and wrapped the robe around her tighter, keeping her eyes on the two bodies rolling across the floor. Gabe twisted his position so his knees were planted in Jack's sternum, and she knew it wouldn't be too much longer.

Clothes that belonged to Piccoult's mistress hung neatly in the closet, and she pulled out a pair of designer jeans and a top that draped open in the back. She had a pair of strappy heels on her feet and her hair braided by the time Gabe finally got tired of fighting. He picked Jack up by the front of his shirt and threw him against the wall.

An obscenely expensive looking glass plate sculpture shattered against the writing desk it had been hanging above. Jack and Gabe were both breathing hard, and blood dotted the corner of Jack's lip. They stared at each other for a long time, and she knew they'd worked with each other long enough that words didn't have to be spoken for them to have an entire conversation.

"Grace, I need to talk to you," Gabe finally said.

"You can talk to me with the rest of the team. Your thirty minutes is up."

"Grace—"

"I don't want to talk about this now. I can't. I'll apologize to the others. I know they deserve that, but I don't feel like being dissected by you right now. Just give me some time."

His lips tightened to a thin line, and she knew if she'd been standing closer he would have grabbed her and hauled her into the bathroom where they could have some privacy, but she was already past Jack and into the main sitting room, and he didn't have any choice but to follow.

"This is Dragon checking in," Ethan said through the com link. "Everyone okay out there?"

"Stand by," Gabe said. "We'll wait until everyone joins us."

"Grim Reaper back online," Logan said. "I'm at the door of your suite."

Grace took a deep breath and straightened her shoulders. She'd made a mistake, and she'd face the others like a big girl. She opened the door for Logan and met his gray eyes as he walked over the threshold.

Jack and Gabe had come into the room behind her, and Jack tossed Gabe a beer before he grabbed one for himself—the hostility gone as if it had never happened. Jack turned a chair around and straddled it, and Logan stood by the door as if he was waiting to make a hasty exit. Gabe stared at her a long moment, and for the first time since she could remember, she couldn't read his expression. It was the face of the man she'd been married to that last year he'd worked for Tussad. The face of a man who had secrets.

"Is someone going to tell us what's going on?" Ethan asked impatiently.

"I want to apol—"

"No," Gabe said, interrupting her. "This is my op. My mistake. I'm the one who owes you all an apology." He stood with his back to the glass balcony doors that overlooked the city, his expression grim. "There are personal issues I knew could come up on this mission, and I knew that Grace might not be able to make it through the op without her past weighing down on her. This is my fault, and I take a hundred percent of the responsibility. And at this point I have to think of the team and the mission."

Grace's hands clamped into fists, and something terrible ripped at her insides. Gabe's gaze was steady on hers, as if the others weren't in the room at all, but he wasn't looking at her as he had twenty-four hours ago.

"You're the best sniper I've ever worked with, Grace, but until you let yourself heal, you're a danger to this team. I'm sending you back to headquarters. Once Jack and I have secured the painting, you and I will talk this through and see what we need to do. But I can't take the chance with the rest of the team."

Cold fingers of fear licked down her spine. She'd always chosen to isolate herself—to be alone because she wanted to. It had always been her decision. Now he was taking that away from her. And then there was the fact that Gabe had made her love him again and was pushing her away because things were getting too hard to deal with.

"And what about all of your promises, Gabe? You're the one who wanted me here. I was doing just fine on my own."

"You can lie to yourself all you want, Grace, but that doesn't change the facts. I brought you here because I love you, and it's time for you to stop running. I brought you here because you need me as much as I need you."

"And what about Tussad?"

"I'll deal with Tussad another day. Once we're not neck deep in shit in the middle of hostile territory. Did it ever occur to you that revenge might not be the best option?" he asked, frustration clouding his voice for the first time. "Because it's sure as hell occurred to me. Maybe if you could let go of the past, you could have a future that didn't involve you having a breakdown during the middle of a mission. Maybe you could have a normal life again."

"What the fuck is a normal life?" she yelled, hating the fact that her control was slipping. "You want to go back to what we had before? Where your entire life was a constant lie? One you didn't feel the need to share with me? Can't you ever think of anything besides the next mission? When did she stop mattering to you, Gabe?"

She knew her words were harsh, and she meant to lash out and cause him pain. It might be childish, but she was hurting too.

"Jesus, Grace," Jack said, shaking his head. "You're not playing fair."

"Stay out of this, Jack. Nothing is ever fair. I know what matters in my life. And I know what I'm living for. Tussad is mine. And taking him out of this world is worth spending an eternity in hell. It can't be much worse than spending it here on Earth."

"Listen to me, Grace. If you want to fight, then we'll fight. But not here. Not now. Tussad is another issue and another op. You and I are another issue. I know someone who can help us when we get back to headquarters. But right now, you need to do the best thing for the team, and go home."

Numbness settled over her body, and she could feel the color fade from her cheeks. She wanted to scream. She wanted to let free the rage that was pummeling against her rigid muscles. To release the pain that was seizing her lungs until every gasp of oxygen felt as if it could be her last.

"Fine," she finally managed to say. "You're the boss." She turned on her heel and headed to the bedroom to gather her rifle.

"Grace," Jack called out. "Don't do anything stupid. Just go home and wait for us there."

She arrowed him with a look that made him come to his feet and move the chair out of the way.

"I don't have a home, Jack. I never did."

CHAPTER NINETEEN

Gabe watched the bedroom door and cursed himself a thousand ways to Sunday. Would they never have it easy? What had he done in this life to deserve this?

The others were deadly silent as they listened to the snick of Grace's rifle case closing. She came out of the bedroom as cold and calm as she'd ever been, her wig straightened and back on her head. Her face was devoid of emotion, though she was pale as a ghost.

"Logan will drive you to the airport," Gabe said. "The plane will be ready to take off as soon as you arrive. My security team will meet you at the airport in London to see to your safety. I'll have another of my pilots come back and retrieve the rest of us after the op is finished."

Logan never showed much emotion, but the look he gave Gabe made sure he knew his displeasure. But Logan knew how to follow orders, and he nodded his head sharply.

"I don't think so," Grace said with a cynical smile. "I can take care of myself."

Cold fear snaked through his body as she took the watch off her wrist and slipped the earpiece out of her ear. "We're done here, Gabe. Don't come after me again." She tossed the electronics on the couch and headed for the door.

"It wasn't a request, Grace. And I'll come after you as many damn times as it takes to get through that thick skull of yours. Logan will take you to the plane."

Logan moved to stand in front of her, and before Gabe or Jack either one could intercede, Grace dropped her bag and shot her hands toward Logan. Gabe had to admire her skill, even though he regretted teaching her those particular moves. She used two fingers to slap at Logan's shoulders, chest and neck, and Logan looked stunned as he fell to the floor, his limbs temporarily paralyzed.

"Have a nice life, boys," she said with a salute as she closed the door of the suite silently behind her.

"Well, you have to give her points for style," Jack drawled, sitting back in his chair.

"What happened? Ethan asked. "I can't see anything, dammit. Why is Kill Shot offline? Her heart monitor isn't even registering. You didn't kill her, did you?"

Gabe closed his eyes and straddled the other dining room chair across from Jack. Logan was beginning to get the feeling back in his body, and he turned his head to glare at Gabe.

"Sorry," Gabe said. "You should be fine in a few minutes."

"Except for his pride and his manhood," Jack muttered.

Gabe ran his fingers through his hair and looked at his watch. They still had eight hours before they were scheduled to break into the museum. He pulled his phone out of his pocket and scrolled through the coded numbers he'd assigned until he found the one he was looking for.

"Simon," he said to his pilot. "Grace is on her way to you. You're her only way out of country. Take her back to headquarters. She's to be detained and on restricted access until we return. Do whatever you have to do to get her to cooperate."

Gabe hung up the phone, and Jack let out a low whistle, drawing his attention. "You're digging yourself a hell of a hole to get out of."

"I'll do whatever it takes to keep her safe."

Ethan cleared his throat and said, "So, by using my amazing deductive reasoning skills, I'm assuming that you and Grace know each other a hell of a lot better than we all thought."

Gabe sighed, and knew he couldn't keep the truth from them any longer. They needed to know what they were dealing with.

"You could say that. Grace is my wife."

"Holy shit," Ethan said. "That, I wasn't expecting. How come you're not mentioned in her file? It says she's never married and has no living relatives."

"You'd better stop digging through our files, kid," Jack growled.

"There's no mention of me in any file," Gabe said. "As far as the US government is concerned, I don't exist on paper."

He said his next words quickly—mechanically—as if reciting from the dossier that was put together after Maddie's death.

"Two years ago, our daughter was targeted by a sniper in Tussad's army and killed right in front of Grace's eyes. The trauma has made her—" Gabe searched for the words he wanted, but couldn't seem to think of one that would make them understand.

"She's not the same person she used to be," Jack said softly. "I can see glimpses of the real Grace in there somewhere, but until her hatred of Tussad is resolved, she's not going to get better. She needs professional help."

"I know that," Gabe said, the frustration evident in his voice. "And I'll make sure she gets it once this is over."

"So what do we do now?" Ethan asked.

"Nothing has changed," Gabe said. "We get the painting and move forward with the plan."

***

The only way Grace knew how to deal with being hurt was with anger, but she knew she had to control her emotions until she was out of the country and back on neutral soil. So for that reason alone, she had the concierge at the hotel get a car service to take her to the private airstrip where Gabe's plane was located. She still had a part to play. At least for a little while.

She had her passport and papers ready when the driver pulled into the private area for VIPs. The guard saw her French citizenship and that she was using Piccoult's aircraft, and he let her through with only a cursory glance.

The plane was ready for takeoff, the stairs extended, waiting for her arrival. Gabe would have called ahead, and she was expecting Simon to try something unorthodox to detain her. She knew Gabe would have given the order. It's what she would have done in his position. Simon would try to drug her food or tranq her before they landed.

Her spine began to tingle as she reached the top of the stairs to the entrance of the plane. Simon should have been waiting for her. Unless he was hiding behind the door, getting ready to detain her. She didn't pull the gun at the small of her back. Not yet. She didn't want to incite panic from the airfield guards. But she did palm the small knife she kept in a sheath on the inside of her wrist.

She didn't want to hurt Simon, but she'd be damned if she was going to be held prisoner until Gabe decided she was able.

"Simon," she called out. "I'm giving you a fair warning. It's best to ignore whatever orders Gabe just gave you. I'd hate for you to get hurt."

She crossed the threshold and immediately checked the hidden area behind the door. There wasn't anyone in sight, but the tingles down her spine had turned into full-fledged alarms telling her to get the hell out before it was too late.

Grace reached for her gun just as the cockpit door

slammed open and she was shoved forward. She rolled as best she could in the confined space and came back up to face her attacker as fast as she could—her weapon pointed and ready to fire.

She recognized Shawn Kimball from the file Ethan had put together. He'd already closed the cabin door by the time she'd made it to her feet, and now it was just the two of them. She kicked off her shoes and held the pistol steady, just as he held his steady on her. His smile bordered on madness, and anticipation gleamed in his eyes. She could also see the intelligence. Kimball wasn't someone to underestimate.

He was a big bastard—close to the same height as Gabe and as broad through the chest and shoulders as Jack. His hair was buzzed close to his scalp, and he held his weapon with ease. She could tell a lot about a man by how he held his weapon. And Grace knew before they even began that she was in deep shit.

"Was Simon the name of your pilot?" Kimball asked, his smile cruel. "I'll have to apologize about the mess in your bathroom. Simon was a big man. Lots of blood."

He came closer, and Grace worked probabilities in her mind, trying to find a way she could fire and get out of the way before Kimball did the same. Her conclusions weren't reassuring.

The plane began to taxi, and Grace knew her chances of winning this fight grew slimmer the minute they were airborne. It would be too dangerous to fire then. She dove to her right and fired off a shot, her back hitting the base of the leather couch against the wall and pain shooting up her spine.

"Bitch," Kimball said.

Shit. She'd only winged his arm. The plane tilted as they rose into the air, and she tried to find her balance as she got to her feet and faced Kimball again. They tossed their weapons to the floor at the same time, it being too dangerous to fire shots while in the air—and she grasped the knife in her hand as Kimball charged her.

She swiped out with the knife, slicing at his shirt just as his fist landed in her ribs. The blow knocked her against the cabin wall and stole her breath, and she dodged his foot in a kick that would have broken her neck. Pain radiated through her body, but she had enough sense to keep moving. A moving target was harder to hit. The knife was knocked from her hand, and she kicked out at his knee, feeling satisfaction when it buckled beneath him. It was only enough respite for her to fill her lungs with oxygen and roll to the side as his fist caught the side of her jaw.

"I can't kill you yet," he said, getting to his feet, favoring his injured knee. "But I'm going to make you hurt."

Grace wiped the blood off her face, unsure exactly where it was coming from. "Why don't we just sit down and you can tell me what you want? You look like a reasonable kind of guy."

"Well, sweetheart, that wouldn't be near as much fun."

They circled each other, Grace trying to make her way to her knife that had skittered close to the cockpit doors.

"Where are you taking me?" she asked as he closed in on her.

"Back to London, of course. Weren't those your orders? It seems you and that husband of yours are having communication problems."

Grace stiffened as Kimball so casually tossed out that bit of information. No one but Frank Bennett and Jack had ever known she was married to Gabe. It had been too dangerous—something that could have been used against him if the knowledge had leaked. She had no illusions as to her position in the agency. She knew without a doubt that if it came to protecting Gabe and what he did for the country, then they'd throw her to the wolves in a heartbeat. But somehow this man knew who she was. Knew who Gabe was.

"I don't know what you're talking about," she hedged.

He flexed his knuckles and smiled cruelly. "I didn't recognize the great and mighty Gabe Brennan when I looked at the surveillance photos my men sent me. I've always heard of your husband, of course, and I believe there was a time I worked with him when he was—"

Kimball shrugged his shoulders as if what he was saying didn't bother him, but she could tell by the hatred in his eyes that his experience with Gabe hadn't been a good one.

"We'll just say he was someone else at the time," he continued. "But you—I recognized you in the photo right away. That red hair of yours is a hell of a beacon."

Before she could dodge out of the way, he'd snatched the black wig from her head and tossed it to the ground.

"We have a mutual friend," he said. "I'm sure Mr. Tussad would love to be here right now, but I'm not working for him at the moment. You of all people should understand how important the financial options and benefits are when considering taking a job."

Grace went cold inside. Tussad's name had the ability to paralyze her like no other. "What do you know of Tussad?" Grace asked. She knew she was giving herself away. The anger in her voice couldn't be concealed.

"Don't you want to know how I recognized you?" he asked.

Her fists clinched at her sides, and she put her weight on the balls of her feet, the anger inside of her building like the fiery heat inside a volcano, ready to burst from the side of a mountain.

"I never saw the resemblance between you and your daughter, but Tussad assured me she was yours. You should have known I was there that day. Anyone trained in combat would have felt my gaze. And I looked at you for a long time, Grace."

The predatory look in her eyes and the way his gaze dropped to her breast made the bile rise in the back of her throat, and the heat of her anger was replaced by the cold lash of his words, striking against her body as if they were physical blows. She finally understood what he was saying.

"It was you?" She could barely get the words past her dry throat, and his terrible smile was all the assurance she needed that he was the one who'd pulled the trigger that terrible day.

She charged him with the force of her anger leading the way. Satisfaction coursed through her when she felt the satisfying crunch of cartilage and bone beneath her fist as she struck him in the nose. The pain his own blows inflicted on her didn't register—the sting to her ribs or the blood that dripped freely from her mouth onto her shirt. Her arm hung useless by her side as she battled him, but her anger eventually gave way to unbearable pain, and she dropped to her knees before him.

Kimball grabbed her by the throat and lifted her until her feet dangled just off the ground. "It's going to be a pleasure putting a bullet through your heart," he whispered, close enough that she was able to feel his hot breath against her face. "It's only fitting you should die helpless just as your daughter did."

The game of life and death had ceased to matter to her, but she vowed she'd live long enough to see the man buried in the ground.

"My days may very well be numbered," she said hoarsely, his grasp tightening around her throat. "But yours are numbered as well. I will kill you, Shawn Kimball. That's a promise. And you'll never even know I'm there until it's too late."

She spit in his face and was in no position to dodge as the back of his fist connected with her jaw. The coppery tang of blood filled her mouth just as the darkness closed in on her.

CHAPTER TWENTY

The game had changed.

Shawn Kimball kept an ice pack against his broken nose as he scrolled through the numbers on Grace's phone, comparing them to those on the phone he'd stolen from the pilot.

He glanced once at the woman. She was out cold, her hair matted with blood and tangled around her swollen face. He'd tied her hands and feet and tossed her in the corner. It would be a while yet until she woke up.

Kimball had accepted the job to help William Sloane recreate The Passover Project because the money had been too good to pass up. But he wasn't an idiot. He'd been around Sloane too long not to realize that he had every intention of getting rid of anyone who had ties to this particular job.

But sometimes it wasn't the money. He had enough

money to last ten lifetimes. Sometimes the past just had to be dealt with. And this was one of those times. He didn't have any particular loyalty to Kamir Tussad. Hell, he didn't have loyalty to anyone but himself. But when Gabe Brennan was working undercover with Tussad, he'd screwed up three major arms deals Kimball had been brokering, the US confiscating the weapons and killing several of his business associates.

At the time, Tussad had been merely inconvenienced. He had enough power and enough contacts to sweep the mistakes under the rug and offer new deals. There was certainly not a shortage of men and women in the world who wanted to hold all the power during the next war— because there was always another war. It was the way the world worked.

No, it hadn't been Tussad who'd suffered. Kimball had been the broker for all the bad deals, and it was him who'd been stripped and beaten. He was the one who'd taken well-placed knife wounds—wounds that wouldn't kill, only give excruciating pain. Tussad had eventually come to his aid because he had another job he needed Kimball to facilitate, but his usefulness was the only reason he'd interfered. Kimball would be dead otherwise.

The CIA had thought he was still doing his job for them at the time. It hadn't been hard to feed them lies and give them the occasional victory. So when he'd told them someone on the inside was betraying them, the agency had been in such disarray trying to find the culprit that it hadn't been difficult to break into classified files and see what agents were working undercover in Tussad's organization. He'd been handed Derrick Kyle and Gabe Brennan on a silver platter.

He'd heard whispers of Gabe before, of course. Everyone had heard whispers. But no one really believed he existed. Men like that didn't really exist. But Gabe Brennan did exist, and Kimball had seen it as a personal challenge to make the legend nothing more than a pathetic memory.

Once Kimball had found out about Gabe, he'd known immediately he would have to betray him to Tussad to get the exact outcome he wanted. They'd had to work quickly because Gabe was trained to be aware when things were about to turn to shit. They'd managed to find out as much about Gabe Brennan as anyone knew in less than twenty-four hours. As soon as they'd discovered he had a wife and daughter, it was clear what their course of action should be. And when they dug a little deeper into Grace's background, it was decided that she'd be left alive. Her kinds of talents might be of use in the future.

He laughed despite his throbbing face. She was about to become very useful. And William Sloane was about to get a rude awakening. The Passover Project was about to go on the open market to the highest bidder. And Gabe Brennan was going to help him do it.

He picked up the dead pilot's phone and pressed the button to dial back his last call.

"What's going on, Simon?" Gabe said on the other end of the line.

"Simon isn't available at the moment. He'd have to pick up all of his intestines off the floor first."

There was a slight pause on the other end of the line,

but Gabe didn't disappoint him. His voice was cold and unemotional.

"And who would this be?" he asked.

"Someone who has a deal to offer."

"Ahh, this must be the infamous Shawn Kimball. You've got a lot of varied interests. I found your file interesting."

"Did you?" Shawn asked. "I found yours interesting as well. Of course, I read it before it was wiped from the system. But I remember you well."

"I had a feeling we might have crossed paths before. But I don't think you're the man in charge of this particular operation. Have you decided to take matters into your own hands?"

"You could say that." Shawn appreciated the fact that he didn't have to spell things out for his adversary. It put them on a much more level playing ground. "I've decided my employer isn't the man to handle The Passover Project. I'm even willing to give you his name once we get down to business."

"And do we have business, Kimball?"

"I've been impressed with how quickly you've tracked us down. Killing Standridge certainly put a wrench in things, but you didn't destroy all of his research. I've already found another scientist willing to take up the good doctor's work."

Kimball knew he had Gabe's attention now. "I know you'll have the second part of the formula once you steal the painting."

"You still need the third part of the formula from the second painting. And even then it will only work if your scientist can recreate the first part that was destroyed."

"It's awfully nice of you to warn me of these obstacles. But don't worry. I've had the missing part of the formula all along. My employer was kind enough to already have it in his possession. It seems he's somehow related to the original scientist who created the formula. Genetics are damned interesting. Haven't you ever wondered where you come from?"

"I don't have the time to have the birds-and-the-bees talk with you, Kimball. You've yet to tell me how we have business. In the next few hours, I'm going to be in possession of the last part of the formula you need. It'll be a cold day in hell before I give it to you."

"Don't make promises you can't keep. You'll give the painting to me and walk away."

"Will I? Why would I do something like that?"

"Because I have something I believe you'll want back." Kimball looked at Grace once more, wishing he could slit her throat and send him the pictures. But the time for her to die would come soon. "She's not dead yet. Your wife put up a hell of a fight. Of course, she's still a woman. It wasn't hard to take her down."

He appreciated the fact that Gabe didn't even pause to think as he lied.

"I don't know what you're talking about, Kimball."

"I think you do. We'll make an even trade. You'll give me the painting, and I'll give you back your wife. If you manage to do it within the next sixteen hours, I'll make sure I don't give her back to you in pieces."

"Give me the name of the man who hired you as an act of good faith."

Kimball leaned back in his chair and adjusted his ice pack. Damned if Gabe Brennan wasn't entertaining.

"Sure," Kimball said with a shrug. "If you kill him, it'll save me the trouble. It was going to be a real pain in the ass anyway. I'm working against the clock as it is. You've probably heard of him. His name is William Sloane."

The silence on the end of the phone was very telling. "As in the Speaker of the House, William Sloane?"

"That's the one."

"Interesting," Gabe said.

"Mr. Sloane is under the impression that he would make an excellent dictator. That power can only go the person who controls The Passover Project."

"And what if I refuse to meet your demands?"

"Then I'll keep your woman alive." His voice rang with the promise of truth. "She'll be begging for death by the time I'm through with her. And while I'm at it, I hope you're not too attached to the boy wonder you've got stashed away in that fortress of yours. My men have been busy in your absence. He's only got a few minutes left before he's just another part of the rubble. It's a shame, really. I've heard he's quite brilliant."

For the first time he heard the urgency in Gabe's voice, and he smiled.

"When do we make the exchange?"

"Oxford Park Station at noon. Platform seven."

"I'll be there."

The line went dead, and Kimball wished he'd be able to see Gabe's face when he realized he was too late to save his wife.

CHAPTER TWENTY-ONE

Iran

"Ethan," Gabe said into their com link. "Evacuate now. Sound the alarm so the guards will know, and use the emergency exit. Don't argue. Start running."

He mouthed the word *bomb* to Jack and Logan, and they stared back at him with identical looks of gravity on their faces. They'd been in situations like this before, and sometimes there was nothing you could do but wait and listen.

Gabe listened to Ethan's muttered curses just before the line went dead. He tossed his phone on the table and willed it to ring. He knew it would take Ethan a few minutes to work his way through the underground tunnels that ran beneath the building and get to the safe house he'd designated for any agents who might be in trouble.

The phones wouldn't work in the tunnels since they

were made of reinforced steel, but ten minutes passed—and then fifteen—and he still hadn't gotten the all clear from Ethan.

"Fuck," Jack whispered. "Who was on the phone, Gabe, and what the hell was that conversation about? Listening to your end wasn't reassuring."

"Shawn Kimball," Gabe said. "And he has Grace. He wants the painting."

He tried to keep his emotions locked away. Grace needed him, but he couldn't slow his frantic heartbeat, and he couldn't help but imagine what Kimball was putting her through. His fist tightened at the thought, and he struggled to ignore the pounding in his skull. He couldn't lose her again. He wasn't strong enough to deal with it. And for the first time he could remember, he was about to say to hell with the mission and put something else as his priority. Something he should have done a long time ago.

His phone buzzed on the table, and Gabe let out a slow breath when he saw the number. He hit speakerphone and waited to see who he'd be talking to.

"Son of a bitch," Ethan said, his voice higher pitched than usual. "That was a hell of a bomb. For a minute there I didn't think I was going to make it. I thought the tunnels were going to cave in on me."

"Where are you?"

"A coffee shop for now," Ethan said. "They've closed off all the streets in a half-mile radius around the detonation site, and it'll be a while before I'll be able to make it to the safe house. The city is going crazy with panic."

"A coffee shop is fine. Just stay put."

"I've got my laptop, but I don't know how I can help you with all these people around."

"Logan will have to do it from inside the hotel room. You need to stay hidden. Put the computers away and just act normal for a change until you can get to the safe house."

Jack interrupted them, his voice harsh. Gabe knew they were in for a hell of a night. Sometimes friendship only went so far.

"Get back to Kimball wanting to trade the painting for Grace. Do you want to elaborate on that?" he asked.

"Kimball has taken over The Passover Project from his employer. I was informed during our conversation that he already had a new scientist working on recreating the first part of the formula. And he also mentioned that his employer had the other painting with the hidden formula right from the beginning."

"Which means that we can't under any circumstances let him complete the formula," Jack said with warning.

"We'll have time," Gabe said. He was only speaking to Jack now. He had to make Jack understand. "If Kimball follows his MO, he'll auction the weapon and sell it to the highest bidding terrorist. I know from experience it takes a couple of weeks to set up an auction like this. Not to mention the added time it will take for Kimball's scientist to complete the formula. We have time," he said again.

"You're speaking in code, Gabe," Logan said. "And skirting the issue. What are you not saying?"

"You heard me mention William Sloane," Gabe said. "It turns out he's the one who initiated the recreation of the weapon. Kimball said he's a descendent of the original scientist, and we all know that he's very powerful in Washington. He's not afraid to throw his weight around to get what he wants, but no one has the balls to come up against him. He'll be President after the next election."

"So you're saying we're going to what? Kill him?" Ethan asked. "What about Kimball?"

"Jesus, Ethan," Jack said. "You're in a public place. We've talked about this before. Keep your mouth shut and just listen."

"I locked myself in the bathroom. I'm all alone."

"This is perfect," Jack said, dropping into a chair and running his hands across his scalp. "So we get to take out the Speaker of the House, whose security is as good as, if not better than, the President's, inciting a national panic and getting our asses in a whole hell of a lot of trouble."

"One problem at a time," Gabe said. "Kimball's the bigger threat now."

"Why?" Ethan asked. "He doesn't have an auction if he doesn't have a weapon. Seems pretty simple to me."

"I don't think Gabe's idea of saving the world and ours are the same any more," Logan said.

He'd been the quietest up until now, listening and processing in his silent way, but his eyes spoke volumes. Logan was pissed. And he had every right to be.

"Kimball wants to trade Grace for the painting, and Gabe wants to accommodate him. It's what he meant when he told Jack there was plenty of time. He wants to give him the weapon and then try to stop him once the auction location is determined."

"Weren't you the one who lectured me on the importance of the whole as opposed to the individual?" Ethan asked, the anger in his voice evident. "SOP says we have to leave her behind. We can't turn over a portion of a weapon that could wipe out civilization for her."

"Agreed," Logan said. "You don't have a choice here. You have to let her go."

"Would you?" Gabe asked, speaking directly to Logan.

They never talked of Logan's past or the horrors he'd been forced to live through. Of the wife who'd died screaming his name for help. The puckered scars of fire covered a good portion of Logan's neck, back, and arms. He was the best explosives man Gabe had ever worked with, but no one was perfect. "If you had the chance to save her," Gabe said softly, "would you do it? Or would you walk away?" He wasn't talking about Grace any longer, and he could tell by the shadows that came into Logan's eyes that he knew it too.

Logan stared at him silently—defiantly—but Ethan wasn't afraid to break into an awkward pause.

"Hell, no," Ethan said. "This is bullshit, Gabe. You seriously think her life is worth everyone else's? I know she's your wife, and I'm sorry about that, but she knows the risks. I'm voting with Logan on this one. What about you, Jack?"

He looked at Jack and watched his friend close his eyes, knowing what was coming.

"Gabe," Jack started to say.

"This mission is aborted," Gabe interrupted. "The Collective is disbanded. Thank you for your work, gentlemen. Go home."

"I don't understand," Ethan said. "You're telling me you're going to throw all this away for her? You're going to risk the safety of the world for one woman?"

"You can't possibly understand, Ethan," Gabe said. "It's not about *one* woman. It's about *the* woman. There's a hell of a lot of difference. If you're lucky, you might understand it one day."

"This is pointless. You can't get the painting without us," Ethan argued.

"Sure I can," Gabe said, pulling the laptops in front of him. "Go home. All of you."

Gabe caught Logan's smile, and knew he understood. Jack groaned from across the table and muttered several inventive curses.

"Like hell I'm going home," Jack said. "Someone has to watch your back. I'm in."

"Me too," Logan said. "But you'd better have one hell of a plan."

Ethan sputtered from the phone on the table. "You've all lost your minds. This is insanity."

"Goodbye, Ethan," Gabe said, moving his finger toward the phone to disconnect.

"Wait, wait," Ethan said. "Can't you even give a guy a chance to think?" He sighed heavily across the line. "I guess I'm in too. Though I want it noted that I reserve the right to say I told you so."

"So noted," Gabe said. "Now let's go get that painting. We've got to be back in London by noon tomorrow."

***

2am

Darkness had crept across the city with reluctance, edging out the harsh sunlight as if night and day were fighting their own inevitable battle. Yellow lights flickered from buildings and parking garages, and traffic was sparse.

The air turned cold and replaced the terrible heat of the day, and a rolling wall of sand came into the city just after midnight. Already, visibility was almost impossible. Car alarms blared, and everyone was tucked safely in their homes for the night. The only bad thing was that Logan had no more visibility through the outside cameras they'd placed than anyone else might. All they had to go by was their GPS units and night-vision goggles.

"We're going to be in trouble if this storm lasts long," Jack said. "The replacement plane will be grounded."

"One thing at a time," Gabe said, staring straight up the side of the museum walls.

He could only see a few feet in front of him, and he didn't like the idea of climbing the side of a building mostly blind. He and Jack stood on the side opposite the main road, the lake at their backs. They were both dressed in black—ski masks pulled down over their heads—and the outside guards had taken their watch indoors because of the storm, so all that stood between Gabe and the painting was three stories of glass.

Gabe looked down at the black gloves that covered him from the tips of his fingers to his elbows. "Are you sure these are going to work?" he asked Ethan.

"Pretty sure," Ethan responded. "As long as you're touching glass. I haven't figured out how to make them stable against other materials yet."

"You're pretty sure?" Jack asked incredulously. "Why are you never completely sure?"

"Well, you're only going up three stories. I've found the gloves have a tendency to lose strength around five stories, so you should be okay."

"You should have let him blow up," Jack said to Gabe.

Gabe ignored them and placed his hand against the window. He immediately felt the pull of the glove against the glass, as if he were dealing with magnets instead of rubber and glass. He mirrored the image with his left hand to make sure both gloves were working properly, and then he began to climb.

His shoulders and arms strained under a rigorous display of pure strength, but he barely noticed the burn as he made his way up the side of the building. Jack kept pace on the window next to him, and neither of them spoke as they made the climb. Not until they saw what waited ahead of them.

"You've got to be kidding me," Jack said.

The glass stopped at the top of the third floor, but

there was a five-foot lip that extended over the roof of the museum that was solid stone. No glass in sight. And Gabe couldn't tell how far the ledge extended up because of their limited visibility.

Gabe detached one of his hands from the safety of the glass and reached up to touch the stone, hoping there was at least a little traction, but the glove slipped off the stone as soon as he tried to grasp it, and his body dropped and knocked against the window lightly so he was dangling precariously by one arm.

"Everything okay?" Logan asked.

"Dandy," Gabe said, pulling himself back up into position, his heart racing at the close call. He tugged at the glove on his right hand with his teeth until it was free and let it drop three stories.

"Shit," Jack muttered, following his lead.

Gabe held himself up with his remaining glove and used his feet against the glass to gain momentum. He pushed up and released his hold on the window just as his fingers clamped around the protruding stone. The rough edges bit into his fingertips and he held on with a prayer as he discarded the other glove and let it drop to the ground. He brought his left hand up to strengthen his hold on the ledge of the building. His muscles bunched and strained, and sweat snaked down his spine as he slowly pulled himself up.

Once he edged over the stone protrusion, he rolled onto the roof and lay there a few seconds on his back.

"I'd like you to work on making the gloves useable in all conditions, Dragon," Gabe said as calmly as he could manage.

"Sure thing, boss. Sorry about that."

Jack rolled onto the roof next to him and muttered the most inventive string of curses Gabe had ever heard before, but they both quickly regrouped. Gabe looked at Jack and nodded, and they made their way across the roof to the skylights that were positioned over the third floor café.

"Ghost and Renegade are in position," Gabe said calmly. "Going into phase one."

Jack took the electric screwdriver from his pack and removed all the screws that held the skylight in place.

"Once you remove the window, Grim Reaper will only have thirty seconds to reactivate the alarm systems using the override codes," Ethan said. "Dammit, I should be the one doing this. What the hell does Grim Reaper know about computers?"

"Ease down, Dragon. It'll be fine," Gabe said. He pulled a small black square from his backpack and tossed it to the ground, catching the tent that popped out quickly before it could blow away. He secured it to the roof and covered the skylights so the wind and sand wouldn't accidentally set off the alarms. No one would be able to see the tent until after the storm cleared, and by then it would be too late. They'd already be gone.

"You ready, Grim Reaper?" Gabe asked.

"As I'll ever be."

"Removing the skylight now."

Gabe and Jack lifted the heavy skylight with little

difficulty, making no sound as they placed it to the side. Gabe counted down the seconds on his watch and breathed out a sigh of relief when he heard Logan's voice.

"Alarm is deactivated, but it's still showing as active in the command center. None of the guards noticed the slight bump in the system."

"Good work," Gabe said. "Stand by while we move to phase two."

The opening left from the skylight was protected with a crisscross of infrared beams, and Jack pulled four quarter-sized metal disks from his bag.

"You sure this is going to work, Dragon?" Jack asked.

"Why do you keep asking me that?" Ethan responded. "It's starting to piss me off. Of course it works. I do not make inferior gadgets."

Gabe took two of the disks and nodded at Jack. He placed one of the disks near the bulb the beam originated from and the other near the receiver on the opposite side. Jack mirrored his image.

"On three," Gabe said. "One, two…"

They simultaneously moved the disks into place, cutting off the beam while giving the receiver the impression the infrared was still in place. The disks were magnetic and held in place without assistance.

"Make sure you don't bump them going inside," Ethan ordered.

"You've got six minutes until the guard makes his rounds," Logan warned.

Gabe and Jack tied the black nylon ropes in the bags to

the pipes that stuck up from the roof and attached them to the hooks at their belts. Gabe slowly lowered himself inside the museum and then tossed his rope back up to Jack once he'd reached the ground. Jack didn't waste any time making his own descent and quickly joined him. He tossed his rope back up into the open space the skylight had left, and Gabe led them into the supply closet to wait out the guard making his rounds.

"Lazy bastard," Logan commented in their ears. "He's not even making a full loop of the top floor. They've got a poker game going in the control room. You're all clear. Get in and get out."

Gabe slid out of the closet and went directly to the west wing where Hitler's paintings were displayed. He pulled his knife from his boot, and it took only seconds to slice the painting from the frame. He rolled it up and stuck it in the tube Jack handed him.

"Uh-oh," Logan said through the earpiece. "That doesn't look good."

Jack and Gabe looked at each other, but didn't answer Logan's warning. They both pulled their pistols and split up, each finding a hiding spot behind large white columns.

"The control room guard just answered a phone call. It looks like Kimball tipped them off to our plans. The alert has gone out to all the guards. I can see both of you on my screen."

"How many?" Gabe whispered.

"Three are coming up the back stairs. They'll come out right behind you, Ghost. Eight are taking the main stairs, and three more are taking the stairs on Jack's side. They'll come out by the café."

Gabe stayed down and moved quickly to the outside of the stairwell Logan had warned him of. The first bursts of gunfire happened on Jack's side of the building, but Gabe knew his friend could take care of himself. The guards hoped to overwhelm him by coming through the door all at once, but their plan backfired on them.

Gabe grabbed the first guard around the neck and fired into the chest of the one right behind him. He kicked out with his leg, pushing the guard he'd shot in the chest so he fell into the guard behind him. The man he had in a headlock struggled until Gabe broke his neck and put one final bullet in the guard that was struggling to move his friend's body off of him.

Those coming up the stairs decided to shoot first and ask questions later. Gabe dove behind the column he'd been hiding behind earlier just as shards of plaster and dust exploded above him. He pulled the knife from his boot and threw it at the first guard he saw, embedding it in his throat even as he was firing his gun.

Several men swarmed him at once, and a gun was difficult to use in close combat. He pulled a Taser from the belt of one of the guards and shot it into his neck even as his foot hit another in the chest and knocked him over the stair railing so he fell three stories below.

He saw Jack get in position on the opposite side of the stairway, and they both worked their way to the center of the staircase, taking out the rest of the guards until it was only the two of them standing at the top of the stairs.

"Update," Gabe ordered.

He pulled his knife from the guard it had been buried in and wiped it on the man's clothes. He and Jack started down the stairs to the lower gallery floors, moving cautiously.

"Two guards blocking each entrance," Logan said. "Police have been dispatched. It's time to disappear. I'm packing up here. I'll meet you at the rendezvous point. Grim Reaper out."

"What can I do?" Ethan asked. "I hate just sitting here."

"Make sure the backup plane I ordered is a go," Gabe said. "We'll be ready for takeoff in twenty minutes. And make sure you talk to the pilot directly. Tell him to take every precaution. I want to make sure he's alive when we get there."

Gabe slapped a full clip in his gun as he heard the sound of boots hitting the stairs and coming toward them. He nodded once at Jack to cover him and jumped over the stair railing, simultaneously firing at two of the guards. Jack covered his back and fired steadily at those blocking the front entrance until they were ducking for cover.

Gabe and Jack ran out the front entrance together, shots echoing behind them. They split off and disappeared into the night and sand just as a dozen police cars surrounded the museum.

CHAPTER TWENTY-TWO

They were running out of time.

All air traffic into London had been diverted or grounded after the explosion of his building, including private planes with high-level security clearance. They'd finally been granted clearance at the military airfield in Kent after Gabe had called in every favor he'd ever been owed. They still had an hour ride by train into the city and a ten-minute walk to Oxford Park Station with only seventy-two minutes left on Kimball's time clock. If anything went wrong, Grace would be the one to pay.

"I've sent an aerial view of Oxford Park to each of your computers," Ethan said. "It's not in a particularly good area of town, and the station is a graveyard of sorts for the old train cars that transported coal."

Ethan had finally made his way to the safe house sometime during the night. His electronic setup there wasn't quite as extensive as it had been at headquarters, but it was close.

Jack and Logan joined Gabe on the train into the city, and they sat in a car that was deserted—mostly because they'd blocked the entrance at each end—their laptops open on the small Formica tables, and maps spread open so they could determine the best route to take once they were there.

"We have to assume the place is wired for explosives considering what he did to headquarters," Logan said softly.

"That's why you and Jack are going to take that nifty device Ethan gave us and look for a bomb while you're searching for Grace."

"You can't think to meet Kimball without backup," Jack said, shaking his head.

"I need both of you searching for Grace. He's going to want to kill her as soon I make the exchange."

"And what are you going to do once you've made the exchange?" Jack asked.

"He's going to want to kill me too. I'm going to try not to let him."

"I'll have the station up on satellite imagery," Ethan said. "Body heat will be traceable. If the area isn't too saturated with people, I'll be able to find Grace if she's there."

Gabe tried not to think about what it might mean if she wasn't there. He wasn't going to give up. And he'd be damned if someone like Kimball was the man to defeat him after all these years.

"Something else you're going to have to be aware of is the 12:05 train," Ethan said. "It's not a passenger train, but it will come through all the same. From what I can tell from the manifest, it's transporting steel and building materials. Four engineers are on board."

Gabe barely heard Ethan in the background of his mind. He ran every scenario he could think of through his mind, and still he couldn't make the outcome end in his favor.

"Gabe," Jack said.

Gabe looked up and saw the understanding in his friend's gaze. He knew Jack had come to the same conclusions he had.

"We're with you to the end, my friend. We'll find her," he promised."

Gabe nodded at the lie. He would find Grace. Whether it be in this world or the next.

***

"Satellite is up and running," Ethan said. "Shit, this place is fucking crowded for a junkyard. I'm counting twelve men circulating the area. I can't tell how heavily they're armed. The metal from all the railcars is screwing with my imaging."

Gabe checked his watch once more and moved faster until he was all but running through the streets to Oxford Park. Jack and Logan had both taken alternate routes, and Kimball would know he'd bring men with him. They were playing a game in Kimball's mind, and Grace had become the pawn.

"Kimball's already at platform seven, Ghost," Ethan said. "He's having a telephone conversation with someone, but it's a secured line, and I'm not able to listen in with the equipment I have here."

"Renegade in position," Jack said. "Northeast corner."

"I've got you in my sights," Ethan said. "You've got a man at three o'clock and another at nine."

"Have you found Grace?" Gabe asked.

"Possibly," Ethan answered. "I've got a weak heat signal dead center of the lot, and four guards are surrounding the area. Her heat signal isn't good, Ghost. She's either hurt really bad or she's locked inside one of the train cars and it's messing with my equipment."

"Help Logan and Jack," Gabe ordered. "Be their eyes. I'm going offline."

"But—"

Gabe flicked the button on his watch and welcomed the silence. He'd slowed to a walk as he crossed each platform, his backpack slung over his shoulder, and his breathing was even, though his heart was racing in his chest. He saw Kimball in the distance but didn't hurry to catch up to him. The only way this would work was if he timed everything just right. He'd have to trust Jack and Logan to take care of Kimball's men on the ground.

"So you're the infamous Gabe Brennan," Kimball said, looking him over slowly from head to toe. "You look different than the last time we met."

"As I recall, you were going by the name of Kenrick the last time you did a job for Tussad."

"You've a good memory. It's been two years since I've used that name. I believe your daughter was the last job I did for my good friend Kamir. I had to go underground for a while after her death. You were very angry, and you must have used every resource you had to track me down. But I was always a step ahead of you."

Gabe didn't allow any emotion to show at Kimball's words. That's exactly what the man wanted, and control was important right now. But he now knew with certainty that he was looking into the eye of his daughter's murderer. Something in Gabe's expression must have given him away because Kimball's smiled faded, and he put his hand in the pocket of his windbreaker where his gun was.

"You know, you're something of a bogeyman in agency circles," Kimball said.

"I'm just a man, Kimball. Like anyone else."

"I doubt that," he said. "Do you have my painting?"

"It's close by. Do you have Grace?"

Gabe watched in satisfaction as Kimball's jaw clenched in frustration. He was surprised Kimball had lasted as long as he had in the CIA, showing as much emotion as he was. An emotional agent was a dead agent.

"What do you mean, 'It's close by'?" he asked. "You were supposed to bring it here."

"Where's Grace?" Gabe asked again.

Kimball smiled and took a step closer, and Gabe

watched the hand in Kimball's pocket, not moving at his enemy's obvious threat.

"She's in one of the railcars, surrounded by enough explosives to level this entire place to dust. And you've wasted precious time by not bringing the painting with you. You'll never find her in the next ten minutes because I'm not letting you go until I have that painting in my hands."

A train whistle blew in the distance, and the sound of gunshots echoed around them, Jack and Logan giving him the distraction he needed.

"Take your hand out of your pocket, Kimball. If you kill me, you'll never get the painting."

Kimball shrugged and did as he asked. "It doesn't matter. My men are busy taking out your team, and you've only got eight minutes left to get me the painting and find your wife before she's nothing more than dust. It's over and you know it. There's no way out of this."

"You underestimate my team."

The train grew closer, and Gabe shifted his body weight ever so slightly. "Here's what we're going to do, Kimball," Gabe called out loud enough so he could be heard over the approaching train.

The wooden platform rumbled beneath his feet, and rocks bounced along the tracks. The train wasn't moving fast, but it was moving fast enough.

"You and I are both going to walk away from here today with exactly what we want. There are other days for me to kill you. It'll be the last reprieve you ever get from me."

Kimball's eyes widened in understanding as the train came by, and Gabe tossed the backpack he was carrying into an open railcar. Fury and panic raced across Kimball's face as he began running so he could grab hold of the train before it left him.

"She's dead, Brennan. This game is over," Kimball yelled back as he disappeared down the tracks.

Gabe pulled his weapon from the small of his back and flipped on his com link as he began running.

"Where is she, Ethan?" Gabe yelled into the link. Long-forgotten prayers circled through his mind as he took out one of Kimball's men with a single shot to the head. Ethan had seen her heat signature. She wasn't dead yet. She couldn't be.

"Veer right," Ethan said. "You've got a man gaining behind you, and you're about to intercept another coming around one of the railcars."

Gabe slid feet first to his left and twisted so he had the man behind him in his sights. It only took one shot to bring him down. The man coming from around the corner had to spend precious seconds searching for him, even though he'd heard how close the shots had been fired. Gabe hit his target before the man could even glance down in his direction. He rolled from beneath the railcar and kept running.

"Shit," Logan muttered. "I found the explosives."

"Can you disarm?" Gabe asked.

There was a slight pause before Logan answered. "Maybe."

Which meant no in Gabe's estimation.

"It's the next car on your left," Ethan said. "Check in, Renegade. You've been awfully quiet."

"I'm here," Jack muttered. "Asshole wouldn't die. I'm headed toward Grace."

"You and Logan clear out now," Gabe ordered. "I'll get Grace and we'll meet at the safe house. Is this the one, Ethan?"

The railroad car was burnt orange in color and rusted with age. Graffiti littered the sides in lime green and black, and the door was closed and bolted with a padlock.

"That's the one," Ethan assured him.

Gabe shot at the lock and tossed the remains to the ground. Jack skidded around the corner at that moment and helped him push back the heavy door.

"I ordered you to clear out," Gabe told him.

"It looks like I didn't listen."

"Almost there," Logan said under his breath. "This is a sophisticated bastard."

Gabe vaulted into the railcar and almost didn't see Grace huddled in the corner. Her clothes were in tatters, and blood and bruises covered her body. He held back the cold rage that wanted to take over—the urge to throw his head back and scream at whoever had let this happen to her—but instead he fell to his knees beside her.

He felt for the pulse in her throat, saying a prayer as it beat steadily under his fingers and thankful that she wasn't conscious to feel the pain he was sure to inflict on her.

"Damn," Logan said. "Less than two minutes on the timer. Get out of there."

"Go, Jack. That's an order," he said before Jack could tell him no. "You too, Logan."

Gabe didn't know where to touch Grace. There didn't seem to be a spot on her body that wasn't damaged, but as gently as he could, he lifted her in his arms and hopped out of the railcar, trying not to jostle her too much. He growled as he saw Jack waiting for him with his weapon out, ready to guard his back as they made their way out of the station. He didn't bother to yell at Jack for disobeying orders. There wasn't time.

They ran through the maze of railcars and across the dilapidated platforms, the air completely still, as if it knew its very existence was in danger. They ran with a strength neither of them knew they possessed, and still it wouldn't be enough.

"Logan, are you clear of the area? Report."

There was silence on the other end until Ethan spoke up. "He turned off his com link a few seconds ago, but the satellite imaging shows he's still with the bomb."

They couldn't have more than a few seconds left, and they still weren't clear of the blast zone. Gabe tucked Grace closer to his body and headed toward the opposite side of the train tracks, his body drenched in sweat and fear.

He'd just placed Grace in a steep ditch and covered her with his body to protect her from debris when Logan came back on their com link.

"We're clear," Logan said, his breath a touch unsteady.

"She's neutralized."

Gabe rolled to his back and looked up at the gray clouds that gathered in the sky, his breath heaving in and out of his chest. The sky around them gave a great whoosh, and it was if the air started breathing again. He'd never forget what the grass felt like beneath him or how eerie such complete silence was.

Gabe turned his head and saw Jack sitting next to him with his knees drawn up and his head down as if he were in prayer. Maybe he was.

"I swear to God, Jack, the next shit missions I'm sent are going to be assigned to you and Logan. When I give you an order, I expect you to fucking obey it."

"I'll gladly take whatever shit job you throw my way," he said, nodding. "To tell you the truth, I could use a low-key babysitting job. Preferably by the beach somewhere."

Gabe laughed before he could help it, the adrenaline in his body beginning to ebb. He'd be shaking like a woman if he didn't laugh. Or crying. He looked at Grace and took her hand gently in his, but as quickly as he'd let his guard down, it was back in place in an instant. The sound of shoes scraping against gravel had his gun out and pointed across the tracks.

He lowered it as Logan walked toward them with a bag tossed over his shoulder—probably what was left of the bomb—his jeans torn and bloody at the knees and his gun held down at his side. Jesus, they'd cut it close. And they sure as hell wouldn't be sitting there if Logan hadn't just saved their asses.

The soft squeezing against his hand jerked his gaze

down, and he saw a thin slit of green through Grace's swollen eyes.

"Sorry." Her voice was barely more than a whisper, and he leaned down, his hand touching her brow in comfort. "It was my fault."

"No, sweetheart," he said. "It was mine. But I've got you now, Grace. And I promise I won't let go. No matter what happens."

Her grip grew surprisingly strong just as she said, "Please don't make me go to a hospital." Then her hand went slack in his, and she was out cold again.

He sighed and bent to pick her up again. It was a damned shame he was going to have to disappoint her so soon. She was going to be mad as hell when she woke and saw the hospital was exactly where he'd taken her.

CHAPTER TWENTY-THREE

Four weeks later...

Grace felt the pull and stretch of every muscle in her body as she upped the speed on the treadmill one more time. Her hair was dampened with sweat, and the black sports bra and shorts she wore were soaked through. She knew Gabe was watching her from his own workout in the corner of the small room that had been designated as a gym. He'd done nothing but watch her the last few weeks.

The safe house was on the opposite side of town from headquarters, almost an hour away, and they didn't have all the comforts of the other building. Or the security. Not that security had done them much good before.

The safe house wasn't in a good part of town. The building had an outside appearance of being nothing more than an abandoned brownstone with rotting wood and chinks missing from the mortar. But outward appearances were often deceiving, and the core of the building was strong and secure. It was three levels, and they weren't afforded nearly the privacy they'd had at headquarters. There was a common living area on the second floor, and Gabe had opened the walls and put the control room there as well, so it was just one big space.

Jack and Logan slept in the rooms on the first floor, and Ethan pretty much slept with his computers. That left the top floor for Gabe and Grace.

Gabe had barely taken his eyes off her for the last month. He'd barely spoken to her, either. Not to mention he'd made it very clear that making love was out of the question. She'd had no choice but to push her body past its limits once she was able to get out of bed, or she'd try to kill him.

The cuts and bruises had healed over the past weeks. Only a light discoloration decorated her shoulders and back. And while her body had been healing, she'd had time to think as well. It was hard to admit that she'd been headed down the path of self-destruction. She'd disappointed her team and Gabe, but worst of all, she'd disappointed herself. She knew what she had to do. And she knew she needed to make Gabe listen. Because she needed him to be her support—her strength—through this. She hadn't been ready to accept his help when he'd first found her in Colombia. But she was ready now.

She slowed the machine to cool-down mode and grabbed a towel off the rail to dry her face. Gabe turned his attention back to the weights he was lifting when he saw her watching him, pretending he hadn't just spent the last hour scrutinizing her every move.

"Gabe," she said, waiting patiently until his gaze met hers.

He didn't stop his reps, and she accepted the slow curl of lust that spread through her as his muscles bulged with every movement. His body was a finely crafted instrument, and she never got tired of knowing that it belonged to her, scars and all. He finally met her eyes, but his expression was shuttered.

"You don't need to push yourself so hard, Grace."

"I'm fine. And I need to push myself as much as possible. You know it's only a matter of time until we hear Kimball has scheduled the auction."

He went back to his workout, trying to dismiss her as he'd done so many times in the last few days. He didn't want her thinking about Kimball. As far as he was concerned, she needed to stay tucked in bed until the entire mission was over.

"It's time to talk, Gabe. No more excuses. I'll meet you upstairs."

She hurried out of the gym before Gabe could try to stop her or insist she wasn't strong enough. They were going to get things worked out between them. And then they were going to make love because she honestly didn't think she could stand the torture of being so close to him and not having him a second longer.

Since Gabe had rescued her, she'd had no choice but to share his room because it had been easier for him to take care of her. There was a spare bedroom on the top floor, but the thought of going back to her own living space wasn't as appealing as it had once been. He'd stopped sharing the bed with her once she'd been up and moving around on her own. It was damned irritating.

She used his shower, the smell of his soap and shampoo a comfort as she rubbed it across her skin. The hot water beat down on her tired muscles, but also made her aware of how sensitive her skin was to any kind of touch. Each drop of water was a caress, and it took every ounce of willpower she had not to move her hand to the juncture of her thighs.

She turned the water off with a flick of her wrist and stepped out onto the mat. Her gun was just where she'd left it on the back of the toilet seat, and she grabbed a towel off the rack and dried off quickly. Gabe never made any sound when he moved, but she knew he was out there, waiting for her.

She dressed in soft cotton pants and a tank top. The best she could do with her hair was to brush the tangles out and let it air dry. She grabbed her gun and carried it with her into the small living area they'd been sharing.

He stood in the kitchen with his back to her, wearing a threadbare gray T-shirt and old jeans. His hair was damp from his own shower, and he measured coffee as efficiently as he did everything else.

"What's this all about, Grace? I need to get down to the control room and talk to Ethan."

She put her gun on the table and went to him in the kitchen since he was determined to make this as difficult as possible.

"I need to say what I have to say," she said. "And I need you to listen." She saw his quick nod, even though he kept his back to her.

Her throat was suddenly dry, and she wasn't quite sure where to start. How to start.

"I know you lost Maddie too, but I need to make you understand." His shoulders tensed at the mention of their daughter's name, but she forged ahead. "As much as you loved her, you never felt that life inside your body. Never felt her growing and stretching, or that instant connection that takes every terrible thing I've ever done and washes it clean because I know in my heart she's the one thing in this life that I've done right."

She held up her hand when he turned around and she saw he was going to speak. Her hand shook, so she put it down quickly, but she got what she wanted. Gabe's lips pressed together, and he nodded again for her to continue.

"And then she was born, and it was a completely different kind of miracle. She was so perfect, Gabe. How could she come from two such imperfect parents?" She licked her lips and tasted the salt of her tears. She hadn't even realized she'd been crying. "I can't tell you what it feels like to have to fight so hard to bring her into the world only to sit there helpless as she was taken out of it."

She couldn't quite bring herself to look him in the eyes. "I hated you for a while. I hated myself. To the point where I didn't care if I lived or died as long as I avenged her death. I've been struggling on my own for these last two years, determined to forget you and deal with the pain on my own in the only way I knew how. What has the government made us, Gabe? What kind of person am I that my first thought is to go out and kill?"

"The kind who has a conscience. The kind who takes chances because others choose to look the other direction when it comes to right and wrong. We know what real sacrifice is. And we live with it because there's no other option." His voice was soft and full of emotion, but she couldn't meet his gaze. Not yet.

"This hate is like a disease," she said. "I can feel it creeping over my skin and devouring my soul. It scares me, and I hate the person I've become."

"Give yourself a break, sweetheart. I still love you as you are. The woman you used to be is in there somewhere, but she's never going to be the same. She'll be stronger. Because she's a survivor."

He moved toward her, and she tried to back away. To get everything said before he touched her and she fell apart. But he wouldn't let her. He pulled her into his arms, and she broke. Sobs violently shook her body as she soaked his shirt with her tears. Two years of pain, and hate, and loathing tore free until the sounds that came from deep inside her no longer sounded human.

Gabe knelt with her on the floor and rocked her as he would a child, his own tears falling silently against her neck. She didn't know how long they stayed that way, but when the tears were gone, her body continued to shake with fatigue and the grief that had finally made its way to the surface.

"I don't want to be this person anymore, Gabe. I can't be this person anymore. I won't survive it."

"And do you want to survive?"

He tilted her face up until she was looking directly into

the blue depths of his eyes. They were wet with emotion and held their own silent grief. Grief that had nothing to do with Maddie and everything to do with the pain she'd caused him.

"Yes. I want to survive. I want to live again. With you."

"Then you will." He kissed her softly on the lips, and she shuddered against him as the weight began to lift from her shoulders. "We're going to do it right this time. There are still going to be trouble spots ahead of us. But we'll do it together. No more running for either of us. I think it would be a good idea to see a grief counselor. I think it's time for us to heal."

The tears she thought were gone slipped down her cheeks. "I'd like that, but what if it doesn't work? I'll kill you if you ever tell anyone this, but I'm so scared. What if I keep having these breakdowns?"

"Then you do, and I'll be there to help you through them. Don't worry about what you can't control. All we can do is our best and fight through it together."

They looked at each other a long while until she finally found the courage to say the words she'd never stopped feeling.

"I love you, Gabe." She touched the ends of his hair and rubbed the silky strands between her fingers, then trailed her way down his neck and up to the coarse beard at his cheeks. She wanted to memorize every texture of this moment. "I just thought I should tell you."

He kissed her softly, his lips tasting and savoring as if it were their first kiss. It was the kiss of new beginnings, and the slow, dizzying feeling of falling in love all over again.

She didn't know how they got from the floor to the bedroom, only that everything around her was a hazy dream. She'd remember the love and tenderness he was showing her for the rest of her life, and the way he looked at her as if she were the only woman in his universe.

They undressed each other slowly, his calloused fingers bringing chills to her skin with every caress. And when they were naked, he lowered her to the bed so they were skin against skin. The hair on his chest rubbed against her nipples and made her breasts ache, and she could feel his hardness pressing against the juncture of her thighs.

Grace moved against him, begging without words for him to fill her, but instead he began to kiss his way over every inch of her body, worshipping her with his mouth and hands. He licked and stroked until she was like liquid fire in his arms, and then he rolled her to her stomach and kissed every bruise and scar on her back.

"Please, Gabe. I need you so much."

He nipped one last time at the base of her spine and then turned her over. He moved between her thighs and she lifted her legs so they twined around his back. Her heart pounded, and her lungs couldn't seem to remember how to breathe properly as she felt him prod against her entrance.

"Open your eyes and look at me, Grace."

Her eyelids were heavy, but she heard the plea in his voice and did as he asked. The stark need on his face was almost her undoing. Her eyes burned with unshed tears.

"This is forever, sweetheart. I love you."

She couldn't get the words past her throat, but she

inhaled sharply and held his gaze as he pushed inside of her slowly. She felt every ridge of his cock against her inner walls, and her nails dug into his shoulders. He was determined to move at a slow pace—to savor the moment—but she was just as determined to get what she wanted.

She arched against him, her back bowing, and she was climaxing before he was inside her to the hilt, convulsing around him in fine tremors that made him grit his teeth and the muscles in his neck go rigid with his restraint.

"Jesus, Grace." He held perfectly still, trying to get himself under control. "I want this to last, sweetheart."

He leaned down and kissed her again, soft lips and the gentle invasion of his tongue as it rubbed sinuously against hers. And then he began to move his hips in tandem with his tongue and all thought left her head. This wasn't a fast coupling or the frantic mating of two lost souls. It was making love at its core, for two souls that had just been found.

Their fingers entwined, and their gazes held steady even as their bodies slicked with sweat and heartbeats raced. Grace felt the tingles of pleasure gathering low in her womb, as if her skin were too tight for her body. Flutters of pleasure skittered across her sensitive flesh, and she cried out as he began to move faster, plunging inside of her from hilt to tip, making sure he claimed all of her.

"Gabe," she cried out, locking her legs around him and arching into him as her orgasm started from the tips of her toes and the top of her scalp and then raced like lightning across her skin until she exploded into a million pieces of pleasure.

He shouted her name as he came inside of her and buried his face against her neck. The last thing she thought as she drifted off to sleep was that it was nice to finally be home. She'd missed it.

***

They didn't speak much over the next two days. There was no need for words. But they touched often and made love as if their lives depended on bringing each other pleasure.

"We're going to eventually have to go downstairs," Gabe said, skimming his fingers down the gentle slope of her breast and watching in fascination as her nipple hardened under his touch.

"Jack will let us know if Ethan gets a lock on the auction. We're just waiting at this point. We don't even know for sure that his scientist was able to recreate The Passover Project. There haven't been reports of other testing sites."

"That's what worries me. It'll be much harder to isolate The Passover Project as a murder weapon if it's only killing one person instead of many. I've got Ethan looking for high-profile unexplained deaths."

He pulled the sheet down so she was completely exposed to him. God, she was beautiful, and he felt himself start to get hard again. He should be exhausted, but found he suddenly had energy to spare.

"Can I ask you something?" Grace said.

Gabe could tell by the tone of her voice that the topic

was something she'd rather not have to talk about. He rolled to his back and pulled her on top of him, loving the feel of her hair as it slid like silk over his chest.

"I'm serious, Gabe. This is important."

"You can ask me whatever you want and I'll give it to you. I'm desperate here." He held her hips and positioned her over his cock, using the pressure of his fingers to push her down. But she held steady above him, not letting him get what he wanted just yet.

"Do you think we can get married again?"

He froze in his attempts and looked up to see if she was serious. Her face was flushed with a combination of desire and embarrassment, and she wouldn't quite meet his gaze.

"I know it's probably not necessary at this point, but I thought—"

"You're right. It's not necessary."

He tried not to smile at the disappointed look that came over her face, and he held her steady on top of him when she tried to go back to her side of the bed. The nightstand that sat next to the bed held a number of important things he always wanted to have on hand. His gun was one of them. His wedding ring the other.

Gabe sat up and pulled the drawer open. Grace struggled against him in earnest now, and he held her in place with one arm as he felt around inside the drawer for what he was looking for. He pulled the silver chain out and held it up in front of her face so she'd see the wide silver band that dangled from it.

The band was plain, with no adornments, and he always wore it around his neck because it was too dangerous to wear a ring in the field. She froze in his arms, and her eyes widened in shock.

"Where's yours?" he asked.

"I threw it away, you jerk."

She punched him in the arm and struggled to get out of his lap once again, and he couldn't help but laugh.

"Like hell you did," he said, adjusting her legs around his waist so he could slide deep inside of her. She inhaled sharply at his intrusion, and her breasts rubbed against his chest with every shuddering breath she took. He held perfectly still and kept his fingers clamped to her hips like a vise so she couldn't move.

"Where is it, Grace? I know you still have it."

"In the bottom compartment of my rifle case," she finally said.

Gabe gave a crack of laughter and then groaned as it made him move inside her. He stood up and held onto her as he made his way to the kitchen table where her rifle case sat.

"Put me down, Gabe. Why are you doing this?" she asked, struggling against him. "If you don't want to get married again, it's not a big deal."

He sat her down on the table and pinned her thighs when she tried to push away from him. Tears glittered in her eyes along with an angry fire that would get him a right hook in the jaw if he wasn't careful. He took her mouth in a slow deep kiss and stroked inside of her once—twice—

until she was pliant in his arms.

"I never said I didn't want to get married again. I just said it wasn't necessary." He found her ring, a smaller replica of his own also hanging from a sturdy silver chain, in the bottom compartment of her rifle case. "Because we're still married."

"Wha—"

"I see you're speechless for once." He fastened the chain around her neck and kissed her again. "I'm sorry to say it, but I shredded your divorce papers."

She laughed and threw her arms around him in sheer joy. "I love you, Gabe. Thank you for not giving up on me."

"My pleasure, sweetheart."

Gabe kissed her again, and her legs tightened around his waist while his shook with desire. He didn't think he'd be able to make it back to the bed, so he lowered them to the carpet and laid flat on his back. She was like a goddess above him—her head thrown back in surrender and his ring flashing like fire as she rode him with complete abandon. All thoughts of control were lost as he felt her clamp around him and cry out his name. All he could do was follow.

CHAPTER TWENTY-FOUR

"I found your test subject," Ethan yelled through the door, pounding against it just to make sure he was heard.

"We'll meet you downstairs," Gabe called back, grabbing for his pants.

"I guess it's back to work," Grace said. "I want to help, Gabe. I know I disappointed the team before, but I can still do something."

He looked at her long and hard, but she'd put her shields back in place, and he couldn't see any hint of the vulnerability he thought he'd heard in her voice.

"I can't make any promises."

She nodded in understanding, and he breathed a sigh of relief. They dressed quickly in black cargos and matching T-shirts, arming themselves to go one floor below just as if they were going out on a mission. Old habits were hard to break.

"You two look rested," Jack said lazily as they entered the second floor off the main staircase.

Grace ignored Jack and went to stand over Ethan's shoulder, and Jack and Gabe shared a silent look. She hadn't spoken to Jack at all since she'd been rescued from Kimball. Part of her was embarrassed that he'd seen her so out of control, Gabe knew, but another part of her was hurt that he didn't back her up when Gabe told her to leave Iran. They'd work it out eventually, but there was tension in the air. Only Ethan seemed oblivious to the fact.

Jack was straddling a chair and playing a game of solitaire on the coffee table while Logan was working in the protected area they'd set up for him so he could safely play with explosive materials. He wore clear goggles and seemed to be concentrating intently on his task, but Gabe knew he'd heard every word since they'd walked in.

"What do you have, Ethan?" Gabe asked.

"Check out screen one." Ethan pulled up files from his computer and displayed them on the wall screen. "Speaker of the House William Sloane was speaking at a college about job growth in front of a crowd of more than three thousand people when he suddenly fell ill and collapsed on stage. The paramedics on scene originally thought it was cardiac arrest, which I guess technically it was if you're talking about all your organs turning into soup."

"Ethan," Gabe said, tiredly. "Stay focused."

"Right." Ethan put up photos of varying states of Sloane's body as the evening progressed on screen two. "Sloane was still conscious and communicating as they airlifted him to the hospital. By the time they were halfway there, the medics stated in their report that he began to bleed profusely from his ears, nose, and mouth. Sloane was dead by the time they landed."

"I guess Kimball is getting rid of his competition," Jack said. "He's not going to want anyone around who knows what The Passover Project is capable of."

Ethan brought up another screen that had nothing but jumbled letters and numbers on it, and he typed in a long series of codes until words formed. He was locked into the investigating agent's computer, reading his report even as the man was adding to it.

"Homeland Security has already filed Sloane's death as top-level security and they're testing the body, or what's left of it, as we speak," Ethan said. "They've searched his home and office, but Sloane wasn't stupid. They won't find what they're looking for, and if Kimball's scientist recreated The Passover Project in its entirety, then the doctors testing Sloane's body will find no trace of what killed him."

"If Homeland Security looks hard enough, they'll find Sloane's ties to Standridge. There are too many connections between his corporations and the experiments. Even his interest in Frank Bennett. They'll know he was involved in something he shouldn't have been." It was the first time Grace had spoken since they'd come downstairs.

"Every file you could think of that might possibly lead the agents investigating in the right direction has been wiped clean," Ethan said.

"They'll bury Sloane as a damned hero," Jack said,

tossing down his cards and standing up to join them in front of the screen. "And no one will ever know that the man who was third in line for the Presidency was a terrorist. He would have had control of the world in just a matter of years."

"Now that honor belongs to Kimball," Ethan said.

"Not if we get to him first," Gabe said. "And the end justifies the means. We know the kind of man Sloane was, and he's paid in full for his crimes. We've got to focus on Kimball. What have you got on possible auction sites?" he asked Ethan.

Ethan cleared the three screens of Sloane's death and went back to work at his computer. "I know Kimball has got something in the works. I tapped into his secure phone line and have been piggybacking his calls since I couldn't eavesdrop through conventional means, and I've deciphered his code enough to know that the auction will take place in three days at sunset. What I don't know is where it's going to be."

"What are the options?" Grace asked. "And do you know who's going to be in attendance?"

"I'm putting the list of attendees up on screen one, though I'm not a hundred percent sure that's everyone."

A list of eight names came on the screen—seven men and one woman—and Jack let out a low whistle. "No, that pretty much looks like everyone. The ones on this list are the only ones who could afford to meet Kimball's price."

Gabe took Grace's hand when he saw Tussad's name on the list, and she gently squeezed his fingers in reassurance.

"They'll want to see a demonstration," Logan said. "Sloane's death won't be proof enough for them because the details have been covered up. They'll demand to see what it can actually do. The auction site will have to be secure for several hours so they can see the weapon work from start to finish."

"And they'll want to be comfortable," Grace said. "The people on this list won't give up creature comforts for that long. They'll expect to be wined and dined and given proper accommodations. It'll be like a damned summit meeting for terrorists."

"The first possible location is in Kiev," Ethan said.

"No," Gabe and Grace said together.

"Alexi Sokolov has a home in Kiev," Gabe explained. "He's on your guest list. Kimball won't show partiality by making the auction in one of the attendees' hometowns. It needs to be neutral territory."

"Ooookay," Ethan said. "Here are the other two options."

The wall screens filled with information and photographs, and they all took in the information, processing what they knew about Kimball and the rest of his guests.

"India or Morocco," Jack said. "What do you think, Gabe? I know you know enough about all of these guys to have formed impressions."

"Ethan, do a search for property acquired in the last two weeks, either as a rental or a purchase," Gabe said. "In Morocco," he added. "Kimball will have purchased it after his scientist had completed the weapon. He'll want

271

opulence that borders on ostentatious because this is the first time he's meeting these people as an equal. He's always worked for them before, and he'll want to show off a bit. Eliminate anything worth less than five million American."

"Run a second check on staff," Grace said.

Ethan looked at her in confusion, and she explained. "If he's hosting an event of this magnitude, then he'll need a well-trained staff as well as security. They'll need to know how to keep their mouths shut, but they'll need to be excellent at their jobs. Check and see where William Sloane's staff is now. That would be the easiest transition. Not to mention they'll all be terrified to go against Kimball after seeing what he did to their boss."

"I knew there was a good reason for you to be here, Red," Jack said, pulling at her braid. "You know all about that womanly stuff."

Gabe knew that was as close to an apology as Jack would ever make, and he could tell Grace knew it too by the way she patted Jack on the arm in response.

"Bingo on both accounts," Ethan said. "A twelve bedroom villa was purchased in Tangier eleven days ago. Paid with an electronic fund transfer from an account in the Caymans, and it's worth an approximate 7.2 million Euros. It has an ocean view from all sides of the estate. It also has a white tiger sanctuary and an underwater dining room."

"That sounds ostentatious enough for me," Gabe said. "What about Sloane's staff?"

"I'm getting there. Geez. A little praise every now and

then wouldn't kill you."

"Ethan," Gabe growled.

"Yeah, yeah. Screen two." He flicked his fingers across the keyboard again and a picture of a man in formal attire came on the screen.

"This is Nigel Peters," Ethan said. "His background includes the Royal Air Force as well as extensive training in London's premier school for butlers. He's an expert marksman, and the Royal Family used him for his bodyguard and butler skills for several years before Sloane lured him away. Peters landed in Morocco ten days ago, according to his passport. Several of Sloane's household staff followed Peters."

"The auction begins in three days' time," Gabe said, pacing back and forth in front of the wall screens, his mind racing with possibilities. "How long did it take Sloane to die after his initial collapse on stage?"

He heard Ethan tapping and turned to face him. Ethan chewed at his lip and pushed his glasses repeatedly up his nose as he searched for the answer. "It looks like it took a little over forty-seven minutes from start to finish."

"We need to find out who Kimball would use for his demonstration," Gabe said. "It'll need to be someone of importance, or it won't have meaning."

"It'll be one of his guests," Grace said. "Kimball will want to let them know that he has power. He's not auctioning off one weapon. He's auctioning off a formula that can be recreated at any time as long as they have the proper components. He'll make sure everyone at that meeting knows he will have the ability to control their actions and their own use of the weapon. He's just put himself in the position of being the world's number one enemy."

"Okay, so you have to assume that none of the guests will arrive more than twenty-four hours before the auction," Jack said. "They're not a trustworthy group of people, and they'll want to arrive in time to see the weapon work, and then they'll all plan to leave immediately following. It's how auctions like this normally go."

"All the guests will have to arrive by ferry," Ethan said. "Remember the house is surrounded by water."

"Over the open water is the perfect place to release the formula into the air. They'll all be on deck, and Kimball's done business with all of them before, so he's had plenty of opportunity to get DNA samples. Hell, he probably has a whole arsenal of DNA samples."

Gabe thought of the painting and the bag he'd handed off to Kimball and knew without a doubt that Kimball had his own DNA. Grace's, too.

"We can't fail," Gabe said. "We can't let the weapon go live, even if the target is a terrorist. We still don't know enough about The Passover Project to be sure it won't have residual effects on others in the area. Our mission is to stop the launch and take out Kimball before the formula changes hands."

"So Kimball isn't to be spared?" Grace asked.

"We take him out. And we take out Kimball's scientist. He'll have him close by. All traces of the Passover Project must be destroyed. Logan will help us with that."

Gabe recognized the look on Grace's face. It was the

look she got when she'd run every possible scenario in her head and come up with the best solution. He knew what she was going to say before she opened her mouth because it was exactly the conclusion he'd come to.

"How big is the island, Ethan?" she asked.

"A little over two miles in all directions," he answered.

"I can take the long shot and get Kimball. Whoever launches the weapon will have to be taken out up close and personal to make sure The Passover Project is properly neutralized. But Kimball is too dangerous to engage with one-on-one. I can take him out."

Silence filled the room, and Gabe stood ready to interfere if things got out of hand. He still had the safety of the mission to consider first and foremost, but he also had Grace to consider. He'd asked her to join the team because she was the best at what she did, even though Ethan and Logan had never seen her skill. He was more than prepared to remind them.

"I disagree," Jack said.

Gabe tightened his fists at his sides out of pure reflex but decided to let his friend have his say before he beat him to a pulp.

"I think Kimball will expect you to be there," Jack continued. "He'll know what your strengths are. There's no way he's going to make himself an easy target for you. He'll have someone like Peters launch the aerosol, but he'll stay indoors and force us to come to him if we want him. You can be cleanup if we run into trouble."

Gabe relaxed completely and nodded in agreement at the logic behind Jack's argument. A position like that would take the pressure off Grace in case she worried about having another breakdown, but being given a job had also saved her pride. Jack was probably the most insightful of all of them when it came to other people's feelings, and he was grateful to him for recognizing that Grace needed to be a part of the team right now.

"Do you have an aerial shot of the island?" Logan asked.

"Hang on a sec," Ethan said. "Screen three."

"He's got a helipad and the ferry," Logan said. "I can make sure there's not a way for him to get off the island."

"And I suppose I'm going to be stuck here with my thumb up my ass," Ethan said sourly. "I never get to have any of the fun."

"You're coming with us," Gabe said. "You'll run security from the boat."

"What boat?" Ethan asked.

"I hope you don't get seasick, kid. We're sure as hell not making our entrance on a luxury cruiser."

CHAPTER TWENTY-FIVE

Tangier, Morocco
Three days later…

It was well before dawn when they arrived just outside of Kimball's island villa, and Grace could feel the anticipation in the atmosphere—from the whole team. This was their last chance to get Kimball. Failure wasn't an option.

The only way they could gain access to the island was by water, and they'd taken a Zodiac that was as black as night into the choppy waters. It was designed for easy travel—an inflatable craft that held six comfortably but also had the advantage of having a motor so they could move quickly if needed. It was a little cramped with Ethan's computers and the diving gear, not to mention the cache of weapons Gabe had put in the specially built compartment at the bottom of the craft.

A storm had passed through only hours before, and it

looked as if another could hit at any time. Not even a sliver of moon could be seen in the cloudy sky, and the waves rolled beneath them, rocking the boat up and down and side to side. Even as she had the thought, fat raindrops slapped against her wetsuit and seemed to bounce off the waves.

Grace wasn't sure if Ethan was going to make it after all. He was so pale she could see his reflection and the whites of his eyes in the dark, and he was holding on to the side of the Zodiac with a death grip as his backside bounced in uncoordinated rhythms against the seat.

"The GPS shows we have about fifty meters until we reach the perimeter of Kimball's security," Jack said. "The Zodiac will have to stay there, and we'll need to swim ashore."

Gabe steered the boat so it was hidden behind a large outcropping of rocks—so no one would be able to see Ethan once the sun came up—and he turned off the motor. The rocks would also act as an anchor since the rough water was likely to make Ethan drift out further to sea if he wasn't tied down.

Ethan fumbled with his laptops and satellite imaging, finally getting everything in place. The computers were all protected from the water by the special casing Ethan had built around them. The computer screens were all set to night vision so they didn't give off any light, and they could only be seen with night-vision goggles.

"Equipment check, Dragon," Gabe said through his com link.

Ethan took a big gulp of air and looked like he was

about to start gagging, but he held it together and croaked out, "All satellites are up and running. Heat sensors are a go. There are a good twenty people on the island, assuming that's only Kimball's staff and security team. I've got his electronic security system online. He's got radar that reaches out to just on the other side of this rock. Jesus, I'm going to be sick."

"Aim for the side," Gabe and Jack both called out, each of them completely comfortable on the rough water.

Grace handed Ethan a bottle of water to rinse out his mouth and put it in the elastic pocket by his side, figuring he'd probably need it again soon.

"I'm good." Ethan panted as if he'd just swam the distance from shore. "I'm all right. Let's do a com check."

"Renegade."

"Grim Reaper."

"Ghost."

"Kill Shot."

Ethan gave the thumbs up, and Grace pulled the hood of her wetsuit over her braided hair. She tested her rebreather—a device that would let them all swim to the island without bubbles giving away their location—and she gave Gabe the thumbs up that her equipment was in good shape.

"The storm's going to help us out some," Ethan said just as a slash of lightning seemed to spear up out of the water only a few feet away. The smell of ozone permeated the air and clung to the skin like residue. "It'll give me the chance to knock out different sectors of the security system so you guys can get to your designated hot spots. The weather is supposed to stay like this through tomorrow."

Grace took out her rebreather so she could speak. "Do you think the rain will interfere with the launch of the weapon?"

"No, but it might narrow the range some," Gabe answered. "If it's still raining when Kimball's guests take the ferry, then they'll all stay under the enclosed area. Look for them to launch the aerosol as they transfer from the ferry to the island just to be on the safe side."

Grace made sure the waterproof case holding her rifle was locked tight, and she slung it across her body so her hands would be free. One by one, they rolled out of the Zodiac and into the churning water, and once they were a good distance below the surface, Ethan check the com links once more so they could hear his instructions. He was going to be their eyes for the next little while.

They all gave Ethan the all clear signal and then waited for his signal to let them know the outer security was down.

"You've got five minutes to make it to the next checkpoint," he said. "On my mark."

Grace swam between Gabe and Jack because the power of their strokes allowed her to swim in their current and keep the same pace. They stayed beneath the surface once they reached the sandy slope that led out of the water.

"Hold tight for two minutes," Ethan said. "I'm turning off sector two on the other side of the island just to confuse things a bit."

Grace adjusted her position carefully, using all her strength to keep near the shore. The waves were stronger here and wanted nothing more than to fling her out to sea.

"Okay, sector two is back up, and you now have guards patrolling in some kind of vehicle. They've also turned the spotlights on and are circling the island. You'll have about thirty seconds where the outer perimeter and the sector you're about to step into will both be off."

Grace waited for Ethan's signal, her thigh muscles burning with the effort it took to stay close to Gabe. As soon as Ethan gave the go ahead, Gabe grabbed her arm and pulled her with him to shore. There wasn't time to catch her breath or rest her shaking limbs. They kicked off their flippers—exposing the neoprene shoes that fit their feet like gloves—and they all ran to safety before the spotlights could circle back around.

The rain came down in sheets, and Grace ignored the cold drops as they snaked beneath the neck of her wetsuit. They dove behind a small inlet of rocks and waited for the spotlights to move on before gathering all of the rebreathers and fins and shoving them into the empty bag Jack carried on his back. They'd leave the bag hidden behind the rocks.

Grace flexed her fingers and rolled her ankles so her joints wouldn't become stiff with the cold, and she sat with her back to the rocks to conserve her strength. Coming in and going out would be the most strenuous parts of the mission.

"The guards have gone back inside the security tower

on the south side," Ethan said through the com link. They're tired of driving around in the rain, and I've made the whole system go batshit, so they think it's an electrical malfunction."

"Good work," Gabe said.

Gabe's eyes were cold and shuttered, and the look of his face would have been terrifying to a normal person. She knew what it felt like to have your humanity slide away as the machine programmed to do this kind of work took over. She'd felt it before they'd left the safety of the Zodiac.

"Grim Reaper, you're up," Ethan said. "I'm sending the path you need to take to your GPS. It's a convoluted route that will mix up the sectors that get shut down, but the guards won't be paying any attention."

Logan adjusted the bag of explosives he carried with him and said, "On your count, Dragon."

Logan took off at a run, disappearing quickly in the rain and darkness.

"Grim Reaper has made target," Ethan said after a few minutes had passed. "Renegade is up. Sending your coordinates now. Kimball's scientist is staying in the pool house. You'll take him out first and then follow the second set of coordinates up to the main house."

Jack looked at the GPS in his hand. "On your count."

Grace and Gabe waited patiently for their turn, and she scooted closer to him to steal a bit of his body heat. He felt like a furnace in the middle of the stormy cold. He took her chin between his fingers and kissed her once.

"You're up, Kill Shot," Ethan said. "Sending your coordinates now to the elevated area you told me you wanted. You should have a nice view of the whole island from there."

"Love you," Gabe mouthed as she moved to take her position.

She nodded once and kissed him hard a final time. "On your count, Dragon."

She followed Ethan's coordinates across the island, climbing the steep rocks that led to the top of a manmade waterfall. Boulders and palms surrounded the area and would give her good cover. The rocks were slick against her hands and feet, and she felt the quick sting of a sharp rock as it sliced through her shoe and into her heel. She stayed low to the ground and found the perfect position to set up her rifle behind a large rock that had a wide crag right down the center all the way to the ground.

Grace put her rifle together as quickly in the pouring rain as she did in perfect weather, and she took position behind the infrared scope. She'd have to change scopes once the sun came out, and the change between night and day would be her most vulnerable time. She sighted across the island slowly and was pleased with the location.

***

"You've got to give me an affirmative position for the launch site," Gabe said to Ethan two hours later.

The sun had reluctantly risen, and they were

surrounded by so much ocean that it looked as if the sun was coming directly out of the waves. But the welcome heat of the day didn't chase the rain away. The black skies turned a putrid gray and continued to rumble.

"I can't tell, dammit," Ethan said, the frustration evident in his voice. "It looks as if there are two separate launch sites. Why would he release two batches of the weapon?"

"One has to be a decoy," Gabe said. "Kimball knew we were looking for him, and he'd plan for all contingencies. Send me the coordinates for both launch sites. I've got no choice but to check them both."

"I've got a visual on the ferry," Grace said. "It looks like everyone's on board from my count." She deliberately glanced over Tussad's familiar face and controlled her anger. Some habits were hard to break.

"There's movement on the island," Ethan said. "Household staff is moving inside the main house, and guards are doing perimeter checks now that the storm's not as severe and they can see better. I've marked the image I'm assuming is Kimball as green on the GPS. He's been in the same place all morning.

Gabe ran to the first launch site, knowing his time was running out. Once the ferry reached the island, it would be too late for him to stop it. He heard the guards talking before he reached the first launch site and knew he'd picked the wrong one immediately. The guards were low-level security, and they didn't even hear him as he came up behind them. He shot the first and snapped the neck of the guard next to him before either was able to call out for help.

"Three town cars have pulled up to the docks," Grace said. "Kimball's not in any of them."

"Do you still have a visual on the one you think is Kimball?" Gabe asked Ethan as he ran to the other launch site.

"The target is still in place. Would he still be in bed with guests arriving so soon? It doesn't look as if he's moved."

The launch site was on the other side of the island, and he listened to Ethan's warnings as he called out when guards were in his path. He only had to take out two before he found himself at his destination.

There were once again only two guards, but Nigel Peters stood in the center of the small clearing, the launch code in his hand as he typed in the numbers to activate the weapon.

"Ferry is docking," Grace said.

"Something seems off here, Ghost," Ethan said.

"Are you getting other heat signals nearby?" Gabe asked.

"No, that's what seems off."

Gabe tuned out Ethan and knew he'd have to take out both guards quickly. Peters was trained in combat, and he'd be expecting him. He was more than likely armed as well. Gabe threw his knife at the first guard and shot the second guard even as Peters brought up his own weapon.

Gabe rolled and fired, while Peters returned fire in slow, steady increments, so Gabe had no choice but to head for cover in a direction he already knew was a dead end. He held still behind a thick palm tree and didn't flinch as a bullet sent shards of the trunk into his cheek and neck. All Peters needed was a target, and he'd be damned if he'd give him one.

The report of a long-distance rifle had Gabe dropping to the ground and taking stock of the situation. Peters was on the ground, a perfectly round bullet hole through the center of his forehead.

Gabe looked up to where Grace was positioned over the waterfalls on the other side of island. The shot she'd taken had been from almost a mile away. There were only a handful of people in the world who could make a shot like that. It was a phenomenal gift, but there wasn't time to do anything but embrace the feeling that things were about to go to shit very quickly.

"Get out of there, Kill Shot. You've just given away your position."

"I'm already moving. And you're welcome for saving your sorry ass."

"You can kiss it later. Just move!"

"I can see the ferry from my position," Logan said. "They're unloading, and Kimball's men are escorting the members to the cars with umbrellas."

"I'm with the weapon," Gabe said, looking at the small cylinder buried partially in the sand. The countdown had already begun on the white plastic tube, but there was an abort button just below the glowing red numbers.

He felt the sting in his shoulder before the sound of gunfire registered. Liquid fire raced through his veins, and he could smell his singed skin where the bullet had exited.

He dropped to his knees and ignored the demands through his com link to tell them he was all right. He brought his other arm up to try and hit the abort button once again when a hand pressed against the wound in his shoulder. He gritted his teeth against the pain, threw his head back, and shoved his fist into his attacker's groin. Gabe was losing a lot of blood, and he wouldn't be able to fight for long.

"I'm going to make your death terribly slow," Kimball said, kicking Gabe flat on his back while he walked off the pain in his balls. "You're a pain in the ass."

Kimball kicked Gabe in the ribs and leaned over him, slamming the butt of his gun across the side of his face. He didn't lose consciousness. But it was close.

"What do you think of my suit?" Kimball asked, slapping his across the face. "I know I had your man fooled. You're not the only one who gets to have all the fun toys."

Gabe opened his eyes and took a good look at his enemy. He was covered from head to toe in what looked like sealskin, but Gabe had seen it before and knew it was a complex design of state of the art materials and intricate wiring.

"It completely erases all body heat. As if I'm not really here at all." He pulled Gabe up by his shoulder, squeezing the wound. "Let's move back a bit. The show's about to start."

Gabe watched with impotent fury as the canister launched and the aerosol was released into the air.

"Why don't we go greet my guests? I'm sure most of

them will be thrilled to see you again. But I'm thinking they're mostly going to want to try to kill you. I believe you've done damage to all of their businesses at one point or another."

Kimball looked around them, and his gaze landed on the spot Grace had killed Peters from. "I'm glad he brought you along, Grace. I've been thinking of you these last few weeks. I'm not nearly through with you yet. I know you can hear me. I know all of you can hear me. Make sure you get in a good position to watch your team leader die. Your game's over. Looks like the good guys lose."

There was nothing but silence over Gabe's com link now, and he was grateful for the chance to think without interruption.

"It's funny, you know?" Kimball asked. "All of those years I spent whoring for the CIA, and all I heard was stories about you. I guess you've just never met your match before."

Kimball squeezed at his shoulder again, and Gabe's knees buckled, but he stayed upright.

"Let's go, Brennan. You're going to get to see The Passover Project up close and personal. It'll be a hell of a show."

CHAPTER TWENTY-SIX

"I've closed Gabe out of our circuit," Ethan said through the com links. "Please tell me someone has a plan."

Grace kept running across the island, her pistol in her hand and her rifle slung across her back. It took everything she had not to let the fear over Gabe's safety take control. She could be afraid later. Right now she had to save him.

There was only one other place on the island that would give her the position she needed to have a clear shot at Kimball. The guard tower was just down and to the south of the main house. It was built from stucco and glass to match the villa, and it resembled a turret, though it had a flat roof.

"Grim Reaper, is the fuse lit?" She asked, referring to the explosives he was constructing all over the island.

"We're lit. What do you need?"

"I need a spotter. Meet me at the guard tower at the

south end of the island."

"Roger that."

"The scientist has been taken care of," Jack said. "I'm crawling through the rafters in the main house, and I've got Gabe in my sights. Kimball has him in a room on the southwest side. Kimball's showing him off like a damned prize. No one is talking about the auction anymore. If they leave him alone, I can get him out, but if I go down there now I'll be dead before my feet touch the floor."

The guard tower came into view, and Grace didn't slow her momentum. She brought her pistol up and took out the two guards at the bottom. Logan met her at the stairs, and he covered her as she went up to the top level, dispatching the remaining two guards.

"You're all clear," Logan said.

"Call out if you need help," Grace said as he went back downstairs to guard her back. She opened the sliding glass windows that surrounded the top of the tower and slid out onto what could loosely be called a fire escape. She replaced her pistol at the small of her back and climbed onto the flat roof.

The rain had steadily picked up throughout the morning, and visibility was getting more difficult by the second. She laid down flat, ignoring the wet that seemed to surround her from all sides, and placed her rifle on a stand to keep it stable.

"Shit, I can't see them from here." She looked again through her scope, but all she could make out from the angled corner room was a single arm holding a drink. "You've got to get them out of that room, Jack. I need a better shot."

"Just a minute," he answered. "Something's about to happen."

***

Gabe sat up as straight as he could in the chair Kimball had placed him in, and he stared ahead as the men and woman he'd betrayed before found out his true identity. He didn't make a sound when Gabrielle Montpellier—a woman who was more ruthless than any man in the room and who'd once ordered a bombing at a French elementary school to gain her way into this select group of terrorists— pushed her manicured thumb into the exit wound at the front of his shoulder. He didn't even glance her way as she casually rinsed the blood off her thumb in the glass of champagne she was handed by one of Kimball's staff.

They all took their turns trying to make his pain worse, and he knew they'd eventually get what they wanted. He wouldn't stay conscious much longer if he didn't stop the bleeding.

"I didn't come here to torture this man," a voice said from the back of the room. "I've already had the opportunity to do so, and I'm bored with your party. I want the weapon."

Tussad's voice was as familiar to Gabe as his own, and he held himself rigidly still so he wouldn't go after the man's throat. He wouldn't make it far, and all he'd get for his effort was another bullet in his back.

"I'm so glad you brought us back to our purpose, Tussad. I can always count on you," Kimball said.

"Where is the weapon?" Gabrielle asked. "You cannot expect us to pay your outrageous opening bid without seeing a demonstration."

"Your demonstration will be starting in the next few minutes," Kimball said. "The great thing about this formula is that you can adjust how quickly you want it to respond. It can have a delay of up to twenty-four hours, or it can show itself in a matter of minutes. I think you'll enjoy the results as much as I have. Why don't we all go into the dining room? There are plenty of chairs, and the floor is tile. Things are going to get messy."

"Is Mr. Brennan not our demonstration?" Tussad asked.

"Not for this particular session. Once you get an idea of what the weapon can do, we'll start the bidding. The winner can use Mr. Brennan as their guinea pig. Or should I call you Ghost?" Kimball asked, leaning forward so Gabe had no choice but to look him in the eyes.

The others filed out of the room, but Kimball stayed behind. "Your wife should be dead just about now. And the rest of your team. My men know where they're hiding, and they know about the boat you have stashed just off the island. I'll keep you alive until I get word they're all dead. It seems fitting you should be the last."

Kimball saluted with two fingers and left Gabe alone in the room. He heard the lock snick shut on the outside of the door and Kimball give orders to his guards to keep a close watch. It wasn't until he was truly alone that he allowed himself to slump down in the chair. He was trapped in an oversized media room that had the bad fortune to have white carpet and white suede chairs grouped around small round tables. A large screen sat behind him, covering the entire wall, white velvet curtains flanking each side. A full bar and kitchen sat to his right, and a bank of windows with the shades mostly pulled down sat on his left. There wasn't a lot to work with.

He tapped the button on his watch that gave him direct communication with his command center. Unfortunately, his command center was stuck in a boat several miles from shore.

"Dragon, do you copy?"

Gabe used his good arm to pull the top half of his wetsuit down so his chest was bared and he could see how bad the wound at his shoulder was.

It was bad. Really bad.

"I copy, Ghost. Damn, it's good to hear your voice."

"You'll change your mind eventually. Has everyone checked in?"

He knew by Ethan's hesitation that something was wrong. "Where's Grace?"

"I can't get her to respond on the com link. Grim Reaper, either. Jack's inside the house. He should be coming through your door in just a few minutes. The last thing Grace said before the line went cold was that Jack would get you out."

The pain in his body was easily forgotten, and something else took its place. Something dangerous and dark. He searched through the drawers in the tiny kitchen area until he found a stack of clean white dishtowels. He pressed one of the smaller ones to the wound on his chest and then wrapped a larger one so it looped under his arm. He held one end of the towel with his teeth as he knotted it tightly.

His gun was gone, but he searched the rest of the drawer for something he could use as a weapon. There were no knives, but one of Kimball's staff had left a corkscrew under a napkin. It would have to do.

Gabe heard the grunt and fall of the two guards standing outside his door, and Jack slipped in a few seconds later. He must have looked worse than he thought if Jack's grimace was anything to judge by.

"Do you need help?" he asked, readjusting the crude bandage Gabe had tied around his shoulder.

"I'm good."

"What are we going to do about Kimball? We can't go in guns blazing and make it back out alive."

"We find Grace and Logan, and if things have gone to shit we detonate the explosives and get the hell off this island."

Gabe didn't have to explain to Jack that he wasn't leaving the island without Grace and Logan's bodies, if there were even bodies to claim.

***

"We've got company," Grace heard Logan call out. "Six or

seven headed our direction."

She left her rifle in position on top of the guard tower and slid down the fire escape all the way to the ground. The first guards were running toward them, weapons raised, as her feet hit the dirt. Plaster and mud exploded all around her, and she slid feet first toward her enemy, her pistol raised and firing rapid shots as Logan laid down cover fire.

The area was mostly open, and there weren't a lot of places available to hide, but she hunkered behind a decorative half wall that followed the stone path up to the main house. Gabe's voice rattled in her ear, and she breathed a sigh of relief that he was okay, but she couldn't deal with the distraction right now and turned off her com link. She saw Logan do the same thing and nodded in his direction while she changed the clip to her gun.

Logan was positioned directly across from her behind the other half wall, and she gave him the signal for what she wanted. Once she saw he understood, she flattened her body into the mud and waited for his report.

His gun seemed extraordinarily loud, as if it was somehow amplified by the rain and wind, and time seemed to slow to the point where she could see each of his bullets cut through the air. Logan ducked back behind the wall as shots were returned, and he held up his fingers so she'd know the position of her targets.

There wasn't time to think. She could lose her shots if she wasted those precious seconds. She took a breath and held it as she rolled into the open, firing in the directions Logan had just given her—seven, eleven, one, and four o'clock—from left to right, and then she quickly rolled back to the relative safety of her position.

They waited a few minutes more, and Logan signaled the all clear. "Go," he said. "Finish off Kimball, and lets get out of here."

She nodded and climbed back to the top of the guard tower, flicking the switch on her watch to check in with command.

"Dragon, I'm back in position to take the shot. Kimball's moved the party to the dining area. I have a clear shot."

"Everything okay?" Gabe asked.

She heard the worry and fear and relief in those two words and relaxed as she realized Jack had helped Gabe get out of the house.

"I'm good."

And she realized she really was. Her mind was clear and her hands were steady. But this was going to be a hell of a difficult shot, and she'd only have one chance to get it right. It was close to a mile in distance to the main house—similar to the length of the shot she'd made when she'd taken out Peters—but the wind was going in the opposite direction, and rain was pelting her directly in the face. There were a lot of added variables with this shot that there hadn't been with the other.

"Grim Reaper, what's your position?" Gabe asked.

"I'm spotting for Kill Shot."

"Stay where you are. Renegade and I are going to set off the light show a little early. Take out the target now, Kill Shot. Things are about to get crazy."

"I've intercepted a signal that military aircraft are headed in our direction," Ethan said. "Their attitude is hostile. We've got less than fifteen minutes before we need to be as far from this island as possible."

"Roger that, Dragon. Close up shop and pick us up shore side."

Grace adjusted her aim with every shift of the wind, blanking out the wind and rain and occasional voice from the com link until she was completely alone in her mind and silence reigned. Her weapon hesitated, and her finger flexed, wanting to pull the trigger, as she passed her scope across Tussad.

Her concentration was broken as she watched The Passover Project being demonstrated in front of the curious and terrified crowd. They were all just beginning to realize what kind of position Kimball had just put them in. They'd all be working for him before long.

Tussad fell to his knees on the floor, a fountain of blood coming from his mouth and splashing onto the white tile like red paint. She watched him die without remorse, her idea of justice being well served.

"Kill Shot," Gabe shouted in her ear. "We're waiting on your hit."

Grace kept her eyes on Kimball and lined her shot up once more—her mind blank and the coldness of the kill steeling her spine. She breathed in slowly and held her breath as her finger squeezed the trigger.

"It's a go," she said, knowing she'd made the shot as soon as the bullet left her gun.

An explosion rocked the area next to the house, and

she knew Gabe and Jack had set off the bomb at the pool house where Kimball's scientist had set up a lab of sorts that housed all of his research and the components to the formula. Debris mixed with the rain, and chaos reigned over the island as she dropped down to the ground beside Logan. She slid the strap to her rifle across her chest and took out her pistol.

"Kill Shot and Grim Reaper headed to the pick up location," she said to Ethan.

"I'm in position. Eight minutes and counting until military transport arrives."

"We'll meet you there," Gabe said. "Five minutes."

The helipad exploded within the next minute, and the ferry and docks went up in flames moments later. Seven of the world's most dangerous terrorists were trapped with no way out but by military assistance. They were going to have a lot of explaining to do.

Five minutes passed, and she gave Logan a worried look. He turned the Zodiac so they were backed into shore.

"Ghost, where the hell are you?"

"Right behind you, sweetheart."

Gabe and Jack appeared out of the shadows, running like hell towards the Zodiac. The bandage at Gabe's shoulder was soaked through with blood, and she could tell he was running on pure adrenaline. Logan had the boat in motion just as they cleared the sides.

Gabe collapsed against her, and she felt for the pulse in his neck, trying not to show him how worried she was.

"I'm fine," he said, taking her hand and kissing her fingers. "But I'm probably going to pass out soon. Don't take me to the hospital."

Grace leaned down and kissed his brow, cradling him against her. "Payback's a bitch, my love."

He smiled, and she took his face between her hands and looked into his eyes. "It's over, Gabe. Tussad's gone. I thought I'd feel something—more. But it almost feels as if I've lost her all over again."

"Because you were able to let it go," he said. "We won't forget her, Grace. And we won't forget what he did and how he paid. The future is ours."

She leaned down to kiss him softly, her cheeks wet with tears. "I'm looking forward to it."

EPILOGUE

One Year Later…
Marseilles, France: New Collective Headquarters

Jack was restless.

Maybe he was burned out. Or maybe he was jealous that Gabe and Grace had managed to have their marriage resurrected from the ashes. They'd worked hard to save what was most important to them, purging the demons that had tried to destroy them. They were happy. And he was happy for them. But there was a part of him that knew that kind of happiness would never be a part of his future.

He'd thought of retiring or taking an extended vacation, and he could tell by Gabe's long looks and probing questions that his friend knew he wasn't satisfied. He just—needed something more.

Even now, Jack was only halfway listening to the team briefing for their next mission, his mind finding it hard to settle on any one thing.

"This one is all you, Jack," Gabe said, sliding a black folder in his direction and getting his attention. "We'll all be there as backup, but it's you our target needs to trust. Do whatever it takes to get the information we need."

"He always gets the hot chicks," Ethan muttered.

Jack looked at the picture Ethan had put up on the wall screen and felt lust slam through his system. He read the description that accompanied the photo until he found her name. *Lissa Yamagata.* Her face was exotic—eyes that tilted slightly, high cheekbones, and lips that were luscious and full. Just the thought of her mouth and what it could do had him shifting in his seat to accommodate the painful erection behind his zipper. She was small, only a couple of inches over five feet, and she had a waterfall of silky black hair that fell straight as rain to her waist.

Her mother was an American citizen, but her father was a Japanese warlord. According to the data Ethan had collected, she was brilliant, fluent in several languages, and had a hell of a sword collection.

The team was watching him carefully, waiting for some kind of reaction, and he realized he must have missed the complete rundown of the mission. Something wasn't right, and he met Gabe's stare head-on and without apology for not paying better attention.

"And what happens after I get the information I need?" Jack asked.

Gabe's eyes narrowed, and he leaned back in his chair. "You kill her."

ABOUT THE AUTHOR

Liliana Hart spent five years teaching music in the public education system. She molded America's youth, busted kids for smoking pot in the restrooms, and broke up illicit affairs behind the stage on a regular basis, so she finally decided to hang up her hat and let someone else have all the fun. (Liliana's Addison Holmes Mystery Series, about a small town teacher who gets into a whole lot of trouble, is somewhat autobiographical, but she won't confess to which parts).

Liliana began reading romance novels with all her new found free time, and when she ran out of things to read, she decided to write her own novels. The result was a 150,000 word thriller--a dazzling adventure--where the heroine was a thirty-year-old virgin assassin (Yes, you read that right). She couldn't imagine why people weren't knocking down her door to read it, but she persevered and began writing a second book. She finally got the hang of things, and eventually learned that losing one's virginity wasn't all that romantic after all. All of her books involve some kind of suspense (she just can't help herself), laughter, and a lot of steamy sex.

Since the failure of her first attempt, Liliana's books have won awards such as: The Daphne Du Maurier, The Suzannah, The Linda Howard Award of Excellence, The Maggie, and many others. Her affiliations include Romance Writers of America and Mystery Writers of America. Liliana loves to cook, and is addicted to reading, Internet Boggle, kickboxing, and Bones. She lives in a big, rambling house in Texas with a couple of cats to keep her company. She loves to get emails from readers.

Enjoy the Adventures!

Made in the USA
Charleston, SC
03 July 2013